# BROKEN PROMISES
**FBI Guys 2**
by
**Marie-Nicole Ryan**

*Romantic Suspense Novel*

RYANDALE PUBLISHING

# BROKEN PROMISES

## Marie-Nicole Ryan

## RYANDALE PUBLISHING

Ryandale Publishing
Copyright © 2011 by Mary Varble
Editor, Linda Ingmanson
Cover Art, Elaina Lee, For the Muse Design & Mary Varble
All rights reserved. Ryandale Publishing
All rights reserved.
Second edition: Ryandale Publishing
ISBN-9781393909965


Published in the United States of America
Library of Congress Registration: TX 7-475-211, 12/11/2011

# What they're saying about

## *Broken Promises*

"Marie-Nicole Ryan has a flair for bringing romance to life..." Fallen Angel Reviews

## *Love Me If You Can*

"Marie-Nicole Ryan has done it again in *Love Me If You Can* from beginning to end." Black Ravens Reviews

"This is a mature and complex love story much like real life with ups, downs and in-betweens... I highly recommend this well-written romantic suspense." The Romance Studio

"Great pacing and mystery keeps the reader at the edge of their seat..." Siren Book Reviews

"*Love Me If You Can* is a fast paced read that will keep your attention until the last page. It is the perfect book for both romance and mystery lovers." Melissa's Sizzling Hot Reviews

"*Love Me If You Can* is a quick paced race to catch a killer and maybe even a happily ever after that will keep your attention." Manic Readers

"...suspense plot is fast moving and keeps the readers guessing until the surprising climax." RT Book Reviews

## *Holding Her Own*

"*Holding Her Own*...is wonderfully written, the action in this book flows like the Louisiana bayou." ParaNormal Romance Reviews

"As a romance and suspense, *Holding Her Own* is a delectably perfect blend of both genres, standing out for me as top notch in both areas." Madame Butterfly's Blog

"Fast paced and with interesting characters, this intricate novel has red herrings in abundance. The ambience of New Orleans enhances the story by contributing to several threads." RT Book Reviews

## ACKNOWLEDGEMENTS

I owe a debt of gratitude to my free lance editor, Linda, who helped me, once again, whip a somewhat flawed story into shape.

## DEDICATION

This book is dedicated to my wonderful friends in Canandaigua, NY, Tom and Marti Miller, who welcomed me into their home and hearts. Also a shout-out to Jane and Gloria who have waited patiently for this story set in their wonderful, picturesque town.

## NOTE TO READERS

If you're curious about the first time Alex and Bette met and want more details, check out the short story prequel, PILLOW TALK.

# Chapter One

*The phone rang.*

*"Just ignore it," she whispered and pressed her lips and body against his.*

It rang again.

Alex shuddered awake. To an empty bed and no sign of a woman. Hell, he'd dreamed about Bette again. An unwelcome reminder he'd been too busy to check on her since they'd gone their separate ways. He groaned and reached for the phone. "MacGregor."

"It's Bette. You have to come home."

Was her tone a touch on the hysterical side? That was Bette's voice, all right. "No can do. Things are about to break on this case—"

"No, you don't understand. Listen to me. You have to come home. Your sister is *missing*."

He sat up and rubbed the sleep from his eyes. A never-quite-forgotten dread jarred his gut and spiked his heart rate. He squinted at the clock. Four. And not a sign of dawn.

"What do you mean she's missing? Where's Brad?" Brad was his sister's husband. "Why isn't he calling?"

"He's in New York for a seminar." A note of rising panic was clear in her voice, as well as more than a hint of her Jersey-girl accent.

"Hold on. Take a deep breath. Start at the beginning. What makes you think she's missing?"

"I left her alone in the office last night. Just as we were leaving, someone pulled in and said his cat was ill. She told me to go on home, that she'd take a look at the cat, and then head on to the emergency clinic. Last night, she was supposed to be on call, but the clinic assistant called me after trying Jackie's cell and home phones." She took a couple of gulping breaths. "Omigod, Alex, she never showed up. She's gone—like, vanished into thin air. Someone *took* her!"

"Just calm down. Maybe she had car trouble and her cell phone was dead," he suggested, trying to think of less ominous reasons for his sister's being out of touch.

"No, she keeps her phone charged during office hours. Something's happened. I just know it. I shouldn't have left her alone with him."

"Then, why did you?" An accusatory tone crept into his voice, even if Canandaigua wasn't as dangerous as Chicago.

"I thought it was someone she knew. I mean, I heard her laugh when they went inside."

A nightmare. A freaking nightmare. Why couldn't he still be dreaming? "Have you called the police?"

"Yes. They're trying to find Brad at his hotel."

"And Cody?" His five-year-old nephew must be terrified to learn his mother was missing, if he'd even been told.

"He had a sleepover last night at the Crandalls'. What should I do? Should I pick him up? Take him to kindergarten or wait until Brad gets home?"

He could almost hear Bette wringing her hands. "Call the Crandalls. Tell them what's happened. Have them send Cody to school. The locals will want to talk to Brad." The husband or significant other was always the first suspect in a woman's disappearance. "I'll catch the next flight to Buffalo. No, wait. First, I have to let my boss know what's going on." Asking for personal leave while he was ass-deep in a serial killer case could stall his career with the Bureau for years. Talk about kissing his dream job on the Violent Crimes Task Force good-bye.

Couldn't be helped. No question about it. No way could he endure losing his sister the way he'd lost his brother Andy. His identical twin.

"I'm sorry, Alex." Bette's voice quivered, her throat sounding as if clogged with tears. "I know you're busy, but I just didn't know who else to call. The sheriff's deputy didn't seem too alarmed. The jerk acted like she was probably stepping out while Brad was out of town. I haven't known her all that long, but I know she'd never run around. And she'd *never* miss her turn at the emergency clinic."

"You're right." Trying to clear his head, he stood and yawned until his jaw popped. "Hang tight. I'll call you as soon as I'm on the ground."

He rang off, shook his head, shrugged into a shirt, and tugged on a pair of jeans. He snatched up the go-bag he kept packed. An FBI agent could be sent anywhere on a moment's notice. Being prepared wasn't just for the Boy Scouts. He called a cab. Since this was personal, he'd be on his own for transport and—

Crap! He hadn't called the Special Agent in Charge.

He called and awakened the SAC. By the time he finished giving the SAC a sit-rep, he was downstairs in time to meet the cab as it pulled to the curb.

Still on the phone, he nodded and tossed his go-bag into the backseat. "O'Hare," he told the cabbie and slid inside.

"Yes, sir," he continued with his SAC. "I know it's inconvenient. Yes, I realize I can't function in an official capacity, even if the locals call in the Bureau."

While he rode to the airport, he used his iPhone to purchase a ticket on the next flight to Buffalo. Rochester was closer, but he'd have a long layover in Buffalo. Might as well drive from there to Canandaigua.

The SAC was understanding but made it clear Alex would be replaced on the VCTF if his situation wasn't resolved in forty-eight hours.

Forty-eight short hours to find his sister.

But forty-eight hours was a long time to avoid getting involved with one sexy Bette Smithson. Dark chocolate doe's eyes. Dark brown hair, thick and silky as a waterfall. No matter how much he'd itched to get tangled up in the sheets with her last New Year's Eve, he'd remained a gentleman.

Damn. Who the hell cared about being a gentleman nowadays? No one he knew.

And what'd he done? He'd kissed her *adios*, put her on the plane to Buffalo, and forgot all about her.

Almost.

That one heated—and unfortunately unforgettable—kiss had been a mistake, all right. He'd promised he'd call. And he hadn't. Now he'd be forced to face the woman who plagued his dreams. Dreams like he hadn't experienced since he was a horny teen.

Bette set aside the phone and balled her fists. Good-guy hero Double-O was on the way. He'd find Jackie before anyone hurt her...if they hadn't already. Dammit. Things like this weren't supposed to happen. Not to someone as good and kind as her boss. After all, Jackie was as much a friend as boss. When Bette had landed on Jackie's doorstep, she'd welcomed Bette with open arms and given her a job and a place to live.

Still, there must be something she could do before Alex arrived, which probably wouldn't be for another two or three hours. And only if he caught a flight right away.

Not like New Year's Day, when she'd flown from Nashville to Buffalo. Jackie's husband had braved the ice and snow, picking up Bette at the airport. At least in June, the roads were clear, making Alex's drive from Buffalo a breeze.

Calling Alex took every ounce of courage she possessed and shook her to the core. She wouldn't have called, not in a million years, if not for Jackie. In spite of their brief night together—where nothing actually happened, thank you very much—it seemed they had a connection. At the airport, he promised to call soon. And then he kissed her. Kissed her good, like call-your-best-girlfriend-and-tell-her-all-about-it good.

Apparently, Special Agent MacGregor was just too busy with his new job to keep his promises. Hell. He wasn't the first man to disappoint her. Not by a long shot.

Still, none of that mattered. Not really. Not when his sister was missing and maybe already dead.

*I should've stayed with her.*

But, hell, this was Canandaigua. Upstate New York, for Pete's sake. Nothing much ever happened here. People didn't lock their doors, except maybe in the summertime when the small town was flooded with tourists.

Lined with summerhouses, Canandaigua Lake's ice-blue waters drew boaters and water-skiers. The perfect climate and the hills above the lake were ideal for growing grapes, which made the Finger Lakes area the New York version of Napa Valley. In addition, there were a million and one places to go and things to do, from antiques to boutiques to one-of-a-kind potteries. And for a small town, Canandaigua boasted some very fine eating establishments. Very fine indeed.

Yet in the middle of all this idyllic beauty, Jackie Stinnett had vanished as surely and silently as the early morning mist on Canandaigua Lake.

# Chapter Two

Bette sat on the hard bench, tapping the toe of her sandaled foot against the tile floor of the Canandaigua Police Department. A surly desk sergeant had given her a brief nod and sent her to sit next to two working girls and possibly a serial killer or two. What was taking so freaking long? Didn't anyone care Jackie'd been kidnapped? And what was going on with the two post-ops still at the practice? Someone had to see after them too.

True, she'd already talked to the detective on the phone, but now he wanted an official statement. "Appreciate it if you'd come down to the station, right now," he'd told her. "Right now" had been seven, but her watch currently showed nine thirty, and she was still sitting. Waiting.

"Smithson!" The desk sergeant motioned with his thumb. "Go straight back. First left. Third door on the right. Detective Spitz is ready for you. "

She swallowed the about-damned-time comment she didn't dare make and responded with a meek nod. No point in hassling the cops.

Of course, Double-O, her nickname for Alex, was different. As a Fed, he saw the big picture and didn't have a small-town cop's mentality. With her family's history, she knew a lot more about cops than she cared to admit. Especially to Special Agent Alex MacGregor.

More than likely, there was some regulation against an FBI agent doing the horizontal mambo with a runaway Mafia princess. Not that any such thing was likely to happen, except in her imagination.

Following the sergeant's directions, she quickly found herself in a small interview room complete with a small metal desk and two vacant chairs. Detective Spitz occupied the third chair—actually, he sprawled. Shiny bald with a thick salt-and-pepper mustache like a Schnauzer's, the detective didn't look like any Spitz she'd ever run across. Of course, working in a vet's office, she was more familiar with the canine variety. In other words, the detective didn't have a bushy white fur coat, and his tail didn't curl over his back. Not as far as she could tell.

"Miss Smithson?"

"That's me," she said with a smile guaranteed to warm the heart of many a good pooch. And even some not so inclined.

Apparently, having his heart warmed wasn't Detective Dog's idea of an interview. He gestured for her to have a seat and proceeded to tell her the interview was being videotaped.

What he did *not* do was read her her rights. No Miranda had to be a good thing…for a start, anyway.

Maybe if she sat, rolled over, and jumped through all their hoops, the department would get off their collective asses and find her boss before something bad happened…if it hadn't already.

She leaned forward, her elbows on the table. "First, before we go into Jackie's kidnapping, we have to get this out of the way. We need to do something about the animals in the animal clinic. There are two post-ops who should be ready for discharge this morning."

The detective let out a long sigh. "This isn't our first time at the rodeo, Miss Smithson. The Humane Society has already been called in. They've evaluated the, uh, patients, transported them to their shelter, and notified the owners of their whereabouts." He paused, then leaned forward. "Now, about this so-called kidnapping. If we can start at the beginning…"

She took a deep breath and composed herself. "Well—"

The detective's cell phone rang. He held up a hand. "Hold on.

Gotta take this." He proceeded to nod and "Uh-huh" a few times, while his face grew redder with each passing grunt.

"Appears we have an outside agency requesting to be brought in on the case. Excuse me." He stood, stomped out, and left her alone. She glanced up at the video camera placed high in a corner and gave a halfhearted smile.

An outside agency meant the Feds, and with any luck, it meant Alex had arrived. Dealing with anyone else wasn't high on her list of favorite things to do. Mostly, Feds were a dour bunch, but he was altogether different.

She ran her fingers through her hair. Heaven only knew what she looked like. Not that it mattered in the grand scheme of things. Only someone with a skewed world view would care about her appearance at a time like this. But there it was. She cared.

She started to chew on a fingernail, stopped herself, and fisted her hands in her lap. Nasty habit—biting her nails. As a child, she'd done it constantly, even though her mother painted the tips of her fingers with some bitter-tasting stuff. In spite of breaking herself of the habit in high school, she occasionally, in times of stress, caught herself about to do serious damage to her French manicure.

Outside the interview room, she could make out the sounds of Detective Spitz arguing with someone. Alex, maybe?

The door opened. The detective stomped in, shoulders rigid. Behind him, tall, confident, and looking better than any man had a right to was none other than Special Agent Alex MacGregor. A mixture of relief and something else best left unacknowledged flooded through her. Breathing came easier. Now that Double-O was here, everything would be all right.

"This federal agent here says *you* called him in on the case. Why's that?"

"Maybe because he's her *brother*." Okay, her tone that time was a little on the snarky side. Not counting summer tourists, Canandaigua was a smallish town. Curious he didn't already know

Alex.

"What's your connection to Agent MacGregor?"

"We met...once." Irritated, she shot Alex a *look*. Why wasn't he explaining their connection himself? "He helped me out of a bad situation and got me a job in Jackie's office."

"If it's all right with you, the agent wants to sit in on this interview."

"Of course." She glanced up at Alex's tall figure. He wasn't acting like they had any connection at all. In fact, he was doing a superb job of avoiding her gaze. His stance was rigid, as if he had a poker up his back passage. "No objections. I want to help anyway I can. And I wouldn't have called him in the first place if it hadn't been an emergency."

There, chew on that.

Alex's eyebrow twitched, but beyond that, he didn't react to her sarcastic tone.

Then his stance relaxed. He went so far as to fold his arms across his chest and lean against the wall, but no hint of his smile played about his mouth. His icy-blue gaze caught hers. "Start from the beginning, Bette." His voice was deep and resonant. Her body shuddered a bit, but she clenched her jaw. Not like an uptight and upright feeb and a runaway Mafia princess would ever have any kind of relationship beyond a booty call. And the chances for that were growing less likely by the second.

"*I'll* handle the interview." The detective bristled and assumed his previous position across the table. "You're just here to observe, Agent MacGregor." He smiled, smoothed his mustache somewhat self-consciously, then said, "Start from the beginning, Miss Smithson."

She gave an eye roll but started the story for what seemed like the fifth or sixth time. "It was a little after closing. Jackie was due to head over to the twenty-four-hour emergency vet clinic. The other employees had already left. I'd just finished the accounts for the week. We locked up and walked out into the parking lot together when a big SUV pulled in and parked. I'd already opened my car door, but I heard him say his cat was sick. I asked Jackie if she wanted me to stay and give her a hand, but she said she could handle it, and I should go on home. I left, and that's the last I saw of her."

"What about the man? Can you describe him?"

She shook her head. "Not his face. He was wearing a black hoodie. But he was tall—about Alex's—Agent MacGregor's height but heavier. Not so trim, I mean." She shot a quick glance in his direction. He frowned, head cocked to the side. Yes, indeed he was lean-muscled and trim, like a soap opera star with six-pack abs.

Strong. Capable. And, dammit, even more handsome than she remembered.

"What about his voice? Any accent?"

"Definitely an Upstater. Nothing else distinctive about it."

"Weren't you concerned about leaving your boss alone with a stranger?"

"In Canandaigua? No. In fact, when they went inside, she turned on the lights and I heard her laugh. So, I figured it was someone she knew."

"Where did you go after that?"

"Home. I live in the Stinnetts's basement apartment."

"And when did you discover she was missing?"

"I kept hearing the upstairs house phone ring. Finally, my cell phone rang. It was the assistant at the emergency clinic wanting to know where Jackie was. That's when I got worried. I tried calling her husband—he was in New York City for a seminar—but I kept getting his voice mail."

She met Alex's gaze. Tried to read his expression. Failed. "I called the—uh, 911. After that, I called Alex—Agent MacGregor— early this morning. Around five, our time." She spread her hands on the table. "That's it. That's all I know."

"Could Dr. Stinnett be having an affair and just took off with the gentleman and his alleged sick cat?"

"No." She shook her head vigorously. The very idea. "She'd *never* do anything like that."

"And Mr. Stinnett? Off in New York." The detective wagged his head. "Couldn't be reached."

"Still?" That didn't sound too good. She shot a surreptitious glance at Alex. No reaction.

"Oh, we got hold of him this morning." The detective nodded with a smirk. "He's on his way home."

"Good." She started to rise. "Is that all, Detective?"

"Not so fast. I've another question or two."

Wasn't it Columbo who always had another question or two? She sat, an uneasy sensation crawling along the pit of her stomach. "Okay?"

"What about *you* and Mr. Stinnett? Maybe you'd like to move upstairs and play house with your boss's husband?"

"What? No!" Appalled, she rose halfway, hovered, then sat back down. "And that's a totally asinine suggestion." She cut her gaze to Alex. Surely he wouldn't believe she'd be so conniving.

"Wouldn't be the first time a hot little number like yourself thought she could better her situation by getting rid of her rival."

She shot the detective a fake smile, then batted her lashes. "Thank you so much for saying I'm a 'hot little number,' but you're an ass-hat." This time, she stood and set her hands on her hips. "If you're arresting me, do it. Otherwise, I've told you all I know, and I'm out of here. If you need me again, I'll be at The Villager eating breakfast."

"Have your breakfast, but don't—"

"Leave town? Yeah, I know the drill. Let me tell you something. Leaving town while the kindest woman I've ever known, not counting my mother, is missing—that's the last thing I'd ever do."

She turned to Alex. "I don't know about you, but I'm blowing this joint. Detective Shepherd or Spitz, or whatever the hell his name is, has managed in the space of five minutes to smear your sister, her husband, and *me*. I've had enough. If I'm not under arrest, I'm out of here."

Heading for the door and holding her breath, she hesitated long enough to make sure the long arm of the law wasn't bent on stopping her…at least for the moment.

To hell with Double-O and his stuck-up attitude. What had she expected anyway? Roses and champagne—not.

# Chapter Three

Alex leaned back and watched Bette flounce from the interview room. She'd changed a little since he saw her in January. He gave himself a mental shake. Damn, his priorities were all fucked up. He was here to find his sister, his only living sibling—not get involved with Bette. He raised an eyebrow at the detective. "Well?"

"Well, nothing. Seems like you two already know each other. Not sure I ought to be telling you what I think." The detective rubbed one side of his thick mustache and sniffed. "What I think is that she knows more than she's letting on." He nodded knowingly. "Yeah, she does."

Bette was right. Local LEO *was* a freaking ass-hat. "You're right. I know her, sort of. But you're wrong about her involvement." Dammit. The last thing he wanted to do was elaborate on how he and Bette met on New Year's Eve in a low-rent motel in Nashville during that city's worst snow storm in recent history. No amount of explanation or qualification would keep the detective from going, "Uh-huh. Sure. Know what that was about."

Alex clenched his jaw and eyeballed the detective. "Like Ms. Smithson said, I helped her out of a jam—of the stalker variety. So I called my sister and asked for a favor. She had an opening in her office and offered Bette a job and a place to live."

The detective scratched his shiny pate. "Hm. Maybe this stalker caught up with her and took the wrong woman. Need to look into that. You got any details on him?"

Alex reined in the anger flashing through him. Talk about the locals getting sidetracked. "Some PI in Nashville. Can't remember his name offhand. I figure if he was stalking Bette, he wouldn't confuse the two women. Hold on." He pulled the phone from his pocket and accessed the background intel he'd dug up. "Name's Rodney Jenkins, formerly with Metro. Nashville PD. Followed her. Sat in front of her apartment building. Got her fired from her job. Even broke into her apartment. You know the drill. Basic Stalker 101, and to my way of thinking, ready to escalate."

Enough about Bette. Her stalker wasn't the answer to his sister's disappearance. He leaned forward. "What kind of forensic evidence do you have on my sister's disappearance?"

"We're processing fingerprints, but I got to tell you, there are dozens of samples from the waiting room alone. We're calling in all the employees for samples to eliminate them."

Alex glanced toward the door. "Bette's? Did you take hers?" Damn, they could eliminate hers right away.

"We'll get around to it before the day's over."

"She's probably still in the building. Why drag her down here again?"

Spitz shrugged his burly shoulders. "No rush. Figure we'll see a lot of her before this is over."

"What about tire tracks in the parking lot? Surveillance video from businesses across the street? Was there any blood in the office? Any signs of a struggle?" Damn. Might as well be talking to a post for all the intel Spitz was offering.

"All in good time, Agent MacGregor. All in good time. We're a small department. We're thorough, but it takes time."

"If you call in the FBI, officially all the resources of the Bureau will be at your disposal." God. What a cretin to be in charge of Jackie's disappearance. His stomach cramped and burned with the irony.

"I think we can take care of this on our own. Like I said, we're thorough."

"Have you even set up a tip line?" He clenched his fists to keep from grabbing the local law enforcement officer's shirt.

"Now, Agent. I'm still not sure your sister didn't take off of her own accord."

Alex glared and shook his head. Un-freaking-believable. "She wouldn't just up and leave, not without her son. Just ask anyone. It took three years of fertility treatments for her to get pregnant. No way she'd go anywhere without him." He glanced at his watch. "Time's running out. She's been gone at least fourteen hours. You know the chances of..." The words dried in his mouth.

"Don't you worry. We'll find your sister." This said with a dismissive shrug.

Alex took a step forward, moving into Spitz's personal space, challenging him. "Like this department found my twin brother sixteen years ago? He was found, all right. Nothing left but a pile of bones on Bristol Mountain."

Spitz frowned, his forehead creasing. "I was on patrol then. Remember the case well. But this isn't the same thing." He shook his head. "Nothing like."

"You don't know that. Has anyone bothered to enter the details into ViCAP? Maybe there've been similar cases nearby."

Spitz stood and stuffed his hands in his pockets. "You know, you're starting to piss me off, Agent. Why don't you get along home and check the phone for voice-mail messages from your runaway sister."

He spun and hit the wall with his fist. "Dammit! My sister isn't a runaway. Someone took her!"

"We're through here." Spitz's chin jutted out with his determination. "Now, if you don't mind, or even if you do, I'd like to get back to the case. I'm sure you can find your way out."

Alex sucked in a breath and clenched his jaw. Sonofabitch wasn't going to do a damned thing to find Jackie. "I'll run my own investigation, Detective. You and this department better pray I find her alive and well."

He stomped out and rushed to the fresh air of the city street. The temperature gauge read eighty degrees. Almost a freaking heat wave for upstate New York.

Since Andy had died at fourteen, it'd just been the two of them, Jackie and Alex. And as good as their adoptive parents had been, they couldn't make up for the loss of his identical twin. They couldn't fill the gutting hole left in his soul. Most of all, they couldn't wipe away the guilt of a promise not kept.

No one could.

# Chapter Four

After leaving the police station, Bette headed for the animal hospital. She hopped into her second-hand Corolla and then drove down Ontario, hung a left on Main heading toward the lake, then another left on Eastern Boulevard. Stinnett Veterinary Clinic was located just inside the city limits. Neon yellow crime scene tape was draped around the porch columns, barring the entrance…and making a jarring contrast with the bungalow's moss-green lap siding, cream shutters, and forest-green door.

She pulled into the side lot where she usually parked and found the side entrance was taped off as well. To make matters worse, it was Saturday morning, and four cars were already parked in the front lot just outside the crime scene tape.

Damn.

What were they going to do without a vet? The locum came in only on Wednesdays. Maybe she'd consider coming in full time until Jackie was found. How would they pay the locum? As the office manager, she'd have to worry about that particular issue later. More importantly, when would the authorities let them back into the office?

What if they couldn't find Jackie?

Jeez. Stop it. No negative energy. Positive thoughts. Positive thoughts.

She climbed out of the car and marveled at the mild eighty degree temperature. In Nashville, where she'd lived for eight years before moving to upstate New York, it would already be in the low nineties and humid as all get-out.

Might as well get it over with. Telling clients the doctor wasn't in and who the hell only knew when or *if* she would return wasn't a job she relished. But since crime scene tape wasn't part of the usual parking lot décor, the people waiting in their cars probably already figured something was up.

She walked along the edge of the tape and met the first of the clinic's clients: tall, slender, silver-haired Gloria Mason with her asthmatic and obese Pekinese. Who said dogs and owners looked alike? Not these two.

"What's going on, Bette? Was there a break-in? Someone looking for drugs?" the woman asked.

Bette worried her bottom lip before answering. "Dr. Stinnett's missing. We don't know what happened. Or where she is."

Mrs. Mason shot Bette a hooded sideways glance, then nodded with a knowing expression. "Oh, well, it was her husband. It's *always* the husband."

Bette shook her head. "Mr. Stinnett's out of town. Please. The police are handling it."

"It's like what happened to her brother." The woman let out a theatrical sigh. "Here one minute. Gone the next."

"No, Alex is fine. I just saw him at the police station." The words came out too fast. Too late to bite her tongue.

"I mean the other one. Andy or Andrew—he disappeared too."

"What?" Before she could ask any more questions, another client came up: Tom Miller with his Maltese, Buffy, a darling little creature who could always be depended upon to act out as soon as his owner left the premises.

Bette reached out and rubbed the little white dog's head, then clapped her hands to get everyone's attention. "You'll probably be hearing about this on the news soon enough. Jackie—Dr. Stinnett— is missing. The office is closed until the police department removes the tape. I don't know when that'll be. If you have an after-hours emergency, please call the emergency pet clinic in Rochester."

One of the clients didn't bother to get out of his car but backed out and drove off. The last remaining client was a tall, skinny man she didn't recognize. He climbed from his red pickup and led a small tricolor Sheltie by its leash. He tried to hand Bette the leash, but she backed up and shook her head. "We're closed. You need to take—"

He ran his hand through his shaggy hair. "Can't. Mom's had a bad stroke, and they say she has to go to a nursing home. I work construction all over the east coast, and I'm only home once every three weeks. I can't take care of a dog. My mom set great store by this little dog, but I don't know what else to do with her."

She looked down into a pair of big dark eyes. Eyes that said, "Take me home. Love me."

Unable to resist the unspoken plea, Bette took the leash. "What's her name?"

"Shadow."

"How old?"

"Around two. She's had her shots. Mom had her spayed during one of those shelter spay days."

What was she thinking? How could she manage to care for a pet when everything with Jackie was up in the air? Hell, she might not even have a job. But that was selfish, and here was this dainty little creature staring up at her, trusting Bette would do the right thing.

"I'll take her." She looped the leash around her wrist and sighed.

The man nodded. "Thanks." He ambled back to his truck. She knelt down and held out her hand for the dog to sniff. The Sheltie backed away, typical behavior for the breed, then apparently decided Bette would do after all. The dog wagged a plumy tail and licked Bette's hand.

She hunkered down, pulled the dog to her, and buried her nose in the luxurious fur. The bitch's coat was well brushed and smelled clean. At least she'd been taken care of. For a moment, the release of tension was like a rush of water from the bathtub when the plug was pulled. "Yeah, we'll suit, won't we?" What she'd do with a dog in her small, basement apartment, heaven only knew. Thank goodness her landlord was an animal lover.

At the thought of Jackie, the tightness in Bette's shoulders returned with a rush. The dog grew skittish and backed away. "Sorry, girl. It's not you. It's me."

"Sounds like you're breaking up with her instead of taking her home."

She looked up. Alex stood looming right behind her, all six-feet whatever of him. "Well, well. If it's not Double-O himself."

"Yeah, thought I'd better warn you. That idiot disguised as a detective has figured you for being involved."

"Believe me, I noticed." She stood and looked at the Sheltie, then at Alex. "I must be crazy, but I couldn't say no to those big brown eyes."

"Know what you mean. I—" He shifted from one foot to the other, then looked at the crime scene tape and frowned.

Okay, was it her imagination? Was he actually referring to Bette's eyes he couldn't say no to instead of the Sheltie's?

Still scowling, he paced, stiff-legged, back and forth beside the perimeter tape. "Can't get in to see the scene. Detective Spitz couldn't, or wouldn't, tell me squat about any physical or forensic evidence they'd found. I can't get a handle on the situation. I know one thing for damned sure. My sister wouldn't run off and leave her husband, much less her kid."

"No, she wouldn't." Bette began to pace alongside Alex. The dog heeled perfectly, as if she were competing at Madison Square Garden. Yes, she'd made the right decision. "She's the most direct person I've ever known. Never pulls any punches."

"You don't know what she went through to have Cody. It was three years of torture."

"Actually, I do." She watched him surreptitiously from beneath her lashes. Might as well be a stranger for all the attention he paid. "Jackie told me a bit about it. We'd share a Diet Coke over lunch and talk about stuff." She chuckled. "Okay, most of the time, I talked and she listened. Once in a while, she'd tell me what a dumbass I'd been about this or that—and she was usually right."

"Big sisters are always right. Don't you know?" His tone was flat. Any warmth she might've expected just wasn't there.

She gave a quick shake of her head and fluffed her hair. "I only have the one brother." Why hadn't he told her about *his* brother? They'd spent a lot of time talking that night in Music City.

Hunkering down to pet the dog, she looked up. "So how are we going to find her before…?"

His blue gaze was cool. Too cool. "There's no 'we' in this. I'm not here officially, but that doesn't mean I'm going to sit on my ass and wait for that idiot Spitz to find her. But *you* need to stay out of it. At the very least, you're a material witness. And if whoever took Jackie thinks you can ID him, you're in danger too. Go home. Lock the door and keep your head down."

"Not going to work." She shrugged, rose, and shot him a skeptical stare. "Besides, now I have a dog to walk."

"Right." He raked his hands through his hair. "Great idea. Make yourself a walking target. I can see it now—you're busy bending over picking up dog poop, and some jerk comes along, hops out, and snatches you off the street quicker than I can say son of a bitch."

She squared her shoulders. "Fine. You can stand here and piss and moan all day, but I've got to hit the pet store before I take this little girl home." She headed toward her car, then stopped and turned. "But when you're ready to let me help you… Well, you know where I live." She flipped her hair back, opened the car door, and scooted the Sheltie inside. Jackie would read Bette the riot act if she ever found out she transported Shadow without a cage or some kind of restraining device.

The riot act would be worth it if only they could find Jackie.


Alex shook his head and watched Bette drive away, all sassy and sexy and full of attitude. No, he hadn't been able to resist her on New Year's Eve. Dammit. She'd needed his help that night. Somehow he managed to resist his baser urges, which definitely included screwing her brains out.

She'd challenged him. But no way in hell was he getting a civilian involved—not any more than she already was. His warnings weren't just to hear himself talk. He meant every word.

As much as his stomach knotted at the very thought of what his sister was going through or had gone through already, he couldn't accept the conventional wisdom that she was already gone any more than he could accept the detective's notion that she'd run away.

He walked over to his rental car, got inside, and sat for a moment. This was nothing like what had happened to Andy. He'd made no promises to Jackie.

This wasn't *his* fault.

So why did it feel like it was?

There were so many things he could've done differently. He could've stayed closer to home instead of gallivanting all over the country like a modern knight in a black suit and tie. He couldn't deny his brother's death at fourteen had set the course for the rest of his life. It inspired him to join the FBI, driving him to achieve his goal of working on the Violent Crimes Task Force.

The Task Force cleaned up the slime. Worse than slime— predators of all types, especially those who preyed on children. Every time a case was solved, there were four more to take its place. A freaking never-ending struggle against evil.

This time, it was his sister who was missing. His sister, who held him when he cried himself sick for a solid year. Who told him it wasn't his fault. Evil had raised its ugly head here in rural upstate New York, his home stomping grounds. This time, he wasn't a powerless teenage boy. And this time, he would see to it the results were different.

# Chapter Five

Chew toys, a bed, a big bag of dog food, and a crate. For the moment, those would have to do. Bette surveyed her small apartment. The Sheltie didn't take up much room and seemed eager to please her new mistress. But why on earth had she taken on the responsibility of a pet?

No, that wasn't the question. Truth be told, she'd been dithering back and forth on the issue ever since she went to work at the veterinary clinic. The real question was, why now, when so much was unsettled?

Let's face it. She was a sucker for big brown eyes. Blue ones too, for that matter. Of the human variety.

The floorboards above her creaked. Shadow's ears pricked. Someone was in the house.

Probably Alex.

Might as well go up and help him get settled. She'd already called Cody's kindergarten teacher and explained the situation. She arranged for him to spend another night with the Crandalls, unless his dad came home in time. Where was Brad, anyway? Had he made it to the police station? More important, where was he when she tried to call him last night?

She left the apartment, carefully closing the door behind her to keep Shadow inside, then walked through the basement. She climbed the stairs leading to the first floor and knocked on the door. "Alex?" Without waiting for a response, she opened the door and entered the newly updated kitchen. "Hey! Double-O, need any help getting settled?"

*All right, don't answer. Jerk.* Who did he think he was, anyhow? Just because he was a high-and-mighty FBI agent and she was a mere vet's office manager didn't mean he could ignore her very existence.

"Alex?" She eased into the hall and tripped over one of Jackie's two Himalayans. "Sorry, puss. I know you're hungry." She'd fed them the night before, but with all the excitement over Jackie's disappearance, Bette had forgotten that little detail this morning. Heading back to the kitchen, she snatched a can of cat food from the cupboards and then grabbed up their respective food dishes. The other Himalayan minced back and forth on the granite countertop, wailing her complaint louder than an emergency siren while the male did his best to hurry Bette by slithering back and forth between her ankles.

Glad no one could hear, she baby-talked the two felines and scraped out Meow-meow Chow-mein into two equal portions.

The cat on the counter arched her back and hissed.

"Al—" She turned. Made out a tall form. In black.

Backed against the counter, she had nowhere to go. She raised her arms to protect her face—

A dazzling array of stars. Then nothing.


Alex drove up Gibson Street to his sister's address. He pulled into the driveway of a yellow three-story Victorian. His sister and her family had moved since the last time he was home into one of the houses in the historic district.

Sweet.

Obviously, Jackie made a good living as a vet, and Brad wasn't exactly a piker in the finance department, even if he did work from home. In addition to playing the stock market for a living, his brother-in-law was a damned fine cook, or so his sister said.

Wonder how Brad liked being interrogated by the local LEOs? The authorities always looked to the husband when it came to a missing wife. Images of how many of those women ended up gave him a wave of nausea.

He exited the rental car. Now, where would his sister have hidden a spare key? Colorful summer flowers filled the foundation beds, and heavy stone pots were situated on either side of the top step to the porch. He lifted the edge of the first one, and there was the key—might as well have left an engraved invitation for every burglar in town.

He pocketed the key and stepped onto the wide porch, which extended across the entire front of the house and wrapped around on the right. Baskets of ferns hung at intervals, their lacy fronds stirring in the slight breeze. He shut his eyes and imagined a tall, frosty glass of lemonade and Bette reclining on a chaise… Her large doe eyes filled with promise. Her full lips parted in a smile just for him. Nekkid as a newborn babe. Oh, yeah.

He shook himself. *Get your head outta your ass, man.* No way was he gonna get saddled with a relationship. The cottage, picket fence, and two-point-two kids wasn't for him. He was here to find his missing sister—end of story.

One kiss at Nashville International did not a future make. Never mind how it totally rocked him off his pins. Never mind Jersey had a lush mouth ripe for kissing. Never mind…

He slid the key into the lock, then realized the door wasn't locked. Damn. Of course, Jersey had her own key. He'd seen her silver Corolla parked around back when he'd pulled into the drive. More than likely she was the one responsible for the healthy green ferns. His big sis was good with animals of every size, stripe, and shape, but if you valued your life, you kept her out of the kitchen and away from anything green.

Opening the front door, he heard the sound of a slamming door. "Bette?" He headed down the hall toward where he assumed the kitchen and back door were located and ended up in a sunroom. More ferns. He batted the fronds away and looked out through the french doors along the back of the house. At the rear of the property, a tall figure in black ran and scaled the fence.

Adrenaline surged. Alex sprinted across the sunroom and blasted through the french doors. Bastard had a big lead. While Alex had his head wrapped around images of a certain troubling female, the intruder had taken his advantage and run like a damned jackrabbit.

Across the pavers and grass, Alex beat it to the fence, jumped, grabbed the top of the fence, and scrambled over. He landed on the other side, falling to his knees in the cinder-strewn alley.

"Son of a bitch!" He brushed off his knees and scanned for signs of the intruder. Bastard got away clean.

Whether or not he was involved in Jackie's disappearance—unknown. One thing for sure, coincidence or not, Alex didn't like it one damned bit.

Back over the fence. Not as easy that time. Adrenaline had propelled him before. Might as well see what the intruder got away with. Not that he'd know. Maybe Bette would. Or Brad, when he got home from the CPD.

Bette…

He ran for the house. Where was the basement entrance? Shit. Nothing visible outside. Must be inside. Why the hell hadn't he tried to come home more often? Why was he a stranger in his sister's home?

Because he'd gotten the hell out of town at the first opportunity. Left for college. Then the army and the Bureau. Sure, he'd called Jackie from time to time, but he was usually too busy to come home for holidays. No, too focused on his career. Too many bad guys, too little time.

Who was he kidding? His home town and his dead twin were forever linked. As long as he stayed away, he could focus on work.

But being home brought back the memories as sharp and fresh as the day his brother's body was found.

Once inside, he searched for the door to the basement. No, not in the hallway. Maybe the door downstairs was in the kitchen. Where was the freaking kitchen? House had to have a kitchen, didn't it?

Finally. He tumbled into the stainless wonderland and stumbled over...

"Bette?"

Kneeling beside her still form, he checked for a pulse. Strong and a little rapid. Afraid to move her, he dug out his phone and called 911.

What sounded like an entire fleet of ambulances and patrol cars arrived at the same time, their sirens blaring. Pain lanced through Bette's head and detoured through her eyeballs. Explosion of those necessary organs seemed imminent.

"Ow." She levered up to her elbow. "Make 'em shut up. My head feels like someone just hit me with a sledge hammer."

What seemed like a whole slew of uniformed men stormed into the kitchen. EMTs? Cops? Hard to tell exactly how many with her vision so blurry.

Alex brushed back a lock of her hair, examining her head for a wound with a reassuringly worried expression on both of his yummy faces.

"What happened?" one of the cops asked. "Did you get a good look at him?"

"He hit me. His face—covered. He was tall." She squinted in an attempt to make the blurry men stop weaving around. "Like you." She pointed at Double-O.

"What were you doing?" another cop asked.

"I came up to feed the cats. I turned around, and there he was.

He must've already been in the house when I got home."

"I drove up right after he hit her," Alex told the officer. "He must've heard me come in and ran out through the back, jumped the fence, and took off down the alley. I followed, but he was long gone by the time I made it to the alley. Must've had a vehicle waiting."

"And you are?"

"Alex MacGregor. This is my sister Jackie's house. I flew in from Chicago this morning. She's missing. Maybe you heard...Jackie Stinnett?"

"We heard," the first officer admitted.

Bette groaned, holding her head with her hands. "For Pete's sake, he's an FBI agent. He didn't hit me."

"Looks like she needs medical attention," one of the officers said.

Alex glanced over his shoulder. "They should be here anytime now."

Someone banged way too loud, for Bette's liking, on the front door. She squeezed her eyes shut and let out a low moan.

"In the kitchen," Alex called out.

She held her head with her hands. "Not so loud. Puh-leeze."

Two paramedics rushed into the kitchen. They set about taking her vital signs, shining lights in her eyes, and trying to convince her to spend the night in the hospital.

"No way." She shook her head vigorously—and regretted it. "I just need an aspirin and a little nap."

Alex's two faces were merging into one...almost. "You need X-rays—doesn't she, fellas?"

"Absolutely," the first paramedic said.

The second piped in with, "And someone to check her level of consciousness every hour."

"No rest for the weary—or is it the wicked?" She giggled. "So, a nap is out whether I'm in the hospital or here at home?"

"Yes, ma'am."

God, the EMT was so young and earnest it hurt. She sighed. "Well, does it take four of you guys to haul me to the hospital?"

"There are only two of us, ma'am." Again, so earnest and sincere.

"I *know* that. I was kidding." She rolled her eyes. "I just wanted to know if you were paying attention."

"She always like this?" one of them asked.

Frowning, Alex shrugged. "Pretty much. What you see is what you get."

"I'm in the room, and I'm not even close to being unconscious." She shot Alex a look of pure displeasure. "But he's right. I'm always like this. I hate hospitals."

"X-rays first. We'll discuss the rest later." Alex's unctuous tone was patronizing to the extreme, but she let it pass.

"You bet we will." She even allowed the EMTs to load her onto a stretcher and into the back of an ambulance. Alex started to climb in beside her. "Nope. You'll need your car to bring me back home."

This time, he rolled his eyes. "See what I mean?"

The EMTs were smart enough to keep their responses to themselves. Damned good thing too.

"I just adopted a dog today. And I can't leave her alone. She needs me." She leaned on her elbow and batted her lashes. "Al, baby, before you come pick me up, take her for a little walk. Okay? Don't want to come home to any surprises. Know what I mean?"

"*Al, baby?*" Alex mimicked under his breath, then nodded. "Had surprises enough for one day." But all this and walk her dog? Life sure had a twisted sense of humor.

He watched the EMTs shut the door and climb into the van. He turned to the uniformed officers. "We'll be back whenever the ER doc says she can come home." Alex shot a backwards glance at the house.

The older uniformed officer, a sergeant, nodded. "The detective oughta show up sooner or later. He'll have more questions."

"I'm sure he will, but first I have to walk the dog."

# Chapter Six

After what seemed like many hours, but in reality was only two, Alex brought Bette home from the ER. It took almost signing a contract in blood swearing he'd check her pupils and level of consciousness every hour on the hour and he'd bring her back immediately if she showed any changes.

Sheesh.

"I'm heading downstairs." Rubbing her head, she looked up at him. "I want to check on Shadow."

"You're supposed to rest. So you're gonna put up your feet and let me check on that dog." He tried to keep his tone pleasant, but why, today of all days, did she have to rescue a dog?

"I'll rest. But I'm sure she's hungry." At the mention of food, Bette's stomach growled loudly enough he could hear it. "Hell, *I'm* hungry."

Where in his job description did it include nursemaid and dog sitter? Still, Jersey was the last person to see his sister alive, and if he had to spend the night with her, he might as well have another go at interviewing her. "I thought you had breakfast at The Villager."

"That's just what I told the detective. I went to the office first, just in case there were patients showing up—which, as you saw, there were."

He held his hands up in surrender. "Okay. Okay. I'll call Pontillo's for a pie. What do you like?"

"Anything but—"

"I know…anchovies?"

She shot him a wan smile, nodded, and headed for the basement door. She paused and turned. "And some of those blister-your-mouth-and-stomach hot wings, okay?"

An hour and a half later, the dog had been fed and walked, again, somewhat uneasily, courtesy of Alex. He'd managed to live through the experience without a single snarl or dog bite. The Sheltie was curled up on a worn plaid sofa with her new mistress, who was watching an interior decorating show on HGTV, which begged the question, with Bette's design background, how could she put up with living in such dreary surroundings?

The Victorian's basement was huge, but her apartment was mostly subterranean. High up were short windows for light and air circulation. Still, how would she get out if there was a fire? The apartment didn't meet codes.

Okay. Not *his* problem.

A kitchen-slash-sitting room, a small separate bedroom, and a bath completed the clean and neat apartment. Except for the pizza-and-wings boxes sitting on the counter, everything was orderly.

He gestured with his beer can. "Ever bother you, living down here like a mole?"

Bette rubbed her arms and shook her head. "It's cozy, safe, and comfortable. Why would I need anything more?" She picked up her Diet Coke and drained it. "More, please. I'll need it if I'm not supposed to sleep tonight."

He got up to oblige his patient. Ironic. Here he was, a trained FBI agent, and he was playing nursemaid to a woman with whom he'd spent one miserable night. Not that it was her fault, just the situation. He handed her the can of soda, then picked up the flashlight. "It's time again, Jersey. Let me see your eyes."

The dog stirred and let Alex know he'd disturbed her afternoon nap by curling her lip. Not a growl, mind you. But he got the Sheltie's message. "Don't think she likes me."

Bette made a show of holding her lids open. "It's your imagination. She's just getting adjusted to a new situation."

"Say, are your pupils supposed to get bigger or smaller when I shine the light?" he asked, teasing her. They reacted appropriately and equally. God, he could really get lost in the depths of her gaze if he wasn't careful.

"Hmph."

"You'll do. Now, what day is it?"

"June fourteenth. The President is Barack Obama. Enough questions. I'm fine."

He turned off the flashlight and sat down on an overstuffed, sagging recliner. "I want to try an experiment. Just to see if you remember anything new."

"Okay." Her response was wary. Maybe she doubted his methods. Maybe she just didn't trust him.

"Shut your eyes and think back to last night. "What was the weather like?"

She let out a sigh, then complied. "Warmer than usual but starting to cool down."

"Was it dark?"

"Getting that way. Jackie and I worked on accounts after the office hours were over. There were a couple of post-op patients. We checked on them one last time. Nothing major."

"What about smells when you left the building?"

She laughed. "No smell of disinfectant. There was something blooming, and you could smell that. Not sure what it was—roses, maybe. Wait. The man's SUV—it was running hot. I smelled the burning oil." Her lids popped open. "Does that help?"

"It might if we find the SUV. Shut your eyes again."

"Okay." She drew the word out like a petulant child who needed a nap.

"Any chance you can remember the make? Anything about the vehicle—no matter how insignificant." His jaw clenched as he waited for Bette's response.

Please, let her remember something that'll help me find Jackie.

"It was black. I'm sure of that. And I know that's no help because the majority of SUVs are black." She sat up. "Lots of caked mud on the tires. Like he really used it off-road."

"How much has it rained this week?"

"Not much. Naples had a downpour Wednesday or Thursday, but we only had a sprinkle in town."

"What else?" Excitement grew in his belly. A possible location for the kidnapper. Now *that* was something. "What about the size? Mid or large SUV?"

"Large. Not as big as a Hummer, though."

"Chrome or markings?"

"No. Look, I just was anxious to get home. Actually, I offered to stay and help, but she laughed and waved me on."

"Could the man have been one of the regular pet owners? Are you sure you didn't recognize him?"

"No, I told you already he was wearing a hoodie. Give me a break. I've only been there six months. I may not have met all the regulars."

"Can you think of anyone who had a beef with Jackie? Maybe someone whose pet didn't make it?"

"No. Everyone loved her."

"Tell me again what happened after she went inside."

Bette let out a huff, then continued. "She went back and unlocked the front door. He followed her inside. That's the last I saw of her. Oh, God, Alex, if I'd just stayed with her." She ended her words with a wail.

Her shoulders started shaking, and before he knew it, she was crying her heart out. Feeling helpless, he reached over and patted her shoulder. "It's not your fault, Jersey. You couldn't have known something was going to happen."

Her sobs tore through him. How could this have happened in a quiet town like Canandaigua? How could someone have taken his sister? Why Jackie? Wasn't it enough his brother had died at the hands of some sick bastard?

From upstairs came the sounds of someone walking around and not being particularly quiet about it either. Had the intruder returned?

He glanced upward, then at Bette. Her eyes widened, her sobs hushed, and her body seemed to draw inward. Motioning for her to be quiet, Alex pulled his Glock from its holster on the side table and headed for the door. He paused. "If I'm not back in a couple of minutes, call 911."

She nodded, her expression contorting into a mask of fear. Her thumb went to her mouth, and she started chewing on the nail. Her other hovered over her cell phone.

"Don't follow me."

She let her thumb go to nail him with a drop-dead look. "Don't worry. I'm not stupid. I don't like guns, and I especially don't like them going off anywhere in my vicinity."

"Good," he said. "After I leave, lock the door."

She nodded that she would. Now it was time to find out who the freak was upstairs.

His weapon held at his side, he eased up the basement steps and tried to avoid making a sound. If the intruder had returned, he sure as hell didn't plan on giving the fucker a warning. He placed his hand on the knob. Waited. Listened. All he heard was the sound of his heart pounding like a bass drum. Mouth dry, he swallowed. Turned the knob.

Only to have a weapon shoved in his face by a bald man sporting a mustache. "Hold it right there!"

Alex eased down one step and lowered his weapon. "Detective Spitz," he said wryly. "Nice of you to stop by. Took you long enough."

"What are you doing here?" The detective's face was twisted

into what might be a permanent scowl. Behind him stood a tall and tense uniformed officer.

"Careful, Detective. You wouldn't want your face to freeze like that. As for what I'm doing here, this *is* my sister's house. I've been in the basement apartment with Bette Smithson. She was attacked—you knew about that, didn't you?"

Spitz lowered his weapon. "Of course I know about it," he sputtered. "This is my crime scene. I don't want you mucking it up."

"You could've given us a warning. As you might imagine, Bette's a little on the jumpy side."

"Don't have to give warnings." The detective waved a paper in Alex's face. "I've a search warrant, and I mean to search this house from top to bottom."

He reached for the warrant. Read it. Spitz was right. Some meathead judge authorized a full search of the entire house. "What's the point? Bette was in the kitchen when she was attacked, and my sister wasn't at home when she was abducted."

A smug sneer replaced the detective's scowl. "We only have Smithson's word for that."

So still looking at Bette. Idiots. "Have a warrant for her arrest?"

"No. But we might by the time this search is concluded," the detective said with an unnecessary amount of bravado. "Now, you and Miss Smithson will vacate the premises until such time as we release it as a crime scene."

"But *she* was attacked. Seen in the emergency room. Required X-rays and a CT scan. Do you think she bashed her own head? Don't forget, I saw the fucker take off down the alley behind the house. Now that she's received medical treatment, why don't you get off your ass and interview her about the attack?" He glanced around the kitchen. "There might be some evidence here in the kitchen. Don't see why you need to tear up my sister's entire home."

Honestly, did he have to tell them how to do their job?

"Appreciate if you would do as ordered. I'll take care of

instructing my men."

"Someone needs to." From upstairs, Alex could make out the sounds of drawers being dumped. He shook his head. Jackie would be so pissed off when she came home.

*If* she came home.

# Chapter Seven

Waiting in her apartment, Bette chewed her thumbnail and looked at her watch. It'd been over two minutes. Time to call 911. Her hands trembled as she punched in the numbers. Overhead, she could hear voices. No gunfire yet.

A sharp rap on her apartment door startled her and set her heart racing. The formerly quiet Sheltie barked, quick, loud, and fierce as Cujo.

"Bette? It's okay. Open up."

Alex. A rush of relief flooded through her. The Sheltie yapped and backed up at the same time. "Shh, it's all right," she said in a vain attempt to calm the dog, then ran to the door and flung it open. "You're all right. Thank goodness." She almost threw her arms around him but stopped just in time.

Alex stepped aside, revealing Detective Spitz and a uniformed cop behind him. "Afternoon, Miss Smithson. I have a search warrant for the entire house. You're required to vacate the premises until further notice."

Her chin dropped. "Vacate? Where am I supposed to go?"

"Not my problem."

She schooled her glance away from Alex's. Where she spent the night wasn't his problem, either, and she'd be damned if she dumped any more of her problems in his lap. "Fine. I need to pack a bag. And the dog. I have to take her things. I just bought them this morning, Detective."

The detective motioned toward the uniformed cop, who followed him downstairs with a jerk of his head. "Rollins, see she doesn't take anything of importance. One bag and the dog's stuff."

With his hands set on his hips, Alex loomed over the detective. "She's had a head injury and requires continual observation. You can't just kick her out into the street."

*Think again.* That's exactly what the detective was about to do. "Maybe I can get one of the other girls from the office to take us in." She glanced down at Shadow. Hadn't the poor little Sheltie been through enough without being uprooted from her new home? And now, just as she was getting somewhat settled, they had to move again.

"I'll find us a place," Alex volunteered. "Since I've been kicked out too."

"We'll be fine. We're not your responsibility—"

"Enough!" The detective shouldered his way by Alex and strode into her small sitting room with a swagger. "Just get your stuff together and get out."

Officer Rollins, a gangly redhead with a buzz-cut, followed the detective into the apartment and nodded. "Ma'am, if you'll just do as the detective says…"

"Fine." She glanced around and sighed. "What about Mr. Stinnett?"

"Don't worry about your boss's husband," Spitz said with a knowing leer. "He's down at the station house assisting us with the investigation."

"Just get your shit together, Jersey," Alex said through clenched teeth. "Let's get out of their way. We'll sort out the rest once we find a place to stay."

Alex's color was high, his movements jerky. Clear to see he was pissed off, not to mention powerless to do anything but follow the detective's orders. Come to think of it, she didn't do powerless well either.

She nodded and set about packing a bag under Officer Rollins's watchful but apologetic gaze.

"I'll get the dog's stuff," Alex volunteered.

"Her name's Shadow. Show her some respect. This is probably more upsetting for her than either of us."

A sheepish smile tugged at his mouth. "Yes, ma'am. I'll collect *Shadow's* belongings. My vehicle awaits, your majesties." He bowed with a grandiose sweeping gesture.

"That's a bit much," she said and rolled her eyes. "Don't forget the pizza and wings."

Yet once again Special Agent Alex MacGregor had leapt on his white horse and rescued the fair maiden. Dammit. Playing fair maiden to his brave knight was getting old, especially when it wouldn't be too long before he jumped on his charger—um, airplane—and took off for the Windy City.

But what about Jackie? Would he even stick around long enough to find his sister?

# Chapter Eight

Once they were settled in the Super 8 Motel on Eastern Boulevard, Alex reclined on one of the double beds. Bette and her dog occupied the other, just like last New Year's Eve in Nashville, minus the canine. He should've never lost his head and kissed her good-bye in the airport. But after spending that one long night with her, being a perfect gentleman while listening to the couple next door screw their brains out, he couldn't let her go without tasting her full lips just once.

What a fucking idiot he'd been.

He glanced at his watch and swung his feet to the floor. "Time for another check. Open those eyes."

She folded her arms across her chest and scowled, her perfect mouth in a sultry pout. "Talking to me or Shadow?"

"Give me a break, Jersey. Is this any way to talk to the man who found you a place to stay—not to mention your dog—at great expense, I might add?"

Her eyebrows lifted slightly at his exaggeration. "Wasn't that expensive. I was there, remember?"

Busted. "You have to admit conditions are better than the last time we shared a motel room."

She sat up, and the dog stirred. "It's all right," she said to the dog, then eyeballed him. "If you mean there's no blizzard raging outside and no one's fornicating at the top of their lungs right next door, then yes, I'd have to agree."

He shook his head. Leave it to her to mention the screwing couple. "How quickly some folks forget," he said, trying to tease her out of her bad mood.

"*Forget?* I didn't forget anything. Seems like a certain FBI agent promised to keep in touch. Maybe even come home soon for a visit."

He squeezed his eyes shut. Yeah, finally she'd brought up the elephant in the room. "I know. Sorry." Crap. What to tell her? He'd lost his head? Promises weren't his thing? "Right away, I was pulled into the middle of a case—a big one." Stalling for time, he cracked his knuckles.

She grimaced. "And then…?"

Man, she wasn't cutting him any slack whatsoever. "It ended. I got a promotion—my dream job—the Violent Crimes Task Force." Somehow, he had a gut feeling she wouldn't be congratulating him anytime soon.

"And it took your *sister* being freaking kidnapped to bring you home. Real close-knit family you have here, Double-O. How long's it been?"

"What's that got to do with anything?" He didn't want to admit once he'd left for college, he hadn't been home except for his adoptive parents' funerals. School, the army, and finally the Bureau were demanding of his time. But maybe if he'd been home—and make no mistake about it, Canandaigua was the only home he'd ever known—maybe his sister wouldn't have been abducted if he'd been there to protect her.

He gave a sheepish smile. "About the task force—my boss gave me forty-eight hours. If I don't wrap it up, they'll replace me."

She rose from the bed and set her hands on her hips. "Guess you'd better get off your ass and find your sister, then. Clock's a-ticking."

Anger and a mixture of fear flashed through him. "Like I don't know that. Sit down and let me see your damned pupils."

"My pupils are fine," she said hoarsely. "But you're giving me a major pain in the ass."

Alex took a step toward Bette. The dog jumped to her feet and began growling at him. Just how serious the creature was, he had no intention of finding out. He backed up. "Sorry. Didn't mean to upset her."

"Shelties don't like loud noises." She sat down and cuddled the dog like it was a baby. "Your sister's a vet. Don't you know anything about dogs?"

He clenched his jaw and said through his teeth, "She's the vet. Not me."

Realization dawned in her eyes. "You don't like dogs, do you?" She shook her head and shot him a disappointed, tight little smile. "I'd never trust a man who didn't like animals."

He walked over to the small fridge, pulled out a bottle of water, and twisted off the cap. "It's not I don't like 'em." He took a long swig, stalling. "It's a...phobia."

Her eyebrows shot up. "You're *afraid* of dogs? Like Shadow could do anything more than lick you to death."

Okay, show her the scars. She won't shut up until you do.

He walked over to the bed, pulled up his sleeve, and raised his right arm. "I was nine years old. I was mauled. One hundred stitches. That's right, one hundred."

"Aw, poor baby." She ran her fingers over his jagged scar. He shivered at the lightness of her touch and wished she wouldn't stop.

"Pit bull?"

"No." He downed half the bottle of water. Why couldn't she just shut the fuck up about dogs?

"Doberman?" She gave him a knowing smile.

"No, just drop it." He shoved his hands in his pockets and began to pace.

"Please don't tell me it was something like...a poodle." Triumph spread across her face.

Dammit. Jackie must've told her. "A *standard* poodle. Those are big dogs when you're nine. And this one was mean."

"What did you do to the poodle? It had to be your fault." If she was trying to keep from outright laughing at him, she wasn't trying hard enough. Her dark eyes glittered with amusement, and her lips twitched.

"All I did was cut across the Pearson's backyard, and she attacked me." He raised his arm again. "Did you even look at my scars? Believe me, they were no laughing matter."

"I'm sorry. I had no idea. Yes, your scars are awesome."

"You think it's funny."

"No, I'm very sorry for the little boy who was nearly lunch for a nasty old poodle. But you have to admit it's pretty funny for a grown man, an FBI agent, no less, who no doubt has stared down the barrel of a gun to get so bent out of shape when this darling little dog growls at him." More cootchy-coo baby talk for the Sheltie. Precious little understanding for him.

"It's a phobia brought on by a childhood trauma. Phobias by nature aren't logical."

"Sounds like Mr. Spock or some FBI shrink has had hold of you."

"Enough!" He headed for the door. "I'm going back down to the stationhouse. I'd like to see what they're getting out of Brad."

"Brad had nothing to do with Jackie going missing. I'd bet money on it. They were a happy couple. I lived with them for the last six months. I would know. At least, I think I would." Her expression grew pensive as she began chewing her bottom lip. Her chin trembled.

"Did I say I thought my brother-in-law was responsible? No. General wisdom says to go after the people closest to the vic—" He broke off, unwilling to come right out and call his sister a victim.

"She has to be all right. She just has to." Bette's face flushed, and she suddenly started to cry again, her shoulders shaking. "Never should've left her. My f-fault." The dog snuggled close to Bette and started licking her cheek, but at least the creature wasn't growling.

In spite of everything, he couldn't leave her like this. He closed the distance between them, sat on the bed beside her, and placed his arm around her shoulders. "It's not your fault." Her head rested against his chest. God, her hair smelled good. Fresh as new-mown grass after a spring shower. He shut his eyes and drank in her closeness. She felt so right in his arms. Why hadn't he come home sooner?

Because he'd wanted to avoid this very situation. Bette was different from the other women he'd dated. Feisty yet fragile. She needed someone who'd stick around and give her a real family. Someone who'd grill burgers and hots on the weekend and have his buddies over for poker parties.

And no matter how good and how right she felt in his arms, he wasn't that man.

"Bette," he said softly, aiming to extricate himself from the situation. She met his gaze, her lips parted. And damned if he didn't lower his head and kiss her. Soft. So damned soft. He lost himself in the moment of expectation and of promises unfulfilled.

Hungrily her body melded to his, and somehow they were lying on her bed. His hands were skimming under her T-shirt to her full breasts, and she was tugging at his belt. He grew hard and pressed against her thigh.

"No." She pulled away and started tucking her T-shirt back in her jeans. "Sorry. I lost my head for a second. Didn't mean to attack you like—" She sniffed, wiped her eyes, and said wryly, "Like an oversexed…poodle."

He sat up and scratched his head and tried to catch his breath. Good thing she'd come to her senses. Otherwise, he'd be crawling between her slender thighs right now. And in a heap of trouble. He cleared his throat. "Thought I was the one who attacked you. Thanks for clearing that up."

Her lips parted. No. Not gonna kiss her again.

He sprang off the bed and straightened the collar of his knit shirt. "Going down to the CPD. Be back in a bit." He stopped, turning toward her. "No, I'm not supposed to leave you alone—your head."

"Go on. I'm fine," she said breathlessly. "Maybe the detective has some news."

Before he could lose his willpower again, he nodded and beat it for the door.

She called after him, "Find out from Brad if I need to pick up Cody."

"Will do, Jersey." He shut the door to the motel room behind him and ran for his rental car, opened the door, and slid inside. Finding his sister was what really mattered. No doubt about it, Jersey was a major distraction.

Talk about a close call.


Bette lay back on the bed and shut her eyes, then let out the heavy sigh she'd held back until Alex was beyond hearing. She could almost feel his strong hands on her body. And smell the soap he'd bathed with. His lips on hers. The taste of coffee.

Shadow wiggled closer, nudging her pointy nose under Bette's hand. She stroked the Sheltie's long fur and told her, "You must be extra well-behaved around Alex, you know. He's a little dog-shy. It's up to you to teach him all dogs aren't like that big old bad poodle."

Thinking of Alex as a young boy brought Jackie's son to mind. She reached for the phone and called the Crandalls, where he'd spent the night, and learned Brad's sister had picked him up and would take care of him until his father was available.

Great. At least Cody was taken care of. One less thing to worry about. Another call to Jackie's locum tenens. Apparently, the cops had released the office as a crime scene, and all the overnight patients had been picked up at the Humane Society by their owners.

Jackie's locum worked only part time, but she agreed she would try to keep the office open as long as she could.

*Jackie. Jackie. Where are you?*

She shut her eyes and tried to concentrate. Nothing. No visual images. No messages through the mists of time and space. Obviously, her psychic powers were nonexistent. Hell, even a hunch would do.

If only she hadn't left her alone. Together they could've fought him off. Together they would've stood a chance. As it was, Jackie was likely facing a monster all alone.

There must be something she could do.

Had some unknown someone been stalking Jackie all along, just waiting for his chance to take her? Maybe. After all, Bette'd had a stalker in Nashville, and after meeting Alex that crazy New Year's Eve, he'd helped her get away from the creep.

He'd done more than offer; he'd been a lifesaver. He bought her a plane ticket and sent her to work for his sister. All Bette's money had been stolen by her stalker, the no-good SOB. And since moving, she'd put aside a little each week to repay Alex. This was the first time he'd been home since she first met him in Nashville six months ago. From the way he acted, he hadn't been home in years.

Strange. He seemed to really care about his sister. Why leave and never bother to come home for a visit? Was he so career-driven he could just forget about his family?

It wasn't as if his family was anything like hers.

Less said about them, the better.

# Chapter Nine

The Canandaigua Police Department wasn't accustomed to major crimes, and the lack of activity in the waiting room showed it. Alex showed his federal ID to the desk sergeant and asked to see his brother-in-law. They directed him back to an interview room. He stood in the hall and observed Brad through the two-way mirror.

His usually well-pressed brother-in-law looked like he could use a few hours of sleep. His eyes were a bleary red, and his five o'clock shadow darkened his cheeks. For the moment, he was alone, and his fingers beat a steady tattoo on the table top. The door opened, and Brad jumped as if startled awake.

Detective Spitz strutted into the small room and sat. "Come on, Stinnett. Give it up. What did you do with your wife? How'd it go, you got in an argument and lost your temper? That happens, you know. We all lose our tempers with our wives. Geez, they can really be bitches."

Brad straightened his back and said patiently as if speaking to a child, "I told you, Detective. I was in New York City at a conference."

"Yeah, about that. No one really remembers seeing you from about five o'clock on until we located you this morning. You had plenty of time to get back to your wife's office and do away with her. Hell, maybe you even offed her at home. Have some help from that hot little office manager of hers? Can't say as I blame you if you tapped some of that." With a knowing smirk, Spitz nodded. "Yeah."

Spitz's technique was right-on, and if the detective hadn't been talking about people Alex knew, he would have approved of the line of questioning. But he did know them, and tension gathered in his midsection. His jaw clenched.

"I didn't have anything to do with my wife's disappearance. I love my wife."

Beads of sweat collected on Brad's upper lip. All those telltale glances to the left. He had to be hiding something. But what?

"Okay, Brad," Spitz said, "just so you know, you're not leaving this room until you tell the truth. Where is she? Maybe you didn't kill her. Maybe we can still pull your ass out of the fire on this. Just tell me where you stashed her."

Brad buried his head in his hands. "I don't *know* where she is. I told you and told you. I need to get to my son, please."

"Should've thought about your son before you killed his mother." Spitz shook his head. "Men like you make me sick. Excuse me while I go out in the hall and puke."

The detective left the interview room and scowled at Alex. "You back?"

"I'd like to have a go at him. If he's done something to my sister, I want his ass." He punctuated his remark by hitting his palm with his other fist. He hadn't known his brother-in-law all that well, but what he did know was from high school. Brad had been a dog and a bully. Maybe he'd never grown out of it.

The detective nodded, his shiny head glistening under the lights. "Have at it. He ain't talking. They never do until we catch 'em in an outright lie."

"Thanks." Alex entered the interview room and took a bottle of water with him. "Here." He handed the water to his brother-in-law. Maybe it was time for a little "good cop," since Spitz's "bad cop" routine wasn't working. "Dude, that detective's a real asshole, isn't he?"

Relief flooded his sister's husband's face. "Man, am I glad you're here. They think I did something to Jackie. I was in frigging New York City."

"Yeah? Or were you in New York dicking around just like the detective said?" Okay, so maybe his good cop routine had already left the building. Dammit. He *was* too close to the case.

Brad's eyes widened, and he pulled at his shirt collar. "You know I'd never be unfaithful to your sister."

"How do I know something like that?" Alex leaned back and made himself comfortable. "Can't blame you. Most men wouldn't turn down a little strange if they're out of town and no one's the wiser." He spread his hands over the table like a dealer spreading cards. "Just tell 'em who you were with that night. Jackie never has to know."

Brad wiped the sweat from his forehead. "I'm a good husband. Instead of sitting down to another rubber chicken dinner, I went to the bar for a drink. Just to decompress. I-I never had any intention of meeting anyone."

*Bingo.* "But you *did* meet someone?"

"Yeah. Guess I had too much to drink. Anyway, we ended up in my hotel room."

*Sonofabitch!* "You fucked her?" Of course he did—cheating bastard.

"Yeah." Brad wiped the sweat from him forehead. "Turns out she was a pro."

"Not like you can put that on your credit card."

"Hell, no."

No proof. Just his no-good, cheating brother-in-law's word. "Tell me you at least got her name."

Brad's expression brightened. "Brandi."

"Dude, half the hookers in New York City go by Brandi. You gotta do better than that." He eyeballed his miserable excuse for a brother-in-law. "You better be straight with me." Not for a New York minute did he believe Brad was telling the truth, the whole truth, and nothing but the truth.

"I didn't have anything to do with Jackie's disappearance. I swear."

He leaned across the table, got in his brother-in-law's face, and lowered his voice. "You better not have, because I will kill your ass if you did."

Brad paled and pushed back. "I swear I didn't hurt her. She's the mother of my son. What kind of man do you think I am?"

Alex stood and slapped both his hands on the table, causing Brad to flinch. "The kind who cheats on his wife the first chance he gets." With that, he spun on his heel and left his sorry brother-in-law to stew in the interrogation room.

Outside, he shook his head and spoke to Spitz. "He's still holding something back. Are you running his phone records?"

"Warrant's in the works. But we'll get them." Spitz stroked his mustache. "Think he's got something on the side?"

"Wouldn't be surprised. He admitted to the hooker quick enough. Too quick. Could be more." Time to play nice with the locals. "Mind if I check out his story with the bartender on duty at the hotel that night?"

"Suit yourself." Spitz's expression brightened. "Don't mind at all. This is a small department, and sending someone to the city is a drain on time and manpower."

If Spitz thought Alex was going to leave Canandaigua long enough to interview the bartender, he was sadly mistaken. "You're not getting rid of me that easily, Spitz." He pulled out his iPhone, called the hotel, and talked to the bartender who was on duty the night before. After obtaining a copy of his brother-in-law's driver's license photo from the obliging Detective Spitz, Alex emailed it to the bartender. Unfortunately for Brad, the bartender couldn't corroborate his brother-in-law's presence the night before and obviously couldn't give any kind of description of the working girl he'd supposedly picked up.

Alex shook his head. "No alibi."

"No alibi. That does it," Spitz said. "I got enough to hold him forty-eight hours. "By then, we'll have some of the reports back on the evidence from your sister's house and office."

"Anything promising?" Man, what he wouldn't give to get his hands on his brother-in-law's computer. "How long before we can get back in the house?"

"I'll let you know."

"You took the computers?"

"Sure thing."

Alex smiled and nodded his approval. Even if he couldn't access the family's computers, at least the locals had the brains to confiscate them. "Bette's too?"

"Yeah, hers too."

Good thing he'd left his Bureau-issued computer in his rental car or the locals might've tried confiscating that one too. Not that it would've done any good. At least with access to the federal data bases, he could do some digging on his own. And the first thing he wanted to know was if there were similar cases logged into the Violent Criminal Apprehension Program or ViCAP.

Now what he needed was to get back to the motel and get to work. Bette was probably chomping at the bit to get back into her apartment, but if Spitz was halfway telling the truth, it would be at least a couple of days before she could settle in with her new four-legged companion. At the thought of the dog, Alex shivered. Involuntary, but there it was.


While Alex was out playing special-agent man, Bette took Shadow for a long walk along Eastern Boulevard, then toward Muar Lake. Ducks were swimming in the small man-made lake, and tall trees gave dappled shade and cool respite from the bright summer sun. A small shop sold frozen custard, but she couldn't take the Sheltie inside. Luckily, it had a walk-up window where she could buy a cone of the rich creamy treat. It'd been ages since she tasted frozen custard. Certainly couldn't find anything like it in Nashville.

She licked the cone of latte-flavored custard and sat on a park bench. Shadow gazed at her intently, not quite begging, but there was no mistaking what the small dog wanted.

Watching the ducks swim in leisurely circles was so relaxing. Bette's eyelids grew heavy.

Without warning, the hair rose on the back of her neck. The Sheltie pulled at the leash as if she saw something to chase. Bette straightened, whipped around, looking for whoever was watching her.

No one. At least no one she could see. But she hadn't imagined it. Oh, no. And Shadow had certainly reacted to something as well. Whether it was a scent or a sound inaudible to human ears, she didn't know. Clouds had covered the sun, turning the bright day into one of shadows. She shivered and rubbed her arms.

"Time to go, Shadow."

Somehow, the walk back to their room seemed a lot longer. More urgent. The gloom deepened, and fat drops of rain splattered on the concrete ahead of them. She picked up their pace to a jog, and the small dog managed to keep up through the downpour.

Bette's T-shirt and shorts were soaked by the time she and one very wet dog reached the motel. Just as they dashed inside the motel lobby and headed down the hall, Alex emerged from their room. "Where the hell have you been?"

She scowled. "What does it look like? I was walking Shadow— thank you very much." She rubbed her arms to abate the wet chill. "I'd like to get dry, if it's not too much trouble."

He shook his head but unlocked the door and let them inside. "I was afraid someone might've grabbed you too."

She brushed past him, then turned. "Grabbed me? With this ferocious guard dog?" She held back a shiver. Should she tell him about the weird feeling someone was watching her? More likely it was just her imagination.

She walked into the bathroom and grabbed a towel, then bent down to dry the Sheltie's fur. Once she'd gotten Shadow's coat as dry as possible, she dried the dog's dainty paws, one by one. She straightened and reached for another towel.

"What're you holding back?" Cocking his head to the side, Alex stood with his arms folded across his chest. "What happened while you were gone?"

"Who said anything happened?" Damn. Was the man a mind reader?

"Your expression. Body language. Eyes averted. Hesitation. Come on, Jersey, spill it."

Still holding the towel, she straightened, set her hands on her hips, and glared. "Is this how you interrogate suspects? I really need to get out of these wet clothes." She wrapped the towel around her head, turban style.

"Don't change the subject."

"It's silly…really."

She walked over and plopped on the bed, patting the bedspread beside her for the dog. "We walked down to Abbott's for a frozen custard." She bent and untied her shoes, then toed them off.

"You walked? Why didn't you drive?"

"It's not that far. Besides, Shadow needed some exercise, and so did I, for that matter."

"Okay, you picked a hot afternoon for a walk along one of the busiest streets in town. Go on."

"I was sitting on one of the benches behind Abbott's and just relaxing. Enjoying the shade and watching the ducks. Then the hair on my neck prickled. At the same time, Shadow alerted to something. I couldn't see anything, so I figured she'd seen a squirrel." She gave a self-conscious laugh. "Anyway, I decided we might as well move along and get back here. So, did you see Brad?"

"You just changed the subject again. First of all, you're not to go anywhere without me until this is settled. And yes, I saw my brother-in-law. His alibi hasn't checked out—not yet, anyway." He couldn't bring himself to tell her the truth about what her boss's husband had been up to in the city.

Her brows drew together in a frown. "I'm sure someone must've seen him. You just have to keep trying."

*Yeah, right.* Alex shook his head. "Are you sure there haven't been arguments? Over money or another woman?"

She let out a huff. "I'll have you know I keep to myself, and I *don't* meddle in their business. Now, I'm not saying there's never a cross word, but they're few and far between. Anyway, why are you so pissed off at Brad? I don't believe for a New York minute that he would hurt her."

"I don't have the luxury of your faith in the man. The husband is always a suspect. I've seen cases, time and time again. A woman disappears, and come to find out the husband's unfaithful. And what do you know, he can't prove his alibi. It's a freaking cliché. No, it's worse than a cliché. Nine times out of ten, it's murder." He paced back and forth, his long strides covering the length of the room.

She hopped from the bed, crossed the room, and rested her hand on his shoulder. "I'm sorry. I wish I were more help."

At her touch, he stopped pacing, sank down on his bed, and buried his face in his hands. "It's my fault. I should've come home more often. History's repeating itself—that's the worst part." His blue eyes clouded with despair. His body seemed to shrink.

"What do you mean?"

He chewed his bottom lip for a moment before speaking. "Jackie and I—we had a brother. My twin. He's dead. That was my fault too."

"What? How? But only if you want to tell me. Remembering is obviously painful for you." She wanted to reach out, touch him, but couldn't quite bring herself to do it.

"We were fourteen. At the movies. Can't for the life of me remember what was showing." He shook his head. "Andy liked the movie. I didn't. I went out for sodas and promised him I'd be right back. But there was this girl I liked, playing one of the video games. We got to laughing and cutting up. We left the theatre and walked down to the strip mall for ice cream. When Mom came to pick us up, Andy never came out of the movie theatre."

"What happened?" Then she remembered Gloria Mason's passing remark in the office parking lot, and even the sinking sensation in the pit of her stomach didn't quite prepare her for the grisly details.

"Three months later, they found his body on Bristol Mountain. He was still wearing his ID bracelet. One just like mine. If I hadn't run off and left him in the movie, he'd be alive today."

"It wasn't *your* fault. Did they ever find who killed him?"

"Nah. Police figured it was a predator. Another kid had disappeared in similar circumstances a couple years earlier. Had to be someone local. And really careful."

"I'm so sorry." Helplessness flooded her. More than anything, she wanted to take him in her arms and give him the comfort he needed. Uncertain how he'd take such a gesture, she held back. It was a quick way to get rejected, and that was the last thing she needed to worry about right now.

"It would've happened anyway." She took a deep breath before continuing. "What I mean is that this predator would've taken someone that day or another day. Just like whoever took Jackie could've taken me just as easily. I don't know if you call it fate or karma, but that's just how it is. You said yourself it wasn't my fault Jackie was kidnapped, but I understand how the responsibility weighs on you. It weighs on me too."

"I'm worried he might come back for you." He took a breath. "At the very least, you're a witness."

The realization that Alex was worried about her hit her.

"Witness? That's rich. The police think *I'm* involved, except when they're thinking she ran away on her own. What about Brad? Do you really suspect him?"

"I have to consider him. Thing is, if I'd been around more, I might have a better feel for the guy as he is now. When I was a freshman, Brad was a senior. He was a jock, your basic prick, and a bully, especially to freshmen."

"I see." Had to be some bad history there. And as much as she wanted to comfort him with more than words, she held back. "Surely everyone understood why you couldn't be home more. You're working for the FBI. You're taking down bad guys." Realization hit her. "Your brother—that's why you joined the Bureau, isn't it?"

He nodded, his mouth twisted into a wry half-smile. "Have to admit it gives me satisfaction when we close a case and have a suspect in hand."

A cell phone chimed. "It's mine," he said and pulled it from his belt. "MacGregor." He paled, nodded several times, then set the phone down. He looked at her, eyes wide. "My nephew—he's gone." Cursing, he jumped up and threw the cell across the room.

"How? I thought he was with Brad's sister."

"Don't know, but I'm sure as hell going to find out. Come on. I'm not letting you out of my sight."

She pulled at her half-dry top. "Give me a second to change into some dry clothes. How long will we—" She broke off and looked at the Sheltie.

"Bring her. Just keep her on the leash and out of the way."

"Out of *your* way, you mean." In spite of her snarky words, her mind raced ahead and reeled with the possibilities. Jackie's son was only six years old. "I'm sorry. That was a really stupid thing for me to say. We've got to get over there."

# Chapter Ten

By the time they reached the tree-lined street where Brad's sister lived with her family, the rain had let up, and it looked like every squad car in Canandaigua was on the scene. Alex parked the rental car as close as possible, almost a block away. "Might as well walk the rest of the way." He eyeballed Bette and the Sheltie as they emerged from the passenger side. "I doubt they'll let us in with *her*."

"I can't leave Shadow in the car. It's too hot. I'll wait outside. No problem." There was grit and determination in her tone. No doubt she would.

How someone could let a six-year-old boy get taken, he'd never understand. Wasn't it enough his sister was missing? Did the fucker have to come back and take her kid too? All his training told him this situation wasn't going to end well. His stomach cramped with the images that came to mind. He knew too much. Had seen too much. Too much to sit back and let the locals handle it.

"Hey, you there with the long legs, wait up!"

He slowed his pace, turned, and saw Bette puffing and running with the Sheltie on the leash. "Sorry," he muttered, unable to wrap his head around it all. Here he was, on the verge of losing everyone he cared about. His nephew. His sister. Dammit to hell, it *was* too much.

Bette's arm slid around his waist, offering him a measure of comfort. "I'm so sorry," she said softly. Her eyes shone with unshed tears. "I don't know what else to say or do."

He gazed down at her. "It helps. You know—just—uh, that you're here." He swallowed the boulder-size knot in his throat and realized he meant it. Having Bette here helped on several levels.

But what he wouldn't give to have his task force team on site. Maybe now the locals would realize how understaffed they were and call in the Bureau.

They reached the crime scene perimeter; he showed his badge and ID. The young patrol officer on crowd control nodded and allowed him through but not Bette. He nodded that he understood. "I don't like leaving you alone," he told her, finishing silently because he knew better than to say it out loud, with only a skittish little dog for protection.

Surely, with all the uniforms swarming over the area, she'd be okay. "Stay close," he warned.

She nodded and appeared almost as skittish as her dog. Her gaze flickered apprehensively over the crowd of neighbors drawn by all the police activity. "Guess I'll be okay with all these men in blue around." She chewed nervously on her bottom lip.

"Just stay close." It was doubtful the kidnapper was in the crowd of lookie-loos. Hell, no, he was too busy kidnapping Alex's family members. Even though he was reluctant to leave Bette behind, Alex strode up the brick walk and onto the porch. He stopped at the door and glanced over his shoulder. She was still in sight and talking to a patrol officer.

Opening the front door, he took a deep breath and tried to relieve the tension that had his shoulders tied in knots. He stepped into the living room. Brad's sister Corrine—he remembered her from high school—sat on the couch, bawling her eyes out, while none other than good old Detective Spitz sat across from her, asking questions and taking notes.

Not the best Canandaigua had to offer—or was he?

Alex ran his hand through his hair and clenched his jaw. No point in pissing the locals off any more than he already had. "Detective."

"Agent MacGregor."

Corrine's face brightened. "You called in the FBI? Oh, thank you. Thank you."

"I'm not here officially. I'm—uh, Jackie's brother."

"Of course. I remember you now," she said with a sob. "But you can still help us, can't you?"

"I'll do what I can." He turned to Spitz. "Surely, now there's a child missing…?" He took a deep breath before continuing. "If you say the word, I can have a team here from the Buffalo field office in a couple of hours."

Spitz shook his head. "Way I see it is this—we have an unfaithful husband and a pissed-off wife. She pulled a disappearing act, and now she snuck in the backyard and grabbed her kid. Abduction by a custodial parent. Not a case for the Bureau."

"Then why are you holding my brother-in-law?"

"We aren't. Released him as soon as I heard about the kid being taken."

"Then where is he?"

"I'm here, Alex." His brother-in-law stood in the doorway to the dining room. He was haggard, still in need of a shave, and his eyes were red from lack of sleep. "The police think Jackie's run off with someone," Brad said. "Just goes to show the husband's always the last to know. She's taken Cody somewhere, and as soon as she tires of her boyfriend, she'll drag her ass home and bring the boy with her. Well, she's got another think coming if she thinks I'll take her back after this. I'll sue for custody. Screw her!"

How could anyone be so blind to the truth? Make it two blind men. "What about the man who showed up as she was closing?"

Brad shrugged. "I agree with the police. That dude was her boyfriend."

Before Alex knew it, he closed the distance between them and slammed his sister's husband into the door. He shoved his forearm against the lying bastard's throat. "You son of a bitch! You're accusing *her* of screwing around? Just because you are doesn't mean she would."

"Stop! You'll kill him!" Corrine screamed, then jumped up and tugged on Alex's arm. "Detective, make him stop!"

"Come on, Agent." Spitz grabbed Alex by the shoulders and pulled him off Brad. "Wouldn't want to arrest you for assault. Not that I really blame you."

Alex tamped down the urge to finish the job, released the chokehold, then took a step back.

Brad coughed and gagged, then said, "You're a crazy man. I didn't do anything to your precious sister." He sucked in a deep breath, rubbed his throat, and glared at Alex. "Mark my words, *she* took Cody. And if I'm not mistaken, that's a crime in this state. When you find my wife, I want her arrested. Understand me, Detective. I want my son back, and I want her charged with kidnapping."

Alex clenched his fists and took a step forward. "Shut your mouth. My sister and her son are missing. That's all we know." He glared at Spitz. "Don't care about your theories. Two people are missing. Two people I care a whole hell of a lot about." He turned back to his brother-in-law. "No matter what you think, they're in danger until proven otherwise." His head pounded as if it might explode. He gasped for breath. Never had he been mad enough to kill someone, but Brad Stinnett had crossed the line and pushed every button.

That's what Alex got for staying away so long. His sister never complained about her husband, but a deep undercover assignment had kept Alex from coming home for their wedding. He assumed if his sister thought enough of Brad to marry him that he'd grown out of his hound dog ways. Guess not—once a prick, always a prick.

Stinnett held up his hands and backed into the wall. "Detective! Are you just going to stand there and let him assault me?" When Spitz's only response was a shrug, he said, "That's how it's going to be, is it? All you law-enforcement types stick together. All right. I don't care who does it. Someone just find my kid."

Alex sucked in a deep breath and squared his shoulders. "Why don't you tell me what you did to Jackie? Where is she?"

"And I already told you. I don't *know* where she is!"

Alex leveled his gaze on the detective. "Are you calling in the Bureau now or not?"

Spitz stood, shook his head, and stuffed his hands into his pockets. "That'd be a no."

"Then I'll find them myself." He clenched his fists, mainly to keep from assaulting the useless detective.

"Don't you go messing around. I'll arrest your federal ass if you interfere in my investigation."

"From what I can see, you don't have an investigation. At best, all you have is a theory"—he turned to Brad's sister—"and pardon me, ma'am, for saying so, it's a piss-poor one."

With that, he stomped from the house. If he didn't try to find his sister and nephew, no one would. It was readily apparent the local authorities weren't up to the task.

Outside the yellow crime tape, Bette stood on the sidewalk and relished the deep shade from the old trees lining the street. Jackie's sister-in-law lived in a lovely gray bungalow trimmed in white with black shutters and a red front door. Two spiral topiaries were positioned on each side of the front door. A herringbone brick sidewalk led from the street to the front entrance, as well as circling around the house. White rose bushes lined the foundation, while a Japanese maple with delicate lacelike leaves provided a punch of color.

Remembering she'd almost graduated from interior design school in Nashville, she sighed. Once, she'd hoped to have such a home. Small enough for one, but well-planned and designed and decorated to her specs. But an annoying stalker in the form of a PI had driven her from her home of the last eight years, Nashville. Now, her basement apartment was more than sufficient.

Meeting Alex that miserable New Year's Eve when she was on the run from a stalker had been a happy accident. She'd checked into a low-rent motel on Murfreesboro Road and snagged the last vacant room in a snow storm. The AC unit had leaked and flooded her room. That had been the last straw. She'd boo-hooed and basically pitched a hissy fit. A loud one. Enter one super-agent, Alex MacGregor. He'd knocked on her door and invited her to share his room. The rest was history.

All of which showed what a great guy he was. He didn't deserve all this pain. And having to stand out here on the street, unable to know what was going on inside the house was chafing her shorts. He needed someone at his side.

He needed *her*.

She looked down at Shadow. This precious dog was the best creature. Patient. Calmer than most Shelties. And, if she wasn't mistaken, in need of a walk.

She led Shadow down the street and waited until the Sheltie found just the right spot.

Dammit. Who could've taken Cody? It was too much to believe in coincidence. Bound to be the same person who'd attacked her in Jackie's kitchen. The same one who'd taken Jackie.

Turning around, she led the Sheltie back to the yellow tape in time to see Alex emerge from the bungalow. At the sight of his long-legged figure, her heart sped up. He was unbelievably handsome—tall and lean, tanned, with intelligent blue eyes. Uh-oh. His never-failing smile—the one that warmed her all the way to the pit of her belly—was missing. Not a good sign.

She watched him scan the crowd of onlookers, presumably looking for her. She waved to get his attention. There it was, a quick flash of his familiar smile.

A rush of heat made her insides twitch. Not the best time to think about that. They were living in too-close quarters to let her hormones run amok.

Yet running amok they were.

He hurried toward her, his long legs closing the distance. His frown was back.

"What's wrong?" she asked as soon as he ducked under the crime scene tape.

He took her by the arm. "The local LEOs are useless. We're getting the hell out of here." With the Sheltie trotting behind them, they strode down the sidewalk toward his rental car while he filled her in on what had happened in the bungalow.

Disbelief sank in and shook her badly enough she had to latch on to the car to steady herself. Alex opened her door, and she smiled at him gratefully but stopped long enough to put Shadow in her crate in the backseat. She then eased onto the front seat. Once Alex was seated, she said, "Brad's no longer under suspicion. Okay, I agree with that. I don't care what he was up to in the city. But they think Jackie took Cody?" She gave her head a vigorous shake. "Unbelievable! So what's our next move?"

"Not a lot we *can* do. If you have to know the truth, keeping an eye on you and that ankle biter sort of hampers my investigation."

"Well, too bad." She wrinkled her nose. "People often tell me I'm very observant. I have a good eye for detail—it's part of the design thing."

"Oh, yeah?" He raised a single eyebrow. "Too bad it wasn't kicking in the other night at the clinic."

"No fair," she huffed. "It was getting dark. I'm much better in daylight. You'll see." If it wasn't such a dire situation, she'd pop his shoulder with her fist like she did her brother when his teasing hit home. While Alex might treat her and tease her like a sister, her feelings for him weren't sisterly at all.

He jabbed the key in the ignition, and to hide her flustered feelings, she reached back and stroked Shadow's head through the crate. "If you want to drop us back at the motel, just say so."

He cast a look of exasperation in her direction. "Not leaving you alone. No matter what Detective Spitz thinks, Jackie's in trouble, and now so's Cody." He pulled out into the light afternoon traffic and headed in the direction of Jackie's clinic. "We'll check out the office and parking lot. See if they missed anything."

"Sounds like a plan." She nodded. "Shadow can help too. She's got a good nose."

His eyebrow shot up again. "Oh, *right*. Thought she might have some bloodhound in her." The irony in his tone said just the opposite.

"Don't dismiss Shadow just because she's a pretty little thing. All dogs have a wonderful sense of smell." She thought for a moment, then added, "Of course, it's true bloodhounds have the best noses. What about other search-and-rescue teams in town? Maybe one that isn't necessarily affiliated with the authorities? There's a trainer who brings his dogs to Jackie. He sells his dogs far and wide to different police departments. He might give us a hand. For Jackie."

"We need to get something of hers so the dogs can get her scent. Clothing would be the best."

"We need to get back in the house."

"And the house is still off limits."

"But *I* can get in, if we wait until after it's dark."

"A covert op. I like it." He shot her a wolfish grin, but the serious glint never left his gaze. "Lead me to this dog person."

# Chapter Eleven

With Bette riding shotgun and the dog safely stowed away in her wire crate in the backseat, Alex drove past rolling green hills to a farm west of town. In normal situations, the peaceful surroundings would lower his blood pressure and chill out his grim mood.

"Turn at the next mailbox on the right." Bette pointed to a large red mailbox shaped like a barn.

Responding with a quick nod, he turned into the paved drive she indicated.

"The kennels are around back. Jackie and I did a house call late one night when one of his dogs got into trouble. Almost had to do a C-section by candlelight when it started storming and the lights in the barn went out."

An image he could've done without. He winced.

They drove around an enormous, two-story house and parked in back. A large barrel-chested man strode out to meet them with a wide smile and his hand outstretched. "Henry Rigby," he said. "Bette." He nodded. "Good to see you again. Surely is awful about Dr. Stinnett. Anything I can do to help find her, I'll do it."

Alex grasped the man's hand. "Thanks so much. The local authorities are barking up the wrong tree—that's my contention, anyway. I'd like you and one or two of your best dogs to check out the parking lot and the office. That's where it happened." Whatever *it* was.

"Thought sure they'd call out the canine officer from the sheriff's office. You sure they haven't?"

Alex shook his head and swallowed the bitterness threatening to overcome him. "The authorities' latest theory is that she was upset with her husband and arranged her own disappearance, including taking her son."

"Kind of extreme, if it were true, and I don't believe it of her." He wagged his head in the negative. "No one who knows her would consider such a thing. She's dedicated to her work and all the animals she cares for." Rigby motioned for them to follow. "Only have six dogs right now. Four are young, in early stages of training. My best bitch is ready to whelp. That leaves one, but he's a fine fellow. He's found more than his share of lost hikers and campers. We'll need a sample of Dr. Jackie's scent."

"We'll have that by tonight," Alex said. "Police have cordoned off the house. Even though she wasn't taken from there." They crossed the pea-gravel drive, and he heard the loud baying of the dogs long before they reached the kennels. Steeling his resolve, he did his best to hold back the shiver sliding up his spine.

The Sheltie gave a series of sharp barks but looked as if she'd as soon run as stay. Bette shushed the dog and scooped her up.

*Good, one less canine running around.*

Each dog had its own run and a dog house. They stopped before one. A large, mournful-looking bloodhound emerged, but his tail wagged, and, although he barked, the creature didn't seem overly aggressive.

Alex swallowed hard. "You'll help us, then? Handle the dog?" There must've been a note of trepidation in his tone or some other subtle cue, because Rigby gave a bark of laughter.

"No worries. This dog's too valuable to hand over to an amateur."

Schooling his response to keep from looking like a cowardly dipshit, Alex nodded. "Good enough. Appreciate your assistance. More than I can say." He cut his gaze to Bette, who was crouched beside the dog's run and already talking baby talk to the bloodhound. But the squirming Sheltie didn't appear any happier being that close to the bigger dog than Alex was.

"I'd better walk her back to the car before she gets any more agitated." Then with a mischievous grin, Bette said, "Unless *you* want to hold her?"

*Smart ass.* "I'll pass." He watched the mesmerizing sway of her hips as she walked back to his rental. Almost losing himself. Almost forgetting why he was here. What the hell was he playing at? He had no business leering after her that way. Dammit. He needed to focus. As for his dog phobia—that would have to wait.

Rigby chuckled. "Cute little gal, isn't she?"

"Uh, yeah." He gave a nervous laugh. "Yeah, she is." *So busted.*

They set a time to meet early the next morning. Rigby would bring Duke, short for Albemarle's Duke of Chiverton, and they would begin a real search for his sister and her son. Alex shook his head at the hound's fancy name but kept his opinion to himself.

Clouds rolled in and promised a threat of rain while Bette waited with Shadow in the rental car. *Not more rain.* Wouldn't that make tracking Jackie all the more difficult? Seemed like everything that could go wrong was. Damn Detective Spitz for not organizing a search right away. Valuable time had been lost. Time Jackie and her son couldn't afford to lose.

She'd watched way too many of those forensics shows, both the fancy prime-time and the grittier reality-based ones. The thought of Jackie lying dead in some field left a knot in her throat. And little Cody? Tears welled in her eyes. She couldn't bear the thought of something happening to that darling child. Big blue eyes like his mother's. A thatch of pale blond hair with a mind of its own, no matter how often Jackie damp combed it. The kid possessed a smile guaranteed to melt the heart of any sensible person. But this kidnapper wasn't sensible, was he?

And she was more of a hindrance than a help to Alex's efforts to find them. Oh, he'd been polite enough, even if it was plainly obvious he'd just as soon get rid of her *and* her dog at the first opportunity.

A loud thump on the fender startled her. She jumped. "What?"

"You looked as if you were a million miles away," Alex said, his expression grim as he stood gazing down at her. "That mutt's not much use as a guard dog. She didn't even bark when she saw me coming."

She crossed her arms over her chest, glared, and added a touch of heat to her response. "That's because she knows you. And she's *not* a mutt."

"Right. Looks to me like someone left good old Lassie outside in the rain and she shrank." He opened the car door and eased inside. "Ready for a B and E?" he asked with a look of anticipation in his eyes.

Insulted by his disparaging Shadow's lineage, she balled her fist and jabbed his shoulder. "You're seriously pissing me off, Double-O."

"Sorry. Who knew you'd go all mama bear on me?"

She raised her fist again. He turned and grabbed her wrist and wouldn't let go. "Don't hit me again. That would be a federal offense, assaulting an agent."

She struggled and gazed into his eyes. No anger there, just something indescribable. Her mouth went dry as sandpaper, and her heart hammered. "What? Would you really charge me?"

"I might." He swallowed hard enough she saw his Adam's apple jerk.

In the backseat, the Sheltie whined. Bette glanced over her shoulder. "It's okay." She faced Alex again. "Stop it. You're scaring her."

He gave a small shake of his head but released her wrist. "You and that dog."

"She happens to need me." Bette reached into the backseat and stuck her fingers through the crate. "Don't you, sweetie?"

"How do you know *I* don't need you more?"

Her eyebrows shot up at his suggestive tone, but she chose to ignore it. Besides it might just be wishful thinking, and no way would she risk his rejecting her again. "You might need my help for this upcoming B and E, but most of the time, you act like I'm a major pain in the ass."

A quick eye roll, then he nodded. "Oh, you are—no doubt about it."

About that moment, her stomach growled loud enough Shadow heard it and whined. "Think we could get something to eat? It won't be dark for a while yet."

"Changing the subject, are you?" he said somewhat gruffly. "Is Charlie's still there? I could sure use one of their thick burgers."

"Not changing the subject. Not like I can make my stomach growl on cue. I'm sure Shadow's hungry too. And yes, Charlie's is still there."

"What about her? I'm not taking her along. She'd be bound to bark and alert the neighbors."

"She'll be all right for a while in the motel room. We can move her crate from the car, and with some chew toys, she'll be content. Probably even go to sleep while we're breaking into Jackie's."

"Having a dog's as bad as having a kid."

"Not so. With a dog, you receive unconditional love. You don't get that from your kids—not after they hit puberty."

"Hmph."

"You don't like dogs. I bet you don't like kids either."

Alex clenched his jaw and turned on the ignition. "Let's get something to eat. This conversation is going nowhere fast. Whatever you think of me, I don't hate kids. I just don't plan to have any. Or get married." He whipped the car around and headed back to the highway.

"Thanks for spelling that out, Agent MacGregor. I assure you I wasn't going to propose anytime soon."

"Dammit, Jersey. I didn't mean to imply you were. It's just I have a difficult job, and—"

"A family would get in your way," she finished for him.

"Exactly."

"Surely all agents don't feel that way?"

"Can only speak for myself. Some do. Some don't. I have two friends from the Bureau who're married. My pal Jake is with the Behavioral Science Unit, and his wife Caitlin retired. They already have one rug rat, and he has a teenage daughter from a previous relationship. They live in Georgetown."

"So they made some adjustments. But they *are* making it work, right?" He kept his gaze on the road and away from her.

"He gave up what he loved doing best—undercover work. Being a part of the Violent Crimes Task Force in a major field office has always been my goal. I don't want to give it up, and I wouldn't want to endanger my family...if I had one. I like being alone. Not answering to anyone but the Bureau."

"Again, message received." She chewed her bottom lip and carefully considered her next words. "But your friends, they're happy? And is giving up something for someone you really love a hardship?"

"Don't know, since I have no plans to do so."

"I'm willing to bet my next week's paycheck that you've never been in love, have you?"

"What's that got to do with anything?"

"If you ever fall in love, you'll know."

Dammit. What had she just said? Would he think she was in love with him? She wasn't. Not really. Inability to keep her gaze on the street in front of her and not on him wasn't any kind of indicator. True, the man was hotter than Pontillo's wings. And what being around the man did to her libido didn't bear mentioning.

But she most assuredly was *not* in love with him.

Apparently, he decided to ignore her comment about falling in love. They fell into a somewhat tense silence as they sped past the rolling hills and valleys where a fine mist gathered and eddied among the trees. She shivered and folded her arms across her chest. The scene was just a little too eerie for her taste. Where were Jackie and Cody? Were they at least somewhere warm and dry?

They rounded a curve, crossed the railroad tracks, and before them lay the city limits of Canandaigua with its quaint turn of the century houses and well-kept yards. Bette's stomach growled again.

Alex turned right on Main and headed south toward the lake. "Charlie's still okay with you?" He moved over into the left-hand lane.

"Yeah, fine...whatever. Just leave us at the motel. I'll get Shadow settled for the evening."

"Suit yourself." He turned left on Eastern and drove past the lake and park. Bright summer flowers bedecked the street as did one of the famous decorated horses scattered around town. Wind had whipped up whitecaps on the lake. She shook her head. Likely a storm would wash away any remaining scent trail. More and more, it seemed as if fate was against them finding any trace of Jackie and her son.

# Chapter Twelve

After leaving Shadow at the motel, Alex suggested they should go to Jackie's first and eat later. Alex stood in the alley behind his sister's house and pulled up his hood. Rain had run down his neck, leaving his shirt a soggy mess. Jersey stood beside him, hunched over and shivering. "Sorry," he said. "Bad night for a covert break-in."

Jersey shot him a brave, if damp, grin. "Either that or it's a good one since it's unlikely the cops—I mean officers—will be sitting anywhere but in their patrol cars."

"Good point." What was it with her and law enforcement? Most people didn't have to struggle to call them by their proper designation. Question for another time. Right now, they needed to get inside.

"You have a key, right?" he asked. "Spitz made me hand over the spare one."

She sniffed and wiped the rain from her face. "Yes. I always keep an extra key 'cause I'm always losing them. Can we get a move on before I drown?"

"I'll give you a boost over the fence." He bent down and laced his fingers together. She set her booted foot in his hands and grabbed for the top of the fence as he lifted her. Her leg went over. Voila, she was out of sight. A soft thump. No cries of pain. Good.

He clambered over and dropped to the soggy grass beside her. "Let's do it." Together they raced for the back entrance. "Alarm?" he asked.

"Nah." She unlocked the door, and they were inside.

At least something was going their way tonight.

"Master bedroom's on the second floor along the back," Jersey said and tiptoed along the back hallway. She could pussyfoot around if she wanted, but he aimed to get in and get out. He pushed by her and bounded up the back stairs. The master bedroom was easy enough to find. The local LEOs had trashed it. Whatever it looked like before, he'd seen worse, but that was the result of a tornado— not law enforcement.

Jersey came up behind him and gestured toward one of the closets. "That's hers on the left. I helped with the laundry sometimes." She rubbed her upper arms and shivered.

"You don't have to explain yourself to me. I'm sure Jackie considered you part of the family."

"Just saying. I didn't want you to think I made myself at home when she wasn't around."

"For the dog, we need something she's worn."

She walked over to the closet and opened the door. "They didn't leave much. If I remember correctly, she wore this blue knit top under her lab coat the day before she disappeared." She removed the garment from its hanger and handed it to him to place in a plastic bag.

"Isn't the rain going to wash away the scent and make the search tomorrow more difficult?"

"As you've already noticed, I'm not much on dog handling. Your Mr. Rigby will have a better idea about that. What about Jackie's shoes? Did they leave any behind?"

She flashed him a smile, crouched, and started pawing through the closet. "For work, she has two pairs of comfortable shoes, just alike. Wears 'em on alternate days." Two pairs of boots came flying over her shoulder, then a jubilant, "Yes! Here's the other pair."

"Okay." He added the shoes to the bag, then stretched the kinks from his shoulders. "We're set, then. Let's get the hell out of here."

"I'm right behind you."

"And I'm right behind you. Hands up," a no-nonsense voice ordered. Alex clenched his jaw and turned around. "Nice of you to drop by, again, Detective."

"Can't say I'm surprised to see you skulking around. Good thing the neighbors are vigilant and called to report intruders." The detective stroked his bushy mustache, satisfaction written over his full face.

Alex nodded, tried to keep the sarcasm from his tone, and failed. "Yes, always pays to have nosy neighbors. Small towns are like that."

"From your behavior, I'm guessing the Federal Bureau of Investigation has different rules from other agencies. Around here, obstruction of justice and interfering in a crime scene are serious matters."

"Quit busting my chops, Detective. We're just here to pick up a couple of things for the bloodhound to follow."

"Bloodhound? You're thinking to follow her trail after the rain and twenty-four hours have passed?"

"Hope lives eternal," Alex said wryly. "You've kept me completely out of the loop regarding evidence and the progress of the case. If you'd been more cooperative, we wouldn't be having this conversation, would we?"

"I've a mind to arrest you for trespassing. You *and* this young lady." He cocked a brow in Bette's direction.

"She's not trespassing." Alex clenched his fists, basically to keep from popping Spitz one. "She lives here. Has a key."

Spitz puffed out his chest. "You know better than to cross crime scene tape."

Alex smiled. "None on the door we used to come inside."

"Yeah? If you thought you had every right here, why the black ops clothes and climbing over the back fence?"

Bette shrugged off her hoodie and fluffed her wet hair, which was starting to curl around her face. "Now, Detective. Surely you can't blame us for doing what we can to find Jackie. Like you told Agent MacGregor earlier, you have a small police department, and you're not equipped for this kind of emergency."

She continued, batting her long lashes at the LEO, "Most places would've already called in the search dogs before it rained and called for an Amber Alert. Is there some reason one hasn't been issued? Whether it's his mother or not who took him, he could be in danger. I know Nancy Grace would love to help with getting the word out about Cody. Real good at that, she is." Smiling, she fluffed her hair again and fluttered her lashes at the detective, who started stuttering.

"Well—uh, I—uh—"

Son of a gun. Wasn't she something? In a matter of seconds, Jersey'd flirted and gone on the offensive, then turned on a dime and threatened him with national media exposure. Reduced the arrogant Spitz to a jibbering jackass.

Two could play that game. Alex took a deep breath. "What about the Amber Alert, Detective? A missing six-year-old child. It's not going to look good on your record when all's said and done." Okay, so an Amber Alert was called only when there was a description of a car or license plate number, but right now, he didn't give a flying fuck about technicalities.

"All right!" The exasperation rolled off the detective in waves. "The, uh, Amber Alert is in the works. Takes time, you know. We're releasing the house tomorrow anyway. Didn't find any sign she was taken from here." Spitz turned. Stopped. Turned back. Smirked. "Good luck with the bloodhound."

Alex waited, giving Jersey a cautious glance. Her eyes were wide, and she was holding her breath. A door banged. Good. Spitz had left the building.

"Whew! I thought we were done for," she said. The breath she'd held came out in a ragged rush.

"First time I've seen you in action." He tried to keep the

admiration from his tone but couldn't quite pull it off.

"Go ahead. You can say it. I was awesome." A slow, seductive smile pulled at her mouth. Her luscious mouth. And that mouth weakened his knees…and his resolve. Kissing her until next week might cure him. Or make matters worse.

"Yeah. You played him just right." Glad of the dim light in the room, he steadied himself against the closet door. "I think we've got enough." His moment of weakness over, he strode by her and headed for the hallway. "Probably a fool's errand anyway," he said under his breath.

"No! Don't say that!" Bette grabbed him by the shoulder and spun him around to face her. Who knew she was so strong? Her warm chocolate eyes shone with unshed tears, her hands fisted at her sides as if she was ready to take a poke at him. "We're going to find Jackie and Cody if we have to tear up Ontario County from Victor to Naples."

A sense of hopelessness almost overwhelmed him. Desperate to make her understand, he raked his fingers through his hair. "You don't know anything. The statistics say—"

She stomped her foot. "I don't care about statistics. Stop it! There's already too much negative energy out there." Tears glistened and fell down her cheeks. "You have to keep thinking positive thoughts or you're worse than Detective Dog. You—you're useless!"

Without warning, she collapsed like a doll whose stuffing had leaked out, and started sobbing. Alex reached for her hands, pulled her to her feet and into his arms. Her tears dampened his shirt as she cried. Somehow, holding her, comforting her, felt right, as if comforting her also comforted him. He shut his eyes and breathed in her scent. The pleasing warmth of her body against his sent his heart rate soaring. Damn, his groin tightened. Would she notice? Maybe not.

"Hold on, I haven't given up on finding Jackie and Cody," he said softly. He wiped away her tears. I guess when I get caught up in quoting stats, I'm avoiding how I feel…how much all this hurts."

"Is it working?" She gazed up at him so earnestly.

"Not so much," he admitted. He leaned forward, touching his forehead to hers. "Jersey, I've made so many mistakes. Focused on my career as if that were the only thing of importance. I forgot about family."

"It's not too late. We'll find them." She peered at him quizzically. "Won't we?" She sniffed, then said in a shaky voice, "We'd better get back to the motel."

A deep sense of loss washed over him as soon as she pulled away. Managing a nod was the best he could do. Dammit. What was it about this one woman that touched him on such a deep level and plagued his dreams at night? Sure, she was hot, with a body that took no prisoners. But he'd known a lot of hot bods in his time. With Jersey, it was so much more.

Could it be the air of vulnerability she hid so carefully behind a seductive façade of smartass attitude and sultry eyes? One minute she was distracting and threatening Detective Spitz, then did a one eighty and cried her heart out because Alex had a moment of weakness. Yes, she was awesome. More than awesome. Make it five feet four inches of pure temptation…and heart.

They headed downstairs. He led the way, with Bette following closely behind, out the back door, and found the rain had stopped. "Thank heaven for small favors," she said. "At least we don't have to sneak out."

"Or climb the fence. Leastwise, you don't. I'll bring the car around front."

She sniffed and smiled up at him. "Thanks. My energy level is starting to flag a bit."

"Adrenaline crash they called it when I was in the Rangers."

"Like after the op or battle is over?"

"You got it." He snapped a two-fingered salute. "See you out front." She nodded, turned and went back inside.

He ran across the squishy backyard and vaulted over the fence. His surge of adrenaline hadn't crashed yet. Nowhere near. Holding Bette in his arms—now, that was a close call. But he'd escaped with his dignity intact.

Barely.

By the time they returned to their motel room, Bette was shivering. "Mind if I dry off first? I don't think I'll ever get warm again." She walked past Shadow's crate. The dog's tail beat the cushion with an enthusiastic *thwap*. She stopped for a second and released the Sheltie from her cage. The animal promptly hopped on Bette's bed and watched Alex sit down and take off his shoes.

Alex said, "No problem. That's part of the crash too."

"If you say so. I just think I'm wet and losing body heat."

He whipped off his sweatshirt and used it to dry his dark blond hair, then pulled a dry one from his go-bag. "I'll head to Charlie's and get us some dinner. Any preferences?"

"Anything but fish." She averted her eyes from his bare chest, but not so quickly she missed his six-pack abs. She stripped off her damp hoodie and started to slip out of the black yoga pants, then realized he was watching her and not trying to hide it. Sighing, she halted her striptease and grabbed a pair of cut-off sweatpants and a T-shirt, then headed into the bathroom.

She turned on the water and adjusted the temperature until it was as hot as she could stand. The hot water and steam began to fill the tub and seep into her muscles and finally eased the chill in her soul. At least she could go back home in the morning. She loved her small, cozy apartment and never realized how much until she was forced to live out of her suitcase once again.

And being around Alex all the time... Much more difficult than she'd thought. As far as he was concerned, she was just an impediment to finding his sister. Unwanted baggage. One step above her dog.

Although, for a moment back at the house, she thought she'd felt him harden as he held her. Either she was mistaken or it was just a natural reflex. Certainly didn't mean anything.

Not to him anyway.


How long she'd been in the tub, she wasn't certain, but Shadow started barking up a storm. Was Alex back and that was why she was kicking up a fuss? Surely not. A chill shot up her spine.

No way. Shadow wouldn't bark at Alex like that. Had she locked the bathroom door? Had Alex locked the door to their room when he left? Of course he had. He was a freaking FBI agent, and he wouldn't have risked leaving her alone and naked in the bathroom with an unlocked door.

She left the water running and eased one foot and then the other out of the tub. Checked the door. Good. Locked. Paranoia—yes, it was a good trait to possess.

Shadow's shrill barks intensified, punctuated by low guttural growls. Definitely not Alex. Her heart pounded so loudly she could hear it. Her hands trembled as she grabbed a towel and frantically dried off. As quietly as possible, she slipped into the cut-offs, then pulled the T-shirt over her head. Her gaze swept the small bathroom. What could she use for protection?

Cosmetics littered the small vanity. Not like she could mousse someone to death. Or stab the intruder with an eyebrow pencil.

Mouth dry, she tried to swallow.

*Think.* She crouched and looked under the sink. At home, there'd be cleaning products. But she wasn't at home. Not a damned thing, except a spare roll of tissue.

Note to self: if you live through this, go armed in the bathtub.

Ridiculous, the thoughts that came to mind at the most

inopportune times. Like during a break-in.

As suddenly as Shadow started barking, she stopped. Had the intruder—and make no mistake about it, there *was* an intruder—left or done something unspeakable to her dog?

What about the sliding door to the tiny patio? She hadn't bothered to check it. Had Alex?

She clenched her fists to stop their shaking. She'd just have to face whoever it was alone, but she'd beat the bastard to death with her bare fists if he'd hurt her baby.

Screwing up what little courage she possessed, she eased back the lock, grabbed the knob, and opened the door.


Alex unlocked the door to their room and found Bette sitting on the bed wearing cut-offs, a T-shirt and a big frown. She had the Sheltie cuddled in her arms and was crooning a mixture of baby talk and nonsense. "If you two want to be alone, I can come back later," he said, giving her a leer.

"Where the hell have you been?" She jumped from the bed and raced toward him. "What took you so long? Someone got in here while I was taking my bath."

He breathed in her fresh, clean scent, but his gaze was riveted to her breasts. She wasn't wearing a bra. The damp T-shirt clung to her fuller-than-he'd-imagined breasts, leaving shadows where her nipples poked through the thin fabric. Gentleman or no, he was a man. Should he say something? Yes, but his mouth refused to form the words.

God, yes, he looked, feasted with his eyes on her beauty.

He dropped the sacks of takeout and must've groaned. Sure as hell couldn't form thoughts, much less words. "Uh—"

"Better not've been you who scared me to death," she said.

His chin dropped. Still having trouble with his powers of speech, he shook his head. "Nuh-uh."

The pressure in his groin grew until he had to turn away.

*Count backwards. Ten. No, one hundred. Ninety-nine.* He knelt in time to rescue their dinner from the dog, and then slowly rose and set the bags on the dresser.

*Ninety-eight. Ninety-seven.* His hold on sanity was stronger.

"If your eyeballs are back in your head, I'll tell you what happened." She loosened the T-shirt and plopped down on her bed.

He shut his eyes and turned away. "Sorry. I just—"

"Got a damned good look. That's what you did."

He nodded, walked stiff-legged over to his bed, sat, and faced her across the space between the double beds. "Yeah, go ahead. What happened?"

He listened to Bette's tale of how she'd been in the tub, heard the dog bark and growl, then opened the bathroom door and found nothing...except an open sliding door.

"I can't believe you'd go off and not lock the door behind you!" She sprang from the bed and pummeled him with her fist.

He stood, caught her wrist, and pulled her close to his chest. "I *didn't* leave the door unlocked." His words came out in a rasp. All he could think about was her body and the single thin T-shirt that stood between them. He'd grown hard again as soon as he had her in his arms. Dangerous territory. "You'd better finish drying off or—"

Her brows shot up. "Or what?" Her breasts rose and fell a little more rapidly than before.

He choked out, "I won't be responsible for what happens next."

"That's a cop-out if I ever heard one." She wagged her head back and forth, then mimicked his words. "I won't be responsible..." Then she turned away from him. *Thank heaven.*

"All right," she said with an indignant huff, then got back in his face and challenged him. "Certainly wouldn't want to incite an attack on my honor—now, would I?" She jerked away from him but stopped and glared over her shoulder. "Didn't know I was staying with a voyeur."

Mad was good. Now if he could just keep her pissed off—and out of his arms—he might just survive the next few minutes. "How was I supposed to know *you* were a closet exhibitionist?"

"I most certainly am not!"

"Couldn't prove it by me."

"As you might well imagine I didn't have time to dry thoroughly." She pulled the damp garment away from her breasts. "Get over it!"

With that, she grabbed her overnighter and flounced into the bathroom. He let out a sigh of relief. Being around her was getting harder and harder, meaning he was on the verge of losing control of his cock.

Sassy. Sexy. And fun. What's not to like?

Don't forget your sister and nephew are missing, and the detective in charge of the case is a cretin.

He knelt and examined the carpet in front of the slider. No footprints. Then he straightened, pulled opened the slider, and walked outside. The small concrete patio was wet and didn't show any signs of an intruder—no surprise there. The patios were surrounded by a lush lawn, but in the dark and with the prior rain, he couldn't make out any footprints.

Bette stuck her head out of the bathroom. "Find anything?"

"Nope." Maybe it was never locked. Maybe the dog had smelled a skunk. Who knew what set the creature off?

He shut the slider, locking it for sure this time.

He walked over to the dresser, opened one of the bags of takeout, and started setting out the food. His stomach rumbled. Damn, a man could starve around here. He dipped into a container of fries and snagged one, sat on the foot of the bed and aimed the remote at the television.

A familiar rerun was on while the promised Amber Alert crawled across the bottom of the screen. About damned time.

Hungry enough to eat a small animal, he leaned forward and

grabbed the burger. The Sheltie pranced back and forth, her nose pointed straight up, sniffing the air. "Better be glad your mistress is so fond of you, or I might be eating a hot *dog*." He chuckled at his lame joke.

A door slammed behind him. He turned to see Bette, dressed only in a pair of short, pink PJs, standing with her hands on her hips. "I don't appreciate your attempt at humor. Just because dogs can't talk doesn't mean they don't understand what we say or mean."

Man. He'd expected more clothes not less. Talk about not being able to catch a break. "Aw, come on. I was kidding. You know I was."

"She's hungry, and I'm sure a bite or two of hamburger would suit her just fine."

"Too bad. I brought you chicken. I have the only burger."

"Then give her a bite. No onions. Dogs can't metabolize them."

"Give her some of your chicken."

"You're the one who needs to bond with her. Just give her a nibble."

Grudgingly he broke off a small bite and held it out. "Here you go, girl." The Sheltie went for it with a snap. "Ouch! She bit me." He sucked on his finger. "Vicious dog. Now you see why I don't like 'em."

"You big baby. That was a tiny nip." She shrugged. "Guess I'll have to work on her manners. You could've just dropped it and let her catch it."

"*Now* you tell me." He reached for another fry.

She snorted and grabbed the french fry from his hand. "Don't eat 'em all."

"I'm happy to share my fries anytime."

"That's good because I love fries." She tore off a small bite of chicken and held it out for the dog. "Sit," she said. Tail wagging happily, the dog sat. Bette dropped the treat and the animal caught it.

She shot him a smug smile. "See that's how it's done—at least until I have time to teach her better manners."

"If you say so." He shrugged, keeping his gaze fixed on the television screen—and away from Bette and those dratted pink pajamas.

The news came on. "Oh, finally," she said. "They have the Amber Alert going. Maybe that'll jog someone to come forward." She leaned against the headboard and ate her sandwich, stopping occasionally to give the dog small bites of chicken.

Sitting on the side of his bed, he inhaled the last of his burger. "Time for lights out." He toed off his shoes, but he didn't dare undress further—not with Bette and her pink PJs in the same room. He would sleep on top of the spread just fine. "We have to meet Rigby early tomorrow morning."

No response except, "Come on, Shadow. Let's go night-night." She patted the bed beside her and stretched out next to the canine.

He reached for the light and doused it. Any other time. Any other place. Or any other woman. What he wouldn't give to be curled up alongside Bette. But she wasn't a good-time gal. She was for keeps.

And he never played for keeps.

"Alex?" Soft as a sigh, her voice drifted across the gap between their beds.

"Yeah?" He pushed up on one elbow. *What now?*

"Do you think there's still hope?"

"What's the matter?" To hide his real thoughts on the matter, he tried a glib response. "You the one losing faith now?"

"Trying not to."

He heard a quiet sniff. Was she crying?

"But it just seems like she's been gone forever."

Over twenty-four hours when, according to statistics, it was likely she'd been dead for twenty-one of them. And Cody. For some reason, he felt the need to bolster her mood. "Tomorrow's a new day. We can move back into the house. We'll meet up with Rigby and see what we can do with his superdog bloodhound. Like you said earlier—and loudly, if I remember correctly—stay positive. And something about not inviting negative energy."

"I did say that, didn't I?" She let out a long sigh that almost ripped out his heart.

"Go to sleep, Jersey. Another long day ahead."

"We *have* to find them."

"We will." It wasn't a lie. They'd be found. Bodies usually were…sooner or later.

# Chapter Thirteen

Sunday morning dawned bright and clear with a bit of dew remaining on the grass when Alex and Bette checked out of the motel. They took their bags back to Bette's apartment and left the Sheltie there as well. After hitting the drive-through at Tim Horton's, they headed over to the animal clinic. Rigby was already waiting in his SUV when they pulled into the lot.

Alex drained the last of his coffee and popped the two remaining Timbits in his mouth. "You didn't have to eat 'em all," he said, mumbling because his mouth was full of the doughnut holes.

"I figured you were a health nut with that G-man physique of yours." She opened her door. "At least *I* had a Diet Coke with mine. Saved a bunch of calories too."

He grunted at her "saved a bunch of calories" remark. "Right." Easing from the compact, he waved at Rigby. "Morning." Where was the dog? Maybe in the back of the trainer's massive, dark green SUV. Increasing tension between his shoulder blades reminded him of his phobia. He sucked in a deep breath. *Just a dog. A very helpful dog.*

"You think we've had too much rain?"

"Depends on how much fell in this part of town. A light rain might actually intensify the scent. Did you bring a scent article?"

"We have the blouse and shoes Jackie wore the day before she disappeared." Bette proffered the scent items, which were still in the plastic bag.

Alex shifted from one foot to the other while he watched Rigby open the back of his SUV and release the bloodhound from his cage.

Damn. The dog was bigger than Alex remembered. To hide his discomfort, he asked the dog trainer, "What makes this breed better at tracking scents than others?"

Rigby rubbed his chin. "Might say he's engineered by nature for scent tracking, from the olfactory center in his brain to his long ears."

"Looks like those ears would get in his way," Alex said. "He ever step on them?"

"They aren't there for looks, son." The dog trainer let out a chuckle. "They sorta sweep along close to the ground and gather the scent in the dog's nostrils. And his low-to-the-ground body is just another part of how form follows function. Has to be kept fit too. Dog like this 'un will keep going for miles. Long as there's scent."

"Wow." Alex scratched the side of his head. "What about tracking in the city? I can see how they would do well in an open field, tracking an escaped felon." Why couldn't he just shut up and let the man get on with it? "I'd think they'd be confused with so many cars. And, obviously, she was taken away in a vehicle..."

"You'd be surprised at how well bloodhounds, especially this 'un, can follow a scent trail. Seen some near miracles. Once Duke here finds a trace of Dr. Jackie's scent, he'll follow it. Still depends on how hard it rained over here yesterday." He removed the scent articles from the plastic bag and placed the items at the level of the hound's muzzle. "If he finds her scent trail, he'll take off, and I'll follow his lead on foot. You'll need to drive behind to keep us from getting run over."

Alex nodded.

"She was last seen inside the building?" Rigby asked.

"Yes. That's the last I saw of her. She went back inside and turned on the lights."

"We'll start there then." The trainer led the dog onto the porch and waited for the dog's signal. "Gonna try around back."

"There's a side exit too. That's where Jackie and the rest of us park."

"And where did the man with the cat park?"

Bette pointed at a large oil spot. "Over there. His SUV must've left that."

Alex walked over to the stained pavement. "He took her away in his vehicle because hers remained here. Police took it in for forensics exam. Doubt they found anything of significance."

A loud baying sound erupted from the bloodhound. Alex jumped. Damn it all. Acting like a scared girl every time a dog barked was getting old. Not to mention unmanly.

"All right," the trainer called out. "He's caught scent." The bloodhound followed a path leading from the side door to the oil spot. He snuffled all around the spot and then took off with the trainer following.

"Jersey, let's go!" Alex shouted and motioned for her to hop in.

"I didn't think he'd find a scent trail so quickly. Honestly, I didn't think he'd find one at all." Bette gasped and fastened her seat belt. "Just think. We might really find Jackie and Cody today."

"Let's just see how far this dog can lead us. Never know. We had a lot of rain yesterday. Scent could play out in a block or two."

"Dammit." Bette all but stamped her foot like a petulant teen. "Stay positive. This is the most encouraged I've felt since she went missing."

"Yeah." Better keep his hands on the wheel and his mouth shut. Stay calm and cool headed. No point in sending Bette into another crying jag. Besides, listening to her cry just about killed him.

Luckily, the early Sunday morning traffic was minimal. The dog kept a good steady pace until it hit Eastern Boulevard, then it slowed and cast about as if confused. "It poured over here yesterday afternoon. Remember?" she said. "Shadow and I were drenched."

"Yeah." Disappointment ground through him like a buzz saw. Sharp. Painful. He chewed the inside of his jaw to keep from screaming his frustration. "Knew this'd be a waste of time."

She popped him on the shoulder. Apparently, she didn't care for the resurgence of his negative attitude. "What about those gut instincts you secret agents are known for? Get in his head. Where would *you* take someone?"

"Special agent—not secret agent," he corrected with a growl, then pulled to the side of the road and let the car idle. "I'd take 'em out of town. I'd need privacy." *So no one could hear her scream.* He shook his head and squinted. Being a profiler never appealed to him. Getting inside the heads of rapists and serial killers was ten degrees of creepy.

Bette glanced toward the hills. "See if Mr. Rigby will try Duke with either the High Road or the Low Road. In spite of all the development, there's still a lot of woods and hills up there."

"Yeah, Bristol Mountain. Naples. Wine country."

"So…"

Alex called the dog handler over to the car and explained Bette's hunch and asked for his indulgence.

"Sure." The older man sniffed. "Anything for Dr. Jackie. But you know Naples had two inches of rain yesterday. Good for grapes but bad for tracking."

"I know it's a long shot." Bette shrugged. "I wish the trail hadn't faded so quickly."

"The police department should've called the Sheriff's Department or me in sooner."

"That's just it. They don't believe my sister's been kidnapped. And now they think she sneaked back and took her son as well. Getting them to mount an Amber Alert took some major arm twisting." He glanced at Bette and acknowledged her contribution with a quick nod.

"Not like Dr. Jackie at all." Rigby dug his forefinger in his ear as if it needed a good cleaning, then shook his unkempt gray head. "So is it the High Road or the Low?"

"Let's start with the High Road," Bette suggested, then raised an eyebrow in his direction. "Okay?"

"Yeah." To Alex's way of thinking, she'd chosen wisely. The High Road, so called by the locals, was a scenic branch off Route 21. It ran along the heights of the hills surrounding the lake and had more than one pullover spot where someone could look out over the lake. Too bad development was consuming, one bite at a time, the natural beauty of the area. The High Road was still less developed than the lower route. "That's the way I'd go, if I was of a mind to kidnap someone."

And dump the body.

No small coincidence they would pass where his brother's body had been found near the Bristol Mountain Ski Resort, if they continued that far. Too many memories lay dead and buried that way. Doubtful they could find the exact spot now, but he'd never forget the sheriff coming to the house and how his adoptive mother had cried. How *he'd* hidden in the garden shed and cried until his eyes were red and swollen.

"Alex?"

Bette's hand on his shoulder brought him back from that awful day. "Sorry. Forgot where I was for a sec."

He motioned for Rigby and his bloodhound to get in the backseat. "I'll take you back to your vehicle, and we'll head out."


He gripped the wheel, his hands set at ten and two, his jaw clenched so tightly he couldn't have spoken if he'd wanted to. With Rigby on their six, they took Route 21 out of Canandaigua, then passed through Cheshire before they hit the scenic route, which quickly started to climb, the green hills and farms on one side and the deep blue of the lake on the other. Hell of a lot more houses. Nice houses—hell, some of 'em were mansions.

Why did one of the most beautiful spots in upstate New York have to be forever tainted with unhappiness in his mind? Because of a promise he hadn't kept.

Traffic on the High Road was nonexistent. At the first lookout spot, Alex pulled over, parked, and waited for the dog handler to do the same. Bette opened her door, got out, and peered at the lake. "Gosh, it's so beautiful up here. It's almost like looking at an Italian lake."

The dog handler exited his SUV and released the hound from his cage. Thankfully, there was only the one dog to contend with.

Was it too much to put all his hopes on this one lone bloodhound? With all the scientific equipment and services available to the FBI, would finding his sister and her son all come down to a single dog's nose?

Rigby ambled over to them. "Y'know this is a real long shot, don't you, son?"

"Yes, sir."

The trainer presented the bloodhound with the scent sample again, then led him into the road. Bette gestured that she'd keep a lookout for any oncoming traffic. The creature sniffed but couldn't seem to pick up anything. "It rained up here in the hills yesterday—a real downpour, so my friends at the winery tell me."

Though Alex would rather avoid going within ten miles of where his brother's body was found, he said the words. "Bristol Mountain Ski Resort—what about it?"

"You got some history there. That was a sorry day." Rigby scratched his chin and nodded. "Have to backtrack, but guess it's as good a place as any."

Ten minutes later, Alex stood with Bette on one side, her fingers entwined with his, and Rigby on the other. They watched the stream of traffic turning into the ski resort. Up ahead, he could see heavy equipment moving new ski lift supports into place, and a helicopter buzzed in the sky above. He frowned. "Lot of development since I was here last. Mansions on the ridge heights. Condos lining the lakeshore. What do they think this is—Vail or

Aspen?"

"Too many changes, if you ask me." Rigby spit on the ground. "Now they're tearing down the old ski lifts and replacing them with something newer and faster."

"I sort of understand it. It's a beautiful area, even with all the new building. People like to get away from the city and enjoy nature."

"Nature used to mean camping. Now it's cable television and that danged Wi-Fi." Rigby twisted his face into a grimace. "Well, day's not getting any younger. Want to try Duke again?"

"Many thanks, Rigby. You might as well go on home. He wouldn't bring her here." Alex shook his head. "Too many people. Too much activity."

The dog handler nodded and headed back to his SUV. He stopped long enough to offer his assistance if any new leads arose.

"Was it close by?" she asked. "Where your brother was found?"

He squinted, trying to remember the lay of the land that horrible day. He'd made his adoptive father bring him to the site. The city police, the sheriff's department, and the state police were all there. By then, everyone had known he'd left his twin alone at the movie theatre. No one had said it was his fault. Didn't have to. Their unwillingness to look him in the eye said it all.

Bones. Some scattered but still recognizable as a human body. And a silver ID bracelet—Andy's—discovered near the right radius. The same bracelet Alex had worn on his right wrist ever since the police returned it. Alex's matching bracelet had been buried with his brother.

He pointed toward the ski lift. "He was found about ten feet into the tree line, about halfway up the mountain." He swallowed hard and fiddled with the silver links of his ID bracelet, turning it round and round his wrist.

"Do you want to go a little closer?" Her voice was hesitant.

Was she afraid he'd bite or break?

He stared at the spot and shook his head. "I've said my good-byes." He choked on the words. "Said 'em long time ago."

Her fingers squeezed his, and he squeezed back, taking comfort in her touch.

"If you're sure, then…" She gazed up at him, her dark eyes shining with a hint of tears. "We could just hike up there and…"

"And what, Bette? Relive the worst day of my life? Relive the biggest mistake of my life? Get up close and personal so I can relive it all over again when my sister and nephew are found? Want to be my shrink? That what you want?" He bit back the rest of his anger and strode away from her.

"I know how it hurts to lose someone, Alex," she called after him. "My parents—"

He spun to face her and spit his words like gunfire. "Your parents died in a *fire*. They weren't murdered and left on a mountainside to rot."

"You're only half right." She set her hands on her hips and jutted her chin. "They weren't left to rot, but they *were* murdered."

Crap. What an idiot he was. He clenched and unclenched his fists. "I'm sorry. You never said…"

"You're not the only one who doesn't like to talk or even think about it. So I *do* understand." She blinked rapidly, and her face crumpled.

Crap. She was going to break down again.

Without thinking, he closed the distance between them and slid his arms around her waist. "You don't have to talk about it." He breathed in the lime fragrance of her shampoo. A shot of whiskey would go well right about now. Her breasts pressed against his chest. He swallowed the lump that formed in his throat. "Unless you want to."

"It was…uh, a business rival. At least that's what my brother and I figured. My brother runs the…uh, company now."

He frowned and pinched the bridge of his nose. "Sounds like a harsh kind of business. Do you worry about him?"

"Always. But I had to get away from there. Too many memories. You understand?" She gazed up at him. Her dimpled chin trembled just a little. "Anyway, that's the real reason I left Jersey and moved to Nashville. Fan Fair was just an excuse."

"Running away and reinventing yourself. Careful, could get to be a habit."

"Not like I had a choice the last time," she said with a bit of heat and pulled away.

But he pulled her back into his arms. Damn it all. He didn't want to let her go. She felt too good in his arms. Too right. And too big a risk.

He must've stiffened, because she pulled back a bit and looked up at him with questions in her dark shimmering gaze. "What's wrong?"

He clenched his jaw. No way would he take advantage of the comfort she offered—the comfort he needed. "Nothing."

"For someone who's supposed to be a secret spy man, you're a hell of a bad liar."

He couldn't hold back the smile twitching at his lips. "You're reading me like a book? Is that what you're trying to say?"

"Yeah." She wrinkled her nose. "One with large print."

Why had he let her get so close? How could he explain how much he wanted and needed her right now, and yet in the same breath, tell her he didn't want to get involved? He'd loved 'em and left 'em plenty of times, but she deserved better than being used and discarded. Yet the thought of what it would be like to wake up beside her every morning set his heart to racing.

Smiling, she gazed up at him and caressed his cheek. "I don't need promises of forever, Alex." Her gaze was full of an indefinable something. As if she knew him better than he knew himself.

Damn. Was she reading his mind? "What?"

"Just sayin'…in case you need to hear it. It's okay. I want to be with you too. And it doesn't have to be more than that."

His mouth grew dry as sandpaper. Where was his poker face when he needed one? He looked around, anything to avoid her direct but seductive gaze. In the distance, the old ski lift towers were being dismantled and removed by a helicopter. "Can't keep much from you, can I? Sure you're not a spy yourself?"

"A woman knows these things," she said with a Cheshire-cat smile. "And I believe I qualify."

"No doubt about it. Definitely all woman."

"Then let's go home. We're not going to accomplish anything here."

*Home*. That one simple term was imbued with layer upon layer of meaning. Some trite but no less true. Home is where the heart is. No place like home. All roads lead to home.

"Okay." It came out as more of a croak. Was he really agreeing to go home with Bette at a time when they were both raw and vulnerable? And could they keep it on a friends-with-benefits basis?

He took her hand and led her back to the car. His questions would have to wait. He stopped and backed her against the passenger door. "I'm no good with relationships, Jersey."

"Not my strong point either." She crooked a slim, dark eyebrow. "Are you going to kiss me or not? I've waited long enough."

He smiled down at her. "Hell, yeah." He pulled her close and dipped his lips to hers. Sampled them. He found them soft and sweet. Her mouth opened to his, meeting and mating his tongue with her own. A flood of lust swept through his body. Staggered him. Braced against the roof of the rental car, he lost himself in the heat of her response. Her breasts pressed against his chest and her mound against his cock.

He left a trail of kisses down her neck to the valley between her breasts. He snaked his hands under her T-shirt and tweaked her nipples through a lacy bra. They tightened into firm buds, and the sound of her low moan spiked his lust into the stratosphere.

He had to have her. Now.

He reached behind her and opened the rear door. She scrambled inside and whipped her T-shirt over her head, revealing a bright red bra. He reached behind and flicked open the fastener. Her breasts spilled out, lush, high, and firm. Hungry to taste her, he dived and caught one of her dark nipples in his mouth and sucked it into a tight bead. He slid his hand down the front of her jeans and found more lace. Damp lace.

His cock so hard he could barely catch his breath, he groaned. She parted her thighs while he fumbled with his zipper.

*Fuck.* He pulled back.

Dammit all. How could he be so unprepared?

"No condom," he gasped. "What was I thinking?"

Bette levered to one elbow, shook her head, and shot him a half grin. "For once you weren't, which isn't—or wasn't—necessarily such a bad thing."

He sucked in a deep breath, then counted backward from a hundred. A little self-control could go a long way about now. Federal agents didn't go around screwing in what was basically a public place. Time was running short for his sister and for his job, and all he could think about was getting in Jersey's pants. And fucking her brains out.

# Chapter Fourteen

"To be continued," Bette said, refastening her bra a touch reluctantly. Not only had they come close to doing the deed in the backseat of the car but in broad daylight. What had her papa said? Close only counted in horseshoes and Uzis.

She licked her lips and tasted his morning coffee. They were already swollen from kissing him. "What now?"

Alex zipped his jeans and gave a bark of a laugh. "Hell if I know."

"I suggest we adjourn to The Villager for a late breakfast. After that, I need to check on Shadow. I hated leaving her alone this morning."

He stepped back, and she climbed out of the backseat and into the front. "Old Duke would've had her for his breakfast." He slid into the driver's seat and started the engine, backed the car around and aimed for County Road 64.

"Not a well-trained dog like that. No way." She shook her head and then giggled. "You still have this thing about dogs. Need to get over it, dude. I can't believe the FBI let you graduate from wherever you guys graduate from."

"Quantico. And it was a close call." His hands shifted nervously on the steering wheel. "How about after breakfast, I go down to the station and see how the investigation is going while you make nice with your dog?" He shot her a sideways glance. "If you think you can, stay close to home. You could still be in danger."

"Really think so?" She wrinkled her nose and shrugged her

disbelief. "I admit I was a little jumpy at first, but I don't think I'm a target. I didn't see enough of him to give a decent description."

"He doesn't know that. Just the same…"

"Whatever." Honestly, just because Double-O was a Fed, he saw boogeymen behind every door. In her life, she'd experienced too much. The real boogeymen were the ones you trusted. Like the one who'd had her parents killed. The same one who'd gone to their double funeral and offered his condolences and still hadn't served a day in prison. No doubt her brother would make sure the dirty rat paid…and when he least expected it.

"What's wrong?" Alex's sharp tone brought her back to reality.

"Nothing." Okay, a little more control over her thoughts or she'd be blabbing the entire story before she knew it.

*Oh, by the way, I forgot to tell you my brother's a mob boss in Jersey.*

Now, wouldn't that be a fine way to end a relationship before it started?


The Villager on Main Street was a local hangout for breakfast. The service was quick and the food hot, and if it was a trifle high in cholesterol, no one seemed to mind. Certainly not Bette. She polished off two eggs and three strips of bacon along with four slices of whole wheat toast slathered in real butter and topped with homemade Concord grape jelly.

Alex pointed his fork at her clean plate. "Why didn't you say you were starving?"

She glanced down at her plate. "I guess eating was easier than talking about the elephant in the room."

"I'm on a deadline, Jersey. My Bureau chief expects me back in the office tomorrow, or I'm sidelined from my current case."

"How can you choose your job over your sister? I don't get it."

"I'm not choosing my job over them. I won't go back until

they're found. I owe them that much."

"Brings it all back, doesn't it—what happened to your brother?" She avoided his gaze—no, avoided seeing the pain that had to be there.

"Yeah," he said hoarsely. "It's bad enough when you lose one family member. You don't ever consider it could happen again, and yet it has." He drained his coffee cup and signaled the passing waitress for a refill. "The CPD needs help, and, hell, I need it too. I'm too close. I'm missing something. Just don't know what." He swallowed his last bite of waffle. "That's it. I'll run you by the house and see you later."

"Okay." *See you later?* Great. Just great. It was back to business as usual with him. As if what almost happened hadn't happened at all.

With a frigging visitor's badge clipped to his shirt, Alex strode down the back hall to the detectives' bullpen. Spitz looked up and gave what was at best an approximation of a smile when Alex approached. "Been meaning to call you," he said.

His heart clutched and seemed as if it did a complete flip. Had Jackie or her son been found? He swallowed the nausea that threatened. Puking in front of the local LEOs wasn't something he intended to do. He barely kept the tremor from his voice. "You have news?"

"Not on your sister or her son, but we *have* discovered something very interesting about your girlfriend, Agent." Spitz preened and groomed his mustache with his forefinger. "Something you ought to know."

"She's not my girlfriend." Not officially. He tamped down his irritation. "So tell me anyway."

"We got around to running her prints. Seems she's from New Jersey."

"That's not news." But her prints being on file was. He motioned for Spitz to continue. "What else?"

"Seems like her name's not Smithson either."

"Oh?" Now *that* was news.

"Name's Spinelli. Bettina Maria Spinelli. The little lady is a full-fledged Mafia princess. Her father was head of the Spinelli family out of Jersey until he and her mother were murdered in a—"

"In a fire. I know." Apparently, Bette had another secret or two up her short-sleeved T-shirt.

"Her big brother Gino's head of the Spinelli family now. And he's aiming at being a bigger thug than the old man." The detective chuckled. "She's not exactly squeaky clean herself. Just thought you ought to know who you're dealing with."

"Thanks, Detective." Alex ground his teeth and pasted a smile on his face for Spitz's benefit. Okay, so she hadn't told him everything about her past. He hadn't either at first. But as much time as they'd spent together, she sure as hell could've found time to mention she was *connected*. Come to think of it, she'd dropped a hint about how her brother and his friends would take care of her Nashville stalker if he followed her to New Jersey. But that was back on New Year's Eve, and other than the recent revelation that her parents had been murdered by a business rival, she hadn't elaborated further.

No wonder she'd changed her name. And "not exactly squeaky clean"? What the heck did the detective mean by that? Only one way to find out. Actually, two. Wait until she came clean on her own or pull up her record. More than likely it was some minor kid stuff.

Better be minor.

Or he could ask Spitz, because the man was fairly dancing in his chair to tell him. "You have her sheet?"

Spitz adjusted his reading glasses and read from his notes. "Age eighteen. Our girl shoplifted a pricey purse from one of the big stores in New *Yawk*. Expensive enough to make it a felony, but her father's mouthpiece got her off with a suspended sentence and community service."

"Anything since then?" Held his breath. Tried to keep from crossing his fingers. Succeeded. Barely.

"Nope, clean as a nun's habit."

He rubbed his chin. "So you have nothing on her."

"Just this thing called my gut." The detective rubbed his belly. "She's in on this. Maybe she's after your sister's husband. After all, with her connections, all she would have to do is call her big brother—and badda-bing, badda-boom—someone disappears."

"You're full of crap. If you knew her, you'd know she'd never pull anything like this. She left New Jersey to get away from the life." At least he hoped that much was true.

"I think you've got a whiff and it's affected your brain, Agent MacGregor."

Alex clenched his fists and breathed through the urge to paste the detective with both. "Like I said, *you* don't know her."

"You wouldn't be the first agent to lose his head over a piece of ass. Keep it up and you'll lose your fine job with the Feds."

Alex took a deep breath and relaxed his fists. That way he wouldn't punch the smirking jerk-wad who was tipped back in his chair and looking too pleased with himself. "You need to watch your mouth. No matter who her family is, Bette doesn't deserve your disrespect." He spun on his heel, then stopped at the door and turned back for a parting shot. "Job loss can work both ways. Incompetence isn't a prized quality in law enforcement."

He strode from the bullpen and stormed outside into the sunshine before taking another deep breath. Never had he seen a detective with so little to be arrogant about.

Bette glanced around her cozy apartment and let out a sigh of relief. So good to be home. No motel room for her. She'd seen enough of those since leaving New Jersey. But if they didn't find Jackie, how long would Brad let her keep renting? More to the point, what would happen to Jackie's veterinary practice? Bette wouldn't have a job for long.

Uncertainty meant stress. And stress wasn't healthy.

*Okay. Take Shadow for a walk.* Poor creature must be stressed as well. New home. New surroundings. First the apartment, then the motel, then back to the apartment. She wrote a quick note for Alex and taped it to her front door. "Come here, girl." She picked up the leash and rattled it. "Let's get moving."

The Sheltie scampered over, sat politely, and raised her pointy nose so Bette could attach the leash to her collar.

Once outside in the sunshine and fresh air, Bette stretched for a minute and then led her dog down the driveway and onto the shady sidewalk. "Let's walk up toward Main and then back." Main Street was only about six blocks, but it was far enough to work out the kinks—both physical and mental.

She and the Sheltie took off at a nice brisk pace. Shadow did well on leash for about a block but then grew skittish as a late-model burgundy Cadillac CTS pulled to the curb just ahead of them. "It's all right." She gave a tiny jerk to the leash, intending to keep going.

The car window rolled down, and a man's gruff voice asked, "I'm trying to find the Wine and Culinary Center. Could you possibly direct me?"

She relaxed. Someone needed directions. No big deal. "Just keep straight. Hang a left on Main, and it's on your right. You can't miss it."

"Perhaps you could show me?" The passenger door opened. The driver leaned forward, but his billed cap obscured most of his face. All she could make out was a beard.


Alex found a note on the door to Bette's apartment. "007, I've taken Shadow for a walk. Back in thirty." Where the hell was she, anyway? What was taking her so long?

*Back in thirty.* He glanced at his watch. Why the hell hadn't she thought to put a time on the note? Thirty minutes from when? Must've taken an awful long walk with that damned dog. How long did it take for a dog to find a good spot to pee and take care of business?

"Dammit!" Ready for a fight, he rushed upstairs. After all this time, she was still keeping secrets. What else hadn't she told him?

The hair on Bette's neck rose like tiny daggers of prickly sensation. "Would I show you?" She backed away from the car. "Sorry, my dog and I are out for a walk." She sped up to stay ahead of the car, maintaining a pace both steady and determined. Up ahead, she recognized one of Jackie's neighbors carrying two shopping bags. She waved and ran ahead, with the Sheltie following on the lead. "Hi, Miss Waller. Let me help you with one of those."

The woman smiled, nodded, and handed off one of the bags. "So nice of you, Bette. When will I ever learn? I always buy too much when I go downtown, and then I have to carry it all back."

"I know exactly what you mean. I'm guilty of the same thing." They walked along the sidewalk to the Waller house, and Bette glanced over her shoulder, checking to see if the man and his car were still there. Great. The Caddy had already pulled away from the curb and was driving toward Main Street.

She swallowed the lump lodged in her throat. The incident with the Caddy had set her every nerve on alert. Something wasn't right about its driver. On one hand, she wished she could've gotten a better look at him, but every instinct said, "Run!" Back in Jersey, she'd learned to listen to her gut instincts. So she'd run.

At the front door, Miss Waller thanked Bette more profusely than her good_deed called for. Point of fact, thanking the older woman for saving *her* butt was more like it. Alex was right. Someone was after her too. Maybe because she'd been at the animal clinic that night. Or maybe everything that had happened over the last couple of days had given her a blooming case of paranoia.

Truthfully, she dreaded going back to Jackie's with only the Sheltie for protection. Right now a Rottweiler would be a more convincing deterrent for any would-be kidnappers. Then she held back a giggle. As uncomfortable as Alex was around meek and mild Shadow, a Rottie would have him on tranquilizers.

"Why don't you come in for some lemonade, dear?"

"Well, I have the dog…" she began, not exactly anxious to leave. A glass of lemonade would be perfect right about now.

"Oh, she's such a sweet little thing. Just bring her with you. I'm sure she won't be a bit of bother."

"Thanks. I will, then." She followed the woman inside and surveyed the array of Victorian era antiques. Very good quality, if her eyes weren't deceived. The woman gestured for her to have a seat.

"You have some lovely pieces," Bette said and sat by a rosewood tea table.

Jackie's neighbor brought a tray set with a frosty pitcher of lemonade and two cut crystal glasses and set them on the tea table. "Was that someone you knew in the Cadillac?" She raised a gray brow. "Or was he bothering you?"

"At first he asked for directions to the Wine and Culinary Center, but then he asked me to show him. I was so glad to see you." Then she hastened to add, "Of course, I would've offered to help you anyway."

"I know you would, Bette. And you must call me Jane." The older woman poured a glass for Bette, then one for herself. She sat and shook her head. "I don't know what this world is coming to. First Jackie, then her little boy." She took a sip. "Do you think someone is after you too?"

Bette shrugged. "Who knows?" she said with a deprecating laugh. "Maybe I'm just paranoid. I was there right before Jackie disappeared. I was the last person to see her, except for whoever took her." She sampled the lemonade. Delish. "Would you mind if I called my friend, Alex? He'll pick me up, and then"—she glanced down at the Sheltie who gazed up so lovingly—"we could get out of your way."

"You're no trouble. But I don't blame you for wanting an escort home."

"It's only two houses away, but..." Honestly she was turning into a nervous Nellie. Next, she'd be jumping at the slightest sound. And if she wasn't careful, she'd turn into the little old lady who called the police about hearing burglars.

"No need to explain." The woman stood, picked up a plate of cookies from the counter, and set it on the table in front of Bette. "In the meantime, help yourself. Have a cookie."

Bette took one. The smell of cinnamon sprinkles set her taste buds to jonesing. She took a bite, and the sweet flavor burst forth on her tongue. A small moan escaped before she could call it back. "Cinnamon sugar. My favorite."

The older woman smiled. "From your reaction, I would say so."

Bette leaned forward and said in her most conspiratorial manner. "I know a lot of women, men too, who swear by chocolate, but for me, it's cinnamon. That's what does it for me."

"And does your friend do it for you too?" The woman's brows shot up, and she clapped her hand over her mouth. "Oh, mercy. That just popped out."

Laughter bubbled through Bette, and her cheeks grew hot. "I'm afraid I don't know the answer to that yet. We're just friends, for now. He has a lot on his plate with the investigation into his sister and nephew's disappearances."

"Such handsome youngsters he and his brother were." Miss Waller leaned back, and her gaze grew distant as she spoke.

"Identical, like two peas in a pod. Andy was the quieter of the two, loved computers, and Alex was the one always getting into trouble. They were both smart. Good in sports. After Alex's twin was murdered, he got worse. He was always on the reckless side. He got into some minor scrapes, and yet he's the one who became a FBI agent." She bit into a cookie and chewed with a thoughtful expression.

"I think he felt responsible for his brother's death," Bette said. "It drives him still."

"Sounds as if you know him pretty well."

She nodded and felt her cheeks warming again. "He's shared a little with me. But it's easy to see he hasn't gotten over it. And everything that's happened with Jackie and Cody makes it worse."

"I wager he feels pretty helpless." Miss Waller paused, wiping a cookie crumb from her mouth. "Has to make it worse, knowing what he knows and seeing what he's seen in the FBI."

"It does." Bette rummaged inside her purse and pulled out her cell phone. "Speaking of the man, I'd better call him and let him know where I am. Excuse me."

The woman nodded and topped off their glasses of lemonade. "Go right ahead."

Alex picked up on the first ring and swore at her. "Where the hell have you been? I was ready to call the CPD and report you and your mutt as MIA."

She bristled at the "mutt" remark but let it go. "I'm two doors down from Jackie's in the light blue house with white shutters. I'll explain when I see you." She punched the disconnect button. Just where did he get off talking to her like that? Not that it wasn't kind of nice to have someone actually care where she was. 'Cause it was.

The neighbor smiled politely at their quick exchange. "Good. Tell it like it is. And while you're at it, don't take any guff from him or any other man. That's always been my motto." Then she winked at Bette. "Probably why I'm still a single lady after all these years."

*Single after all these years?* Was a house full of antiques and crocheted doilies what lay in store for Bette's future?

"I'm sure you had plenty of boyfriends in your day."

The elderly woman sat straight, her gray brows arched. "Young lady, I'll have you know I'm not dead yet."

"Oh, no. I didn't mean to imply—" Her misery was ended by the other woman's laughter and a knock on the front door.

Alex.

"Don't." Bette motioned for her neighbor to remain seated. "I'll get it."

She opened the door, and relief flooded through her with a rush. Tall, tan, blue-eyed Alex. Oops. Make that Alex wearing his frownie face. "Come inside. Be extra nice and Miss Waller might let you have some lemonade and cookies."

"Miss Jane, you're looking well." He nodded, saving his smile for the older woman. He settled somewhat uneasily on the settee beside Bette and shot her a sideways glare.

Okay, so he was pissed off. Nothing new about that.

He made nice with his sister's neighbor but didn't have anything to say to Bette. Fine. If he wanted to act like a spoiled brat, he could. Minding his manners, he accepted a glass of lemonade and bit into a cookie. A genuine smile broke across his face. So, she wasn't the only one who loved cinnamon.

He praised the neighbor's baking to the high heavens and then said to Bette in a rather churlish manner that it was time to get back to the apartment for a strategy session.

After thanking Miss Waller for her hospitality, Bette nodded and rolled her eyes just so Miss Waller could see, and that good woman's mouth twitched with a restrained smile.

Bette reined her own impulse to smile. No need to let Alex in on their little private joke. She led Shadow outside, and as soon as they were on the porch, Alex deigned to speak. "I want an explanation. Why are you...?"

"Explanations when we get home." She jutted her chin and sashayed back toward Jackie's house, happy in the knowledge Alex was right behind her and for once she was safe.

# Chapter Fifteen

Bette unlocked her apartment door with one hand and snatched the note with her other and held it under Alex's nose. "See there? I left you a note."

"First, why the heck didn't you just call me and tell me you were going to walk the dog?"

She couldn't resist shooting him a slight smirk. "Because you would've told me to wait for you, and I didn't think Shadow could—wait, that is."

"Second, think you could've put a time on the note? Given me a clue how long you'd been gone? And third, why were you at Miss Waller's house instead of walking the dog? And *why* did you think it necessary for me to come over and get you?" Hands positioned at his waist, he loomed over her—all six feet three inches of him. The man really could loom when he had a mind to.

"Well, silly. You would've missed the lemonade and cookies if I hadn't."

He puffed out his cheeks and blew out a breath. "Had to be more than lemonade and cookies—by the way, they rocked. Explain, please, before I'm tempted to wring your pretty neck."

Delaying an answer, she walked over to the bedroom mirror and preened at his "pretty neck" remark. "Do you really think so?"

"Stop changing the subject. Why the hell were you having cookies at Miss Waller's? Besides, I didn't give you permission to go out without me in the first place."

"*Permission?*" A full-blown shudder ran through her. She took a deep breath. "First of all, I'm a grown woman and used to doing as

I please." She glanced down at Shadow and said firmly, "*We* needed some exercise, didn't we, girl?"

"Again I ask, why weren't you walking her? What happened? Dollars to doughnuts, something did."

"Is it your cop's *gut* that tells you so damned much?" She set her hands on her hips and got in his face, as much as she could, given he was a good eleven inches taller.

"No, it's the dodgy expression in your eyes and the annoying way you answer all my questions with a question."

She wrinkled her nose. "Fine. I'll tell you."

"I *knew* it." He paced in long strides across the limited free space of her sitting room.

The smug expression on his face was aggravating beyond belief. "If you know so damned much—"

Alex stopped mid-stride and turned slowly. Red-faced and jaw clenched, he sucked in a deep breath. "Are you purposely trying to drive me insane? Because I'm close." The words came out with an angry rasp.

She shook her finger in his face. "You just hold on a damned minute. Let me get Shadow settled in the bedroom. Our arguing is upsetting her." She hid her satisfaction at having the final word, led the dog into the bedroom, and unfastened the leash.

"Fine," he called after her. "Wouldn't want to upset the dog, or should I say the *baby*?"

Ignoring his snarky comment, she patted the comforter. Shadow sprang onto the bed and rolled over on her back. After a quick belly rub, Bette clenched her jaw. Nothing else to do now but face Alex and tell him about the man in the burgundy Caddy.

She'd have no more freedom until the kidnapper was found. Not that she minded Alex acting as if they were joined at the hip. Still, with her family history, a Fed was the last person she ought to be involved with. Not that she was ever involved in her brother's business, but there was bound to be at least a rule or two against a government agent fraternizing with a Mafia princess.

She shut the door behind her, walked over to the sofa, and plopped down. "All right. You've had a bug up your butt ever since you picked me up at Miss Waller's. What was that about?"

"You're stonewalling." He sat somewhat gingerly in the wing chair with the frayed arms and stretched out his long legs. "Spill it, Bette. What happened?"

"All right!" she said with some heat. "I figured walking up toward Main wouldn't hurt anything. We'd gone about a block or so when this burgundy Caddy CTS, late model, by the way, pulled to the curb ahead of me. He rolled down the window and asked for directions to the wine center." She reached up and finger-combed her bangs back from her forehead.

"Sounds innocuous enough."

"Then he asked me to *show* him the way and opened the passenger side door. Now, I just have to tell you that gave me a real hinky feeling. The hair stood up on the back of my neck. I mean it really did. I told him sorry, but I had the dog, and luckily, Miss Waller was coming down the sidewalk. I waved like a madwoman and asked if I could help carry her bags. That's how we ended up at her house." The last words came out with a whoosh of relief. She leaned forward and waited for his response.

Frowning, he stood and paced the short length of the room twice before he stopped and fixed his gaze on her. "No more walks for the dog—alone, I mean. We'll take her together." He took two more long strides and stopped right in front of her. He eyeballed her like she was a suspect in an interrogation room. "I learned something else today. When were you going to tell me? Or *were* you?"

Okay, he'd been at the police station. Had they gotten around to running her prints? Was the CPD that efficient? Could she bluff him? "What? Is that bug up your butt still buzzing?" Not a great comeback, but the best she could come up with on short notice.

His jaw tightened. "Bettina. Maria. Spinelli. Daughter of Victor Spinelli. Sister of Gino Spinelli. Crime boss. Guess that makes you Miss Mafia Prin-*cess*."

Oh, crap. Scratch the bluffing option. She opened her mouth, but it was cotton-ball dry. "I left that life behind," she managed to croak and tugged at the neck of her T-shirt. "I wasn't a part of any of it."

"But they have a rap sheet on you."

"I was eighteen. And stupid." She chewed her bottom lip. Why hadn't she fessed up before he found out? Too late now.

"It was a frigging *felony* conviction."

"Barely. Besides, I didn't serve any time."

"Yeah, thanks to your father's mouthpiece, you got off with community service. What did that consist of? Picking up trash for a couple of afternoons?"

She jumped to her feet and set her hands on her hips. "It was a thousand freaking hours, and it was humiliating, not to mention scary as hell. They put me to work in a men's homeless shelter, cleaning their *johns*. Let me tell you, those men didn't have the least idea of cleanliness. And the way they *watched* me. One of them did his damnedest to corner me. Believe you me, it wasn't a typical celebrity's idea of community service—not that I'm comparing myself to a celebrity." A shudder shook through her as the old feeling of panic rose and almost took hold. She staggered and collapsed on the sofa.

His expression softened. He perched on the arm of the sofa and stroked her hair. "Poor little princess."

Luxuriating in the tenderness of his touch, she said, "I learned my lesson. I guess you'd be happier, Agent MacGregor, if I'd to prison and come out a hardened criminal."

He slid his arm around her shoulders. "No, I wouldn't have wanted that. I'm glad you learned your lesson, but Spitz blindsided me with that juicy piece of intel. Have to say he enjoyed it a little too much."

"I didn't want to be that person anymore. Bette Smithson is who I am now. Tina Spinelli was used to having her way. *She* was a spoiled brat, or Mafia princess, if that expression floats your boat. B-but when my parents died—were murdered—in that fire, I knew I had to get away from the life. Before that, I didn't know what my father was. Not really."

"You *had* to know." His tone chided her, but gently, as if maybe he understood her reasons for not telling him everything before now.

"No." She shook her head vigorously. Dammit, he had to believe her. "He was really careful not to discuss business around me and my mother. All I knew was he owned a big construction company and my brother was learning the business from the ground up." She shrugged. "So I was naïve. But I grew up the night they died. After the funeral, I packed the few things not burned in the fire, got on a bus, and headed for Music City, USA."

"So that business about Fan Fair was just smoke?'

"Yes…and no. My first job in Nashville was at the Wildhorse Saloon. For a tip, one of the patrons gave me a ticket to one of the events, and *then* I discovered country music."

So now he knew it all. Every freaking bit.

Good-bye, Fed. Hello, empty bed.

Her heart sort of slipped a notch or two. She watched him stand and walk over to the small, high window and stare outside. Yeah, their one-step-forward, two-steps-back relationship was over before she'd had a single chance to wiggle out of her bikini panties.

Hands in his pockets, he turned and faced her again, his expression as grim as the Reaper's. "What the hell are we doing here?"

*Obviously, nothing.* Afraid to say too much or too little, she opted for a blank stare but discovered she couldn't meet his direct gaze. She turned away, and a lump the size of Rhode Island formed in her throat, making it too difficult to speak.

Alex, confused by her lack of reaction, fumbled for the right words. "Hell, for all I know, you could be involved with someone else."

She whirled and closed the distance between them. Her brows drawn together in a fierce frown and fire in her eyes. "Are you being stupid on purpose? When would I have time for anything like that?"

Crap, definitely not the right words. Try again. "It's been six months… What I mean to say is, I didn't expect you to move up here and become a nun."

She set both hands on her hips and glared. "As you might flipping expect, I have some trust issues when it comes to men. Besides, the one man I thought I could trust kissed me until I was limp and promised he'd call. But no-o-o. No call. *Nothing.* For six months! It took your sister being kidnapped to bring your ass back home."

He backed up, just to get a better view of Bette in full-out, raging bitch mode.

Awesome. Her dark eyes flashed with fire. Her tanned skin flushed with anger. Her lithe body tensed. She hissed and pounced, ready to strike like a cobra with a serious mad-on.

No fangs. Just a pair of small fists clenched and ready to pound his chest. He snatched her wrists and pulled her close. Her body against his set his heart hammering like an Uzi. "I'm here now. Sure you want to waste what time we have together being pissed off?"

"Is that how it is with you? Make hay while the sun shines? Any port in a storm?" Pausing, she took a deep breath and struggled to loosen his hold.

"If you've run out of clichés…"

"Clichés?" She stomped her foot. "If I wanted an English lesson, I'd have—"

"You'd have what?"

"What difference does it make what I would've done? You can't show up here and expect me to fall into bed with you at the drop of a hat."

He frowned and raised a brow. "Forgive me if I'm confused here. You're calling my character into question. Were we not about to get naked in the backseat of my car not so long ago?"

"Well, at least you remember *that* much. Exactly what is the extent of your memory? One hour? One day? Just how often did you think about me or your promise to call?" She gave him a tight smile. "I'd say about—" She formed a zero with her thumb and forefinger and held it in his face. "And here's another *cliché* for you: out of sight, out of mind."

"Not fair. I started a new assignment and jumped in full force. I *thought* about you." No matter how much he accomplished on the job, nothing could banish her completely. Like every frigging night, she haunted his dreams.

"You *thought* about me? That's so freaking lame I might have to throw up." Her body swiveled and one foot pointed toward the bathroom.

*Little faker.* He reached and snatched one of her wrists. "Don't waste the energy. Not on my account." A pulse beat rapidly in her throat. Her chest rose and fell. Her lips parted.

He crushed her close and wrapped his arms around her waist. No struggle this time. Together, their bodies molded and swayed as their lips met. Hers soft and pliant, they opened to the sweep of his tongue. He couldn't get enough, not if he lived to be a hundred.

Her knees buckled. He eased her over to the bed and somehow managed to get the dog to scram. He yanked the T-shirt over her head, then lowered his head and kissed her breasts through the red lacy bra. "God, you're beautiful."

She yanked his shirt from his jeans. With his free hand, he whipped it over his head. Skin to skin. Nothing better.

Her hands splayed down his chest, grabbed the zipper of his

jeans and inched it down. She spied his pale blue silk briefs and smirked. "Well, well, what do we have here? Nice material, Double-O." She reached behind her and opened the drawer of the bedside table. "Good thing I'm prepared." Holding up a condom, she gave him a smug little smile.

He laughed. "So…not exactly a nun."

She made a face and batted her lashes. "Shut up." She ripped open the packet with her teeth and sheathed him.

At her touch, a groan ripped from his throat. Kissing her lips, he snaked a hand around her back and unsnapped her bra, then worked his way from her neck to her breasts. He buried his face in their firm, lush softness. Her small brown nipples peaked and begged him to taste. She squirmed and moaned, then, cupping his ass, she pressed her mound against his erection.

His legs trembled. Time to hit the mattress for real. Still not quite believing what was about to happen, he eased her down. "You're sure about this?"

Her eyes opened, dark and glazed with passion and, amazingly, a touch of humor. "Oh, yeah."

He yanked down her jeans and slipped his hand into her already damp panties. She lifted her hips, and he eased the lacy undergarment down over her firm ass and tossed them on the floor.

He nibbled her knees, and her thighs parted, allowing him access to her core. Working his way north, he flicked at her sensitive nub. She moaned and rotated her hips, then boldly grabbed his erection and guided him into her warmth.

He thrust deep and let her wet heat envelop him. Her silken heat drove him mad to possess her and never let her go.

Her slender legs circled his waist as she rose to meet him thrust for thrust. He pounded into her, giving no quarter. They fit together so perfectly, as if her body was made for his…and his alone. Under his touch, her skin heated like a furnace. She stiffened and moaned when she came. A second later, he shuddered, and his world exploded. He collapsed by her side with a groan.

God, what had he done? Made love to a Mafia princess. Had to be a dozen federal regulations against it. He imagined the scene, introducing the new wife to the boss. Hell, it'd never get that far. Once the FBI ran a background check on her, it'd all be over. Or he'd be out of a job.

Still, Mafia princess or not, they'd made love. Sweet love.

Yeah, think about the loving. Forget about later. He rolled onto his side and faced her. Slowly, she levered onto her elbow and gazed at him with a single raised eyebrow.

# Chapter Sixteen

With her free hand, Bette brushed her hair back from her face but kept her gaze fixed on the man she'd just made amazing love with. "What's wrong?"

His eyes widened, and his chin dropped. "Wrong? Nothing."

"You're stiff as a board."

"I thought that was a good thing"—he let out a nervous laugh—"given the circumstances."

She slowly shook her head. "No. Something's wrong. Your body language—"

"You're going to lecture me, a trained FBI agent"—one of his brows shot up—"about body language?"

"Don't pull that secret-agent Double-O crap on me." She scooted up in the bed, tugged on the sheet, and covered her breasts. "Might as well tell me. What's on your mind, Agent MacGregor?"

"My mind was on *you*, and I was enjoying the view." Sitting up, he swung his legs over the side of the bed but didn't move any farther.

"So, that's how it's going to be? Wham, bam, thank you, ma'am." Sheesh. What in blazes was she thinking? Apparently, no man could be trusted, not even this uptight, oh-so-right Fed. "Okay, I'm ready. Give me the 'it was a mistake' speech, and then haul your fine keister out of my apartment."

He twisted around. His eyes widened with obvious disbelief. "What? You want me to leave?"

"I'm pretty sure your FBI training included the English language. Hell, yes, I want you out of here." Getting madder by the minute, and just so he'd get the point, she sprang from the bed and jerked on her jeans and T-shirt.

Time to move on. Time to make tracks…as soon as Jackie and Cody were found.

"But—" The most aggravating man in the world brushed his hand through his hair, leaving it in a spiky, sexy disarray.

"But *nothing*. You've got better things to do than grabbing a piece of tail. Remember—your sister's missing. *And* your nephew."

His jaw clenched so hard she could almost hear his teeth grit. "Not likely to forget it." Not soon enough for her, he stood and pulled on his jeans. He finished dressing without another word but stopped at the door and carefully avoided stepping on Shadow, whose eyes were wide with confusion. "Got a lot on my mind, Bette. Surely you understand that? Cut me some slack."

"I understand a lot. You screwed me and regretted it the very second after you got your rocks off. Naturally knowing who I really was didn't stop you from screwing me in the first place. After all, you're a *man*. What man's going to turn down a sure thing, huh?"

"You're wrong. That's not how it was." His sheepish expression gave the lie to his words.

Folding her arms across her breasts, she followed him to the door. "We're done. This conversation is so *oh-ver*."

"Maybe so, but you've forgotten one thing. There's someone out there who's made it his mission to screw up my life and take those closest to me."

"Not an issue." Setting her hands on her hips, she raised her chin, jabbed her finger against his chest and then back at hers. "You and me—we're not close."

"Doesn't mean he's aware of our current situation, unless he's bugged your apartment."

Her breath caught, and she gave an involuntary gasp. "You don't think—do you? Heaven only knows how long he was in the house."

"Just hear this—I'm not letting you out of my sight. You've kicked me out of your apartment, but I'm staying in the guestroom upstairs. You will *not* go out without me. When we're apart, you *will* check in with me by cell phone on an hourly basis. Understand?"

Great. Just great. All she needed was to be reminded of her mistake every hour on the hour. She'd already be packing if it wasn't for Jackie and her little boy. They deserved her loyalty, even if Jackie's brother was a Grade A horse's ass.

Shadow chose her moment and jumped on Bette's thigh and wagged her tail. Great. What would she do with her new dog if she took off to who knew where? No way could she leave the gentle Sheltie behind.

"Understand?"

"Yes, I freaking understand." *Control. Dammit. You're not a child.* She sucked in a deep breath, and then let it out slow and easy. "Could you just find the guestroom and get out of my face for a while?"

He pulled his iPhone from his pocket and waved it. "Call me in an hour or I'll be down here like white on rice."

"Spare me the clichés. But since you seem so fond of them, don't let the door hit you on the ass as you're leaving."

He turned, took a step, then stopped and shook his head. His jaw clenched, the muscles working. Apparently, he had more to say but wisely refrained.

No, he picked up his go-bag and headed for the door, his moment of indecision passed. Without a word, he left her frozen stock-still and holding her breath, and slammed the door. The sound was a shock, and with all her pent-up energy drained, she collapsed on the bed. Shadow jumped into her lap and started licking her face. "What the hell have I done, little girl?"

\*\*\*

Alex stomped upstairs and located the guestroom. The white, ruffled bedspread and curtains were more than a little on the girly side, and the walls were a hideous shade of Pepto pink. Still, the room would do as long as he was in town. He tossed the go-bag on the bed, then sat and tested the mattress. Firm enough. It would do.

He'd made a hell of a mistake. One he'd rectify as soon as Jackie and Cody were found. Speaking of which, his supervisor was due an update. His forty-eight hours were almost up.

He pulled up SAC John Riley's number and waited.

"Riley." His boss's voice was a rough growl. Ominous beginning to the conversation, given what Alex was about to tell him.

"MacGregor." Alex sucked in a deep breath and kissed his chances for career advancement good-bye. "I'm not gonna make my deadline."

"Didn't figure you would. Been keeping my eye on the case. Understand your nephew's missing too. You still convinced she was kidnapped and hasn't done a runner with the boy?"

"That's *not* the kind of person my sister is, sir. She's stable. Her vet practice was doing well. Her husband's kind of a prick, but I don't figure him for being involved. These locals don't know what the hell they're doing. They don't consider this a kidnapping case. If you could—"

"You *know* the procedure. The Bureau has to be called in by the local PD. What took them so long to call an Amber Alert?"

"Official take was no vehicle was seen. So no Amber Alert; however, they were talked into issuing one eventually."

"Rough. For your sake, I hope this wraps up favorably and as soon as possible. As for your spot on the task force… While I can't hold it indefinitely, I'll extend your leave by a week. Keep me informed."

"Of course." A sense of relief shot through Alex. Close call. "Thank you, sir." Now there was just the small matter of one pissed-off Mafia princess. A woman he could love, given half a chance. Where the hell had that come from? Love wasn't a part of his career plan. No, Bette was the very woman who would sidetrack his career if his boss discovered her background.

And if that jackass Spitz could find out, the SAC certainly would...*if* it came down to the SAC's need to know.

In other words, if he continued to see Bette, in spite of her current snit fit, sooner or later the SAC *would* need to know. She'd be thoroughly vetted, and the truth would come out. Whether or not she was a part of the Spinelli crime organization might not make a difference to his superiors. True, they couldn't prevent his involvement with her—free country and all that—but marrying her could—and probably would—sink his career.


So Double-O had second thoughts about bedding a dead Mafioso's daughter. Well, screw him! Bette pounded the pillow. Too bad pounding some sense into Alex wasn't an option.

And screw him she had...and enjoyed every blissful minute of it...until his face grew tight as if he were sucking a lemon and he pulled away. If it weren't for Jackie and her sweet little boy, the open road would be next on this chick's agenda.

Relationships—who needed 'em? Not her. Relationships were a one-way street to a place called Motel Misery. The best thing to do was hunker down and take care of her dog. Dogs didn't have second thoughts about loving you. They just responded to love and affection and returned it unconditionally.

Besides, who could trust a man who didn't like dogs? That should've been her first clue to Alex's real character. He was a grown man and way past the time he should've gotten over what had happened when he was a kid. As if Shadow, who didn't weigh an ounce over sixteen pounds, could or would hurt him. As if...

Said Sheltie curled up in Bette's lap and gazed up at her with a devoted doggie expression. She sighed. That she and the Sheltie bonded so quickly still amazed her. As a breed, Shelties were known to be loving and sweet companions, but they tended to be shy and usually took several days to bond with new caregivers, especially if they'd been ill-treated. By all indications, Shadow hadn't been mistreated, and for that, Bette was thankful. There should be some kind of hell reserved for those who abused children and animals.

As for fainthearted men like a certain FBI special agent... Well, he could just go back to Chi-town and—

No, she'd forgotten one important fact. Alex was living through his own hell right here and now. First his twin and now his sister and nephew—no wonder he was edgy and uptight.

Cut the man some slack.

Losing her mother and father in the fire had nearly killed her. Alex had already suffered one loss, and the fear his sister and nephew were already dead and lying in a field waiting for their bodies to be discovered was too much. More than anyone should have to handle.

Maybe she should apologize for being such a bitch.

Or maybe he should apologize for using her.

But maybe she'd used him too.

Okay, time to pull up her big girl panties and take the high road in the relationship, at least until his sister and nephew were found. Since the local cops were basically useless, she and Alex needed to work together. The personal stuff would just have to wait.

# Chapter Seventeen

Upstairs in the guestroom, Alex booted his laptop and accessed the ViCAP database. He entered the parameters of his sister and nephew's disappearances and waited. What he discovered was plenty of disappearances of women Jackie's approximate age and even more of children Cody's age, even a few mother and child abductions together, but not a single documented disappearance of both a mother and child occurring as separate incidents.

As bad as he hated to consider the possibility, maybe Spitz was right in assuming Jackie had dumped her unfaithful husband, run off with the guy with the cat, and then snatched her child at the first opportunity. Given what he'd learned about Brad's infidelity, Alex wouldn't blame her if she dumped the jerk, but why like this? Any competent divorce attorney would've advised her to sit tight, sue for divorce, and take Brad for all he was worth. And if she was actually going to pull a stunt like this, she would've warned her brother upfront.

What was the alternative? Brad was responsible for doing away with Jackie and had their son hidden away. In cases like this, it was almost always the husband. And if that were the case, then his sister was already dead. That thought set his stomach to burning and cramping. Intending to check out the hall bathroom, he set aside the computer and headed for the door. What he needed was some Pepto.

He stopped short as a sharp knock sounded. Mentally, he groaned. What did she want *now*? Another chance to unleash her ferocious and basically unjustified temper? "Yeah?" He whipped open the door.

Bette stood with fist upraised ready to knock again or maybe to bust him in the chops. The dog stood beside her, wagging its bushy tail for all it was worth.

"Sorry." Her eyes widened, and she pulled back her fist.

"It hasn't been an hour." He gave the words a bit of a growl, hoping she'd just go away and leave him the hell alone.

Her damned fine breasts rose as she sucked in a breath. "I came to apologize, you jerk."

"For what? Seeing as how *I'm* the jerk." Ready for her next retort, he clenched his jaw.

"While I won't argue the point"—she wrinkled her nose and continued—"I got to thinking."

"Since when did thinking enter into your *modus operandi?*"

Her eyes flashed with a touch of anger. "You're not making this easy."

"*Easy?*" He tried to tamp down his anger and failed. "Nothing about you is easy. Not since we first met."

"I just knew you'd have to dredge up that night." She shifted her weight from one foot to the other and crossed her arms over her breasts. "I thought maybe I should, like you said, cut you some slack. You're under a lot of stress. Plus, I kept something from you, and you had a right to be pissed off. No matter what happened between us *before*, we need to work together to find your sister and Cody."

"I don't need a partner…" Just barely, he refrained from finishing that sentence and saying a partner who doesn't know her ass from her elbow about investigating a kidnapping.

"Yes, you do." Her chin rose, and her dark eyes flashed, reminding him how stubborn she was, given the chance.

"You and that dog are distractions. Just keep your butt in your apartment, and let me handle the investigation end of things."

"Fine. Where were you going when I knocked on the door?"

"How do you know I was going anywhere?"

"You opened the door the instant I knocked. You had to be standing right there."

"I was headed—" He broke off, refusing to admit to an unsettled stomach. She'd jump on the least sign of weakness, and the last thing he needed was her mockery or sympathy.

"All right, then, head wherever. You should know, since the authorities released the office as a crime scene, I'm going in to straighten up. The locum will need help, and Jackie will need us to keep the practice going until she comes back. Got it?" She nodded as if to emphasize her point.

"Yeah, I got it. And if that SOB comes back for you…?"

"Then I'll aggravate him to death, like I do you."

"Good luck with that. Works for me." Brushing by her, he started down the hall; then a wave of shame hit him, slowing his steps. He stopped and turned. "I didn't mean that."

Bette gazed up, her brown eyes shining with tears. "I know." She closed the short distance between them and slid her arms around his waist, resting her cheek against his chest. "I'm sorry I've been a bitch. I'm sorry I didn't tell you about my family, and I'm so sorry this has happened to yours."

Alex swallowed hard. Bette's anger he could contend with, but this soft, gentle side touched him on a level that unsettled him and left him more than a little confused. This side of Bette he could love. Make a life with.

"Let me help, Alex. I feel so responsible." Her dark gaze was as sincere as any he'd ever seen. "If I'd just stayed with her, maybe the two of us could've fought him off."

Two women, both on the small side, wouldn't have had a chance. He caressed Bette's cheek, then said, "And maybe you'd both be dead."

"No!" She let out a gasp and banged her small fists against his chest. "You mustn't say that word. I—"

"I don't want to believe it either." In spite of their infrequent contact over the years, he loved his sister. She and her son were all the family he had left. And no way would he give up trying to find them, even if it meant searching every square inch of Ontario County.

"We can't give up. You have to let me help you. Even if it's, I don't know, go-for type stuff."

"Uh-huh." He nodded slowly, resigned to the fact that she was going to help whether he wanted her to or not. "You gonna dig holes? Think maybe they're underground?" No joke. Many a "collector" had been found to have a fortified cellar or a modified torture chamber where he kept his victim, sometimes for years. All he could hope was that Jackie and Cody were still alive. His body gave an involuntary shudder at the thought of either being tortured.

"What is it?" Bette's brow furrowed. The concern in her voice rang true and resonated on a deep level. Already she knew him well enough to gauge his reactions. "Let's just say I know too much. Seen too much."

"Guess it's like they say, sometimes too much knowledge isn't a good thing."

"Never more true than in this case." His throat dry, he choked out the words.

"So tell me what you need me to do." She gazed up at him, her expression sincere. "And I don't mean go hide in my apartment." She nodded at his open laptop. "You've already been working on something. Find anything we can use?"

Damn, but the woman was determined to help. "It's more what I haven't found." He moved the laptop from the bed to the dressing table. It'd have to do for a desk. Best not work on the bed—not with Bette in the same room. "I didn't find a single instance of a woman being abducted that was later followed by her child's abduction, except in cases of custodial interference. And that's not the case here." He went on to tell Bette about the FBI's Violent Criminal Identification and Apprehension Program database, or ViCAP, for short, and how he'd only found the more common cases. Basically, nothing with a profile like Jackie's abduction.

"Sounds like to me—okay, just hear me out." She leveled her gaze in his direction. "This isn't what *I* actually think, but I can see why the police *might* think Jackie ran away."

"Because it's the easiest solution. Write her off as a runaway mom. Like they tried to write off my brother as a runaway."

"Did they really?" Shaking her head, she let out an exasperated huff.

"If our dad hadn't been a doctor and one of the town's movers and shakers, they wouldn't have done anything. As it was, one detective got very involved and busted his ass trying to find my brother and, later, whoever took him."

"What's his name? Could he give us a hand?"

"I'll never forget Detective Sergeant Johnny Ross. I'll check around and give him a call. He's probably retired by now."

"Hm." She twisted her mouth to the side. "Did they ever find his killer, or were there more boys taken?"

Smart gal. Asked good questions too. "Like a serial? No, that's the weird part—no more boys were taken. Detective Ross said the area must've gotten too hot for the kidnapper, so he moved on."

"Look, you and I both know Jackie didn't run off." She continued pacing. "Maybe we need to take a deeper look at Brad."

"Brad has an alibi—of sorts." He hesitated, not wanting to tell her Brad's alibi was a hooker who hadn't been found yet.

"Of *sorts*? Either he does or he doesn't."

"It's not that cut and dried." Damn, Bette was great at cutting to the chase. Might even prove to have a knack for investigating. "The local LEOs are still looking into that aspect—at least, they better be."

"You're not telling me something." She cocked her head to the side and eyeballed him.

"Okay. There was a hooker, Brandi, as yet-to-be-found."

"The dirty rat!" She shook her head and fisted her hands. "Don't think I won't be telling Jackie."

"Careful, Jersey." Indeed, her New Jersey accent had resurged, and she was in full Mafia princess mode. Her eyes flashed with anger as she flipped her hair over her shoulder.

She shot him a sideways glance and shrugged. "Makes me wish—just a little—I could get my brother. Y'know?"

He set his hands on her shoulders and stopped her pacing. "I *do* know, and no, don't even *think* about it." Better yet, she should read the no-BS expression in his gaze.

She pursed her lips and shrugged. "My brother doesn't even know where I am."

"You sure?"

She nodded. "Definitely. I let him know I'd left Nashville and why. And you don't want to know what he threatened to do to Rod—" She held up a hand. "Don't worry, I didn't give Gino his name. I just let him know I was okay and back in the Northeast. That, plus I still didn't want anything to do with the family business."

"Good." How he'd ever explain it to his superiors at the Bureau, he wasn't sure. Getting involved with a wise guy's sister was a career killer, the death knell to his life's dream. But he was sure of one thing: Bette's desire to keep out of the family dealings— at least until she threw out her comment about putting a hit on his brother-in-law. What would he do without the Bureau? All through school, that was all he'd ever wanted. He shook his head, wishing he'd never let his Galahad complex get the better of him six months ago. Almost.

"God. What a face. Come on. You know I was kidding about putting a hit on Brad. I'd much rather deck him myself, and then tell Jackie." She chewed her bottom lip thoughtfully. "Do you think she actually knows he's unfaithful or will she be devastated? Honestly, I thought they had a good marriage. Just goes to show, I guess." She pulled out the chair in front of the dressing table and sat, giving her long, dark hair a pat.

Somewhat gingerly, Alex sat on the edge of the bed and smiled at the image of Bette decking his brother-in-law.

Without warning, the dog, which had been behaving fairly well, jumped on the bed and flopped over on her back, exposing her belly with her four hairy paws outstretched. "What?" Glad of the distraction, he darted a glance at Bette, managing to control his urge to flee. "Rude dog. Can't you control her?"

"Little girl just wants her belly rubbed. You should be flattered."

"She's tormenting me." Like her mistress, but not on the same level.

"No such thing. Dogs are smart, and they know people. Even if you're still afraid of her, she's letting you know she's submissive and won't bite."

"Yeah, that's what they all say." His tone rose in a falsetto. "*'Oh, don't worry about her. She won't bite.'* Right! Next thing you know, I'm in the ER with multiple lacerations."

Bette doubled over, laughing so hard she seemed to have trouble breathing.

"I'm serious."

"I know you are. That's what's so funny." This she managed to say between gasps of laughter.

"You and this *dog* are seriously pissing me off."

"I'm sorry. She's just recognizing you as the alpha male."

"Alpha male? Yeah, that's me, all right." He cast a quick look at the dog. "She senses that, huh? Pretty smart of her."

More giggles from the Mafia princess. Man, he had to get that phrase out of his head.

His cell phone rang. The caller ID showed Canandaigua PD. "Sorry to interrupt your hilarity, but I need to take this." His heart raced as he answered, "MacGregor." Good news or bad?

Detective Spitz's flat and noncommittal tone came over the line. "Got a floater washed up on the north bank of the lake. Matches your sister's general description. Appreciate it if you'd come down to the morgue for an identification."

"Oh, God." His heart sped into overdrive.. Mouth dry, he tried to speak. Finally, the words came. "Already at the morgue?" Why hadn't they called him sooner?

"Give us an hour or so."

"Where is she *right now*?"

"Still on the scene. Now listen to me. This is an active crime scene. FBI or not, you don't have any business messing around down here. The coroner's already pronounced her, and she'll be on her way into the morgue before you can get down to the lake. Hear me, MacGregor?"

"Yeah." He disconnected the call, then turned to Bette. "Uh—" His tongue literally stuck to the roof of his mouth.

"No! What is it? *Tell* me!"

He waved her away, shaking his head and not wanting to believe it was his sister's body on the way to the morgue. *Had* to be a mistake. He picked up the car keys. "Gotta go."

"Wait. I'm going with you." She jerked the keys from his hand. "I'll drive."

"What about the dog?" Why he gave a flip about the mutt when his sister might be dead, he had no earthly idea.

"Taking her down to my apartment right now. Won't take me a sec." She headed for the hallway; the Sheltie jumped off the bed and followed. Bette stopped at the door. "Wait for me!"

Once Bette was out of sight, Alex sat on the bed and buried his face in his hands. Images of floaters came to mind. The same desolation he'd felt when he learned his brother's body had been found knifed through him just as sharp and left a new jagged wound. God, this couldn't be happening again.

Not again.

# Chapter Eighteen

Bette turned on the ignition and gave Alex a sideways glance. She'd never seen him so down. Eyes dull. *So* not all there. "You going to tell me where we're headed sometime today?" Her hands shook on the steering wheel. Dammit. "I heard you say morgue. That's where we're going, to the morgue, right? Are they sure it's Jackie? No, it just can't be."

"No. Drive...toward the lake."

"Which side?" She backed out onto the street and headed the car in the direction of Main Street.

"Just head toward the bathhouse—the park, whatever they call it now."

"Okay..." She held her breath, waiting for him to tell her more.

"Should be able to see where we need to go from there."

His tone was so devoid of emotion, she had to drag more information out of him. It just couldn't be Jackie or Cody, please, no. "Please tell me about the call. What h-have they found...?" If she couldn't even bring herself to say the word "body," she certainly couldn't blame Alex for staring ahead and giving a dead-on impression of a zombie. She hung a quick left on Main.

She stayed in the inside lane and again cut her gaze toward her grim passenger. His Adam's apple bobbed as he swallowed. He ran a hand through his hair and shook his head.

Okay, eyes back on the road. The lake was only a few more blocks. She'd know soon enough. Not that she couldn't guess. Or wanted to.

And sure enough, up ahead, Eastern Boulevard was blocked off, and a cop was directing traffic away from what had to be the crime scene. Multiple patrol cars, a black van with *Coroner* on the side, and what had to be every cop car in Canandaigua and Ontario County lined the side of the road.

Seeing all the cops and patrol cars with their flashing blue-and-white lights hit her harder than expected. Too sharply, it brought back memories of the night she'd returned from a girls' night out and found her home a pile of smoking embers. Her parents were dead and already loaded into the *meat wagon*, as one of the cops called it. She swallowed, blinking back the tears. Fat lot of good tears would do.

A block before the police detour, she turned and parked on a side street. She removed the keys from the ignition, then turned to see Alex's bleak expression. "I'm so sorry."

"Don't know it's her. Not yet." Without meeting her gaze, he scrambled from the car and raced toward the lake before she could undo her seat belt.

"Dammit. Wait!" He shouldn't have to face whatever the authorities found—not alone. She jumped from the car and ran after the man. The man who might've just lost his only sister.

Alex's heart pounded, beating loud in his ears. He stopped running only when the patrol officer stopped him at the perimeter of the crime scene. "FBI," he said, whipping out his ID and badge, and then ducked under the tape before the officer, who was only doing his job, could object.

He surveyed the scene, and quickly his gaze focused on the gurney and body bag. Time slowed. Was this what his grand illusions of being an FBI agent amounted to? His sister dead at the hands of an unsub? Would his nephew be next?

Powerless. Dammit, he was powerless. And more than

anything, he hated that someone else had the upper hand and had taken his sister's life.

*No. Not Jackie.* Not until he saw for himself.

A wide form blocked his progress toward the body. Alex held up his arm to shove the detective out of the way.

"Hold on, MacGregor." Spitz shoved back and stood his ground. "You don't have any business down here. Told you to meet me at the morgue."

"Dammit, tell me! Is that my sister or not?"

"Look, I'm sorry," Spitz began. "Should've waited until—"

"Until what?" The rage, the anger, the unfairness of it all burst from him, leaving him shaking and needing to punch someone. Anyone. And Spitz would do fine.

"One of the sheriff's deputies knows your sister—takes his dog there— Anyway, says it's not her. Sorry, but he came on scene a couple of minutes after I called you."

"It's not—is he sure? Let me see. I *have* to see." He dragged in a breath, then moved toward the body, his legs jerking, almost failing to support him.

Spitz jerked his head at the coroner's assistant. "Let 'im have a look."

The assistant unzipped the bag enough for him to see the pale, bloated face of a woman. Fair hair and dull, dead blue eyes. But it wasn't his sister. Someone else.

Relief surged through him. He wanted to dance and sing, but remorse kicked him in the gut. Someone else would grieve tonight. Someone who'd lost a mother or sister or daughter.

But not Alex. Not yet.

A commotion broke out behind him. He turned and saw Bette duck around the patrolman and run toward him. He opened his arms. "It's not Jackie."

Bette threw herself into his arms and hugged him. "Thank God. I was so scared. Are you all right? Do you know who it is?"

He shook his head. "All I know is it's not my sister." He took a deep breath. "Let's get out of the way. There's still plenty of work to be done."

Hand in hand, they walked slowly back to where the car was parked. He restrained the urge to skip. "I feel so guilty."

"Why?" She gazed up at him, her dark eyes filled with confusion.

"Because I'm so damned happy it was someone else. Anyone but my sister."

"That's only natural." She squeezed his hand. He squeezed hers back, receiving an enormous amount of comfort from her simple gesture and her very presence.

They walked the block back to the car, picking their way along the bumpy sidewalk where the roots of hundred-year-old trees had broken through the concrete. "I was so afraid," he finally admitted. "All the way down to the lake, I imagined how her body would look. Fortunately, that woman hadn't been in the water very long. At least her family won't have to view a body that…" He paused, then continued, "She'll still be recognizable…to someone. You wouldn't believe the horror the relatives of some victims have to identify." He shook his head. Given that the physical description of this woman was similar to Jackie's, was there a serial killer just starting up in the area? But that didn't fit with Cody's being abducted so soon after his mother.

He felt a shiver pass along her arm. She slowed her pace. "And you were visualizing the worst-case scenario?"

"Yeah," he said with a nod. "That's where my mind went."

She squeezed his hand, tighter this time. "Me too." Her tone softened and soothed as she admitted her earlier doubts.

By now, they'd reached his car. He held out his hand for the keys. "I'm all right. I'll drive."

"You sure?" She shot him a quizzical expression. "I don't mind driving your car at all. It's much nicer than mine."

"Keys, please." He kept his tone playful and opened the passenger door. "Thanks. I'm glad you were with me. What an ass, worrying about my career. My sister could still be just as dead as the woman they just fished out of the lake."

"I know your career's important. I *get* it." Her cheeks colored, she averted her gaze. "I—uh, just didn't think my family would matter, and then when it seemed like it might, it was too late. You already knew."

"Thanks to Spitz."

"Yeah, good old Detective Dog." She frowned, slid inside, and he shut the door.

When he entered the driver's side, she patted his knee. "Don't worry. I'm not going to ruin your career. We had a quickie. That's all it was. Nothing more. Nothing less."

He swallowed the hard lump of emotion forming in his throat. "Ever since my brother was found, all I ever wanted was a career with the Bureau."

"Chill. You don't owe me any explanations, Double-O. I'm a big girl. It's not like I was a virgin. Besides, we both had a good time." She lifted her shoulders in a casual shrug.

What a woman. With those few brave words, she'd released him from the necessity of continuing their relationship. Gave him his freedom. Once his sister was found, all he had to do was walk away. From Canandaigua. From family. And from Bette.

But could he? Could he just tuck tail and run from everything that reminded him of the greatest losses in his life? Hell, yeah, he could.

Wouldn't be the first time. How many girls had he loved and left before they got too close? Wouldn't be the last. But somehow, Bette was different. He more than liked her. He *trusted* her. One of life's little jokes: the one he didn't want to leave was the one who could torpedo his career.

\*\*\*

Bette entered her apartment, half expecting Alex to turn and go back upstairs. But he seemed in no hurry to leave. He straddled a ladder-back chair and patted his knee. Shadow placed her two front paws on his thigh, and he rubbed her head.

Now, that was new. Bette walked over to the counter and checked the coffee pot. "Want some coffee? Won't take long."

"Yeah. Guess I will." He shrugged. "You know, this dog of yours isn't so bad."

"Told you," she said over her shoulder while she ran cold water into the glass pot and then poured it into the receptacle. Measuring the coffee and dumping it into the basket, she wondered how far he'd go in making up with Shadow. "She has a name."

"Yeah, *Shadow*. I know."

She leaned back with her elbows on the counter and watched the two. "She's a good dog."

"Just don't expect me to talk baby talk."

"Just don't complain when *I* do."

Shadow jumped down from Alex's thigh, circled the room, and picked up one of her toys. She brought it back to Alex and stood looking at him with her expressive eyes.

He frowned. "What's the matter? What does she want?"

"She wants to play. Tug-o-war or fetch. Either will do fine."

He reached for the stuffed toy, and the dog pulled back. "Hey, she's strong."

"Careful. Don't pull too hard."

"I'm not pulling. She's the one pulling like a tug-o-war machine."

The coffeemaker bubbled and hissed, signifying the coffee was finished brewing. Bette poured a cup for Alex, who'd just managed to wrest the toy from Shadow, and then retrieved a Diet Coke from the fridge.

"Now throw it. She loves to fetch." Alex tossed the toy, and

Shadow scampered to retrieve it. Bette set the cup down on the side table.

"Thanks," he said. "I need it. Intravenous would be even better. It's not every day you think your sister's body might've just washed up on the lakeshore."

Damn, the man really had a gorgeous face. She swallowed, refusing to acknowledge just how much she was attracted to him or how much she cared. "Glad I could be there for you. And doubly glad Detective Dog was wrong. That jerk should've been more certain of his facts before he summoned you to the morgue. Honestly, he's clueless, and that's not a good condition for a detective, now, is it?"

She turned and aimlessly started straightening paper napkins on the small counter. Anything to keep her hands busy and her mind off a certain agent's hot bod.

"Bette."

At the sound of her name, she whipped around and sucked in a startled breath. In spite of the fact Alex was sitting astraddle the chair, Shadow had somehow jumped into his lap, had her front feet planted on his shoulders and was licking his face. His expression wavered between abject fear and tentative acceptance.

"Make her stop." His tone was soft and pleading; his hands gripped the back of the chair.

Biting her lips to hold back her laughter, she clapped her hands. Shadow stopped bathing Alex's face, turned in Bette's direction, and promptly curled up between his thighs.

"Get her off. Please."

"You are seriously phobic, aren't you?" She sighed. "Okay, Shadow. Down." She pointed to the floor, and the dog obliged. "See, she's very smart. All you had to do was ask her. Never have I seen a supposedly alpha male act so un-alpha."

She slipped onto his thighs, facing him. "I don't think Shadow will mind if I take her place." She leaned forward, intending to kiss his brow. Instead, he took her face in his hands. Her breath caught. "I thought—"

"Stop thinking, Bette." He winked. "You saved me from that creature. I don't know what I would've done without you."

She extricated herself from his lap and the chair and got to her feet. "You are such a *liar*. And a damned bad actor too."

"Is that animal of yours is properly licensed. Maybe I should take you in for—"

Feet planted apart and hands set on her hips, she glared. "Take me where? For what? For rescuing a dog?"

"No." His gaze caught hers and held fast. "I'd rather take you to bed."

Now, what did he expect her to say to that? Bette swallowed the knot in her throat. "That's just great. You're ready for another booty call, and you used my dog to play on my sympathies."

"Booty call?" He shook his head. "Not so. You were there for me this afternoon. Don't know what I would've done if it'd been Jackie. I needed you."

"Let me get this straight. A *booty call* is your way of saying 'Thanks'?"

Shaking his head, he stood, moving the chair aside. "It's my way of saying… Hell, I don't know."

She folded her arms across her chest. No point in making things easy for him. "If you don't, neither do I."

"Bette, I don't know what it is about you." He stroked her cheek with his finger. Such a tender, unexpected gesture surprised her. Still, she didn't draw back when he continued with a half grin, "But there's something—"

She held up her hand to stop him and straightened her back. "Careful, Agent MacGregor, you're venturing into dangerous territory. You've a career to think about. Correct me if I'm wrong." Attitude wasn't enough to keep him at bay. His presence drew her like hot fudge on vanilla ice cream. Inexorably. Completely. Oh,

God.

"Liked it better when you called me Double-O. Remember New Year's Eve?"

"As if I'd forget."

"You were blazing hot that night. No wonder I couldn't sleep."

"You certainly didn't act like I was." No, indeed. He'd been an all-too-perfect gentleman.

"Didn't seem right to take advantage of a lady in distress."

"Like you want to take advantage *now*?"

"Mutual advantage." He swallowed hard. His Adam's apple bobbed with the effort. "No strings."

"Such an attractive offer—not." She tried to turn away, but he hooked a finger under her chin and raised it.

"If you want me to leave, I will." His gaze held hers, daring her, or was he pleading to stay?

Her feet seemed rooted to the floor. More than anything, she wanted to lose herself in his arms and the rest of his hot body. She swallowed, trying to bring some moisture to her mouth.

He inched closer. Close enough that the spicy smell of his aftershave tickled her nose. Close enough that his body heat enveloped her and drew her ever closer into a web of desire.

Close enough that his lips brushed hers. Resistance be damned. She surrendered to his strength...to his intensity...and to his questing tongue. Her head spun, and her bones weakened, accomplishing a fine imitation of Jell-O left out a little too long.

A half moan, half sigh escaped as her tongue met his. She grabbed his shoulders, and he swung her up into his arms, her legs encircling his waist.

He carried her into her bedroom and kicked the door shut before the dog could follow. His mouth never left hers as he laid her on the bed. She pulled his knit shirt over his head as he snaked a hand underneath her torso and unsnapped her bra.

"Pretty good at that," she said into his mouth. "Must've had some practice."

He made an unintelligible response which sounded suspiciously like a snort, then said, "Ain't going there, Jersey. This is about you"—his head dipped to leave a trail of kisses down her neck— "and me."

She pulled away enough to lever up on an elbow. "No strings, remember?"

"Right." He drew the word out as if reluctant. "No strings."

"Then forget the 'you and me' crap. This is just about *now*. That's all."

"You're one tough broad." He slipped her T-shirt over her head and pulled away her bra for good measure.

She marveled at the perfection of his chest and ran her hands languorously over his shoulders and down his chest to the waist of his jeans.

"No rush. I want to look at you," he said, pulling her closer to him. "I want to touch you all over."

Beneath him, Bette gave a tiny snort into his shoulder. "Wasn't that a song back in the day?"

Propped on his forearms, Alex made a face and shook his head. "What am I going to do with you, Jersey?" Then he gazed down at her with a devilish light in his laser-blue eyes. "I know."

A warm thrill coursed through her. What did the man have in mind?

His mouth fastened on a nipple, causing it to tighten into a nub. She grasped the sheets with both hands. "Comes with the territory, being a Mafia princess and all." How she managed to respond coherently at all was a minor miracle. The warmth of his tongue and the light scrape of his teeth on her nipple set her thighs to quivering and heat pooling between her thighs.

He lifted his head and sucked in a breath. "Not going to forget *that* fact."

His ironic tone hit her like a sucker punch. Neither one of them was likely to forget her background. Not now. Not ever.

He unzipped her jeans. She lifted her hips, allowing him to work them down. Burying his nose at the apex of her thighs, he slid her jeans and panties down her knees and calves. Her thighs trembled at his intimate touch. "No fair," she gasped and kicked off her jeans. "You're not nekkid yet." She rubbed Alex's erection through his jeans.

"I'll fix that quick enough." He stood on his knees and slid down the zipper.

She could make out the jut of his cock through the thin material of his silk briefs. Her mouth dried. She reached and jerked down his jeans and briefs in a rush. Freed from restraint, his cock pulsed when she caressed it.

"Hold on." His plea came out in a raspy groan.

She looked up at him, her heart pounding like a snare drum. "I am."

"No, I mean hold up. Hell, I don't know what I mean. Take it easy, or this'll be over before we're started."

"Wouldn't want that." Bette reached for a condom at the same time he did, his warm hand covering hers.

"No, we wouldn't."

She sheathed him while he stared down at her, his eyes darkening to deep sapphire blue. "Not at all," he mumbled as he took her nipple into his mouth and sucked.

He slid two fingers inside her while massaging her clitoris with his thumb. Hips squirming, she moaned with need. She grasped his shoulders and opened herself to him. He cupped her buttocks, centering himself, thrust home with one sure stroke.

She answered his thrusts with her own, biting his shoulder to keep from crying aloud. Deeper. Harder. Faster and faster, they tangled and entwined until neither could resist the overwhelming tide that washed and exploded between them.

Alex's breath was ragged, and perspiration glistened on his

forehead as he sagged against her. His eyes were half closed, but she saw the emotion as he gazed down. He kissed her and breathed, "I love you, Jersey. God help me, but I do."

He *loved* her? Was he out of his mind?

True, no man had ever taken her to these heights. But why count on what could never be? She wasn't about to ruin his career. And there wasn't a damned thing she could do about her family, especially since Gino was still a major player in Atlantic City.

A clean break. That was what she needed. As soon as they found Jackie, Bette would take Shadow and head to LA or Seattle. Or anywhere but where she was likely to run into Alex MacGregor. And yet, the thought of never seeing him again brought tears to her eyes.

*Be strong.* "This can't happen again," she murmured into his shoulder.

He levered up on one elbow. "Don't know why not."

"Nothing's changed. You're still a Fed, and I'm a mobster's daughter."

His brows drew together as if he were considering his options. "Maybe something could be worked out."

"*Something?*" She shook her head. She could see the doubt written in his eyes, no matter what he said. "You're dreaming."

He swung his feet to the floor and winked. "Let's continue this conversation in the shower."

The last thing in the world she needed was a round of shower sex. She chewed her bottom lip. "I don't think so. You go ahead. I've got stuff to do."

"More important than…" His eyes widened with disbelief.

"Afraid so." Best she got away now while she still could. Rather than spend the rest of the day in his arms—no, that was way too dangerous. Too dangerous for her heart.

She wasn't sure where her future lay, but it certainly wasn't in Special Agent Alex MacGregor's bed, his arms, or, least of all, his heart. No matter what he said in the heat of the moment.

"Fine, but if you change your mind..." He lifted the corner of his mouth as if he thought he could change her mind with his charm alone.

"I won't." She hopped from the bed, snatched up her fallen clothes, and pulled on her panties. She felt his gaze lingering on her breasts and crossed her arms. "Go on. No free peepshow."

Heading for the shower, he laughed, waving his hands in a gesture of surrender. "All right, if you say so."

She exhaled a sigh of relief, her thighs trembling with the urge to follow him. Swallowing the lump in her throat, she steeled her resolve. Booty call was over. Work was calling her name. Even if it was Sunday, she could straighten the office. No doubt the cops had left a mess with fingerprint dust and crap.

Okay, so she was running.

Big deal. Running away was something she was good at.

# Chapter Nineteen

Guilt was a bitch. What the hell had she been thinking? Making love while Jackie was still missing. Bette waited until she heard the shower running and quickly wrote Alex a note, telling him where she was headed and why, then propped it on the beat-up coffee table.

After fastening Shadow in her backseat crate, Bette headed to the office. The locum would appreciate Bette's efforts in the morning. As she neared the office, she flicked on the turn signal, then turned into the parking lot. At the same time, her cell phone chimed.

She waited until she parked before answering the unfamiliar number showing on the screen. Curiosity got the better of her, so she answered.

"Bette! I'm so glad—got you. I need—help." A burst of scratchy static. "Quick. Be—he—back."

"Jackie? Is it really you?" Stupid. Of course it was. In spite of the poor reception, static and dropouts, she'd know her boss's panicked voice anywhere. "Are you all right? Is Cody with you?

"We're—deserted wine—side Naples. Hur—not—time. He's com—"

"Which—?"

A cry of pain followed by a sharp click, then the mocking whine of the dial tone.

Bette's heart slammed until it threatened to rip from her chest. Okay. So, the too-stupid-to-live heroine always took off on her own and then needed the hero to come charging to the rescue. Not this time. Maybe only part of the cliché was true. She certainly hadn't imagined Jackie's voice on the phone. That much was true. Maybe she'd made the call under duress, and it was a trap.

Even so, she had to follow up. Forewarned was forearmed, right?

*No, first call Alex.* Together they stood a much better chance of finding and rescuing his sister and nephew. Time to check in with him anyway. She hit his number on speed dial.

No answer. It rolled to voice mail. "Fat lot of help you are. I just heard from your sister. As far as I can tell, she's in an old deserted winery outside Naples. Jackie told me about one, so maybe you'll know which one I mean. Sure hope so, 'cause I'm not waiting around. I'm heading up there right now to have a look-see. Hope to see you soon—like really soon."

Okay, so now she'd officially gone into too-stupid-to-live territory, but who the hell knew where Alex was or how long he'd be. She swallowed the lump in her throat. It was their first solid lead, and she couldn't just sit around and wait.

She turned on the ignition and whipped the car around.

High Road, here I come.

The High Road was a picturesque twisting two-lane road with the hills on one side and glimpses of the lake far below. The air was clear, and even with the AC on full blast, the interior of her ancient Corolla was definitely on the warm side. Might as well roll down the window and breathe fresh air instead.

While she drove, she considered her options as well as her chances of finding the right old winery. It couldn't be Widmer's because, while it was closing, it wasn't deserted by any means. If she remembered Jackie's quick Canandaigua history lessons correctly, there was at least one other winery which had stopped production back in the early nineties.

She reduced her speed and peered over the steering wheel for a sign of the little-used road. There it was. She braked and turned into the road which was more of a double-rutted track than a road.

Damn. Bringing the vehicle to a stop, she banged the steering wheel in frustration. Maybe this wasn't the right road after all. A weathered wood gate barred her from further progress. The canopy of trees was densely grown and shut out the sun, but it seemed as if there was a clearing ahead. What could it hurt to check it out?

She got out of the car and released Shadow from her crate. "Come on. Let's see what we can find. Alex ought to show up sooner or later." Sooner preferred.

She eased her way through the gate, and the dog followed. They hadn't gone more than a few yards when a crawling sensation inched its way up her neck. Someone was watching.

Shadow yipped as the leash was ripped from Bette's hand and a strong arm wrapped around her neck. She clawed at a hairy forearm and gasped for air. He dragged her backward. Her feet scrabbled for purchase, but her efforts were wasted. And there wasn't a soul in sight to help her.

His grip on her neck tightened until her vision grew fuzzy and Shadow's barking grew dim.

Then, nothing.

Alex emerged from his long solo shower, drying his head with a thick towel. The bedroom was empty. He wandered into her sitting room. Ditto. Where the hell was Bette?

Maybe she'd taken the dog out? He glanced around the room and spied a piece of paper propped against a can of Diet Coke. "Dammit!" What was she thinking, going out alone? Bad enough he was falling under her spell, but he couldn't even take a shower without her running off to get into trouble. Straighten up the office—right. She wanted to get away…from him.

Just as well. Every time they made love, they grew closer,

making their eventual parting more difficult. She felt so right in his arms. But their being together wasn't going to work in any shape or form.

He shook away the memories of their lovemaking. He tried calling her cell. Busy. Okay, time to get his ass in gear. He redressed and raced for his rental car, cursing the fate that put them in the same town.

Five minutes later, he reached the vet's office, but Bette's car wasn't in the lot. *Dammit.* He picked up his cell phone to call her again and give her a piece of his mind, but found she'd already left him a voice mail. *Double dammit.* Might as well listen and hear what she had to say for herself. Her message—talk about a good news and bad news situation. Elation that she'd heard from his sister—such as it was. And Bette was on her way to the rescue.

Damn!

But did she use her head and wait for him? No, she and that dog had likely headed off on what at best was a wild-goose chase. The worst-case scenario didn't bear thinking about.

Before he could turn around and head for Naples, his cell phone rang.

About damned time she called. But no, it wasn't Bette. In fact, he didn't recognize the number. Possibly, it was one of his feelers calling back. "What?"

"I have them," the voice said in a raspy whisper.

"Them?" Alex's mind raced while he strained to hear the caller's voice. Maybe he could determine the sex or an accent. But no way to tell either from a whisper.

"All three of 'em."

*Three?* Bette too? The kidnapper had Bette? Was that how the kidnapper knew Alex's cell number? Somehow he had to get the call triangulated.

"Did you *hear* what I said?"

"Yes, I heard. What do you want? How much?"

"We have to meet, but only after I'm certain you aren't being followed."

"I have to know how much. I'm not rich. It'll take time to pull the money together."

"One million each. Your sister. Your nephew. And your girlfriend."

"That's a hell of a lot of money. See here, dude, I'm a low-level federal employee, and I don't have anything like that."

"From what I hear, your sister's husband has plenty stashed away in offshore accounts. Surely, he wants his son back, even if he doesn't care about the others. It's a package deal. Three mil for three people *you* hold dear. I'll call again."

"No! Wait—"

The connection went dead.

He pounded his fist on the steering wheel. All right. No choice but to call in the Bureau. No way could he come up with three million dollars at the drop of a hat. He needed surveillance equipment. His phone—they could triangulate the call.

He made four calls. One to Spitz. One to the retired Detective Ross who, according to his daughter-in-law, was out of town. One to the Buffalo field office. And finally one to the home office in Chicago. A ransom demand called for manpower. No way could he muddle through this on his own.

It was clear the kidnapper was escalating. He'd taken three people. It couldn't be a coincidence. Three people Alex cared about were in the hands of someone. Someone who harbored a personal grudge? Someone here in the town he'd avoided for at least the last ten years. Why? Who could he have pissed off so badly they found it necessary to kidnap everyone he loved?

Loved? His sister and little Cody were a given.

*And Bette.* Yes, he loved her, in spite of her prickly temper, love of all things canine and questionable family connections.

Screw it all. It didn't make sense. None of it. Maybe *he* was the one the kidnapper wanted. Maybe Jackie, Cody, and Bette were just bait, which begged the question: if they were bait, were they dispensable?

Bigger question: was it possible they were already dead?

Who could hate him this much? Could it be the same person who was responsible for killing his brother?

Dark. Bette opened her eyes and still couldn't see a damned thing. Something rough and scratchy rubbed against her cheek. Her head pounded like Big Ben was striking twelve.

Movement. Lying on her side, her body was jostled as if the vehicle was being driven over a rough road. The smell of rubber and oil. Must be in the trunk. Okay, where was the trunk release? All modern cars were supposed to have them. If she could just see. She tried rubbing her head against the trunk floor. Anything to get the hood off. Hands tied behind her. Okay, if she could just get her legs to move, maybe she could kick out one of the tail lights. Someone might see she was being held prisoner in the trunk.

A *prisoner*. The sickening truth sank in, and she had to swallow back the urge to throw up. Every woman's worst horror was being kidnapped. Kidnapped by some rapist who would torture and kill her and leave her body for insects and animals to snack on. And where was Shadow? Had the bastard just left the little dog to run loose and get lost in the woods?

She'd watched too many of those forensics and true crime shows. Her heart pounded and raced, drowning out Big Ben. Could this get any worse?

Of course it could. The vehicle slowed and stopped. Then moved forward after about a fifteen second pause. Waiting for an automatic gate to open? She counted the time intervals, trying to determine distance. Another thirty seconds and the vehicle shuddered to a stop. The driver's door opened with the slightest of sounds, then the crunch, crunch of his slow footsteps in the dry brush. Taking his time, was he? Must be secure in his surroundings. Okay, better make the most of her ears, since she couldn't see a damned thing.

The trunk opened. She sucked in a breath of fresh air. Filtered by the hood, the smell of pine and cedar filled her nostrils. Sounds of birds. Insects buzzing. A dog barking. Not Shadow. No, a big one, by the sound of it. Still in the woods. That figured. Fewer witnesses to whatever horror was about to take place.

*Her* horror. Oh, God.

Before she could roll on her back and kick whatever body part she could, he scooped her up like a sack of potatoes and slung her over his shoulder. He was damned strong, and he strode calmly to wherever the hell he was taking her.

Her hell. Oh, God. Alex, where are you?

She wiggled and pounded his thick-muscled back with her fists, but nothing deterred him. Swallowing her fear, she found her voice. "You won't get away with this. They'll find you, and you'll spend the rest of your life in prison."

He didn't respond. Likely he recognized her threat as a vain one. *If* Alex ever found him. Big word, "if." *If* Alex noticed she was missing. Of course, he would. She was supposed to call him on the hour. How long had it been since she'd been grabbed?

Her captor stopped. Next came the sound of metal scraping. A lock? Then the sound of a door swinging open. Sounded like a heavy door too. He adjusted her dead weight against his side, closed the door and started downward. Cool, damp air.

*No. No.* Not imprisoned in some kind of basement or cellar. She'd never see the light of day again. She counted the steps— fifteen. Fifteen steps and a metal door between her and freedom.

He stopped and set her on her feet. "We're home now," he said. Something familiar about the sound of his voice and yet not. It had to be the same man who pulled up and asked Jackie to see about his sick cat. Were she and Cody already dead? And now it was her turn? "Jackie! Cody!"

"We're here, Bette." Jackie's voice. Hope surged through her. Breathing became easier. They were still alive. So what did he want with her?

"Quiet!" he ordered, then whipped the hood from her head.

Light. Dim, but still it hurt her eyes until they adjusted.

Her captor loomed over her, bulky and muscular. Dressed in black. She raised her gaze. Full sandy beard. Blue eyes. So familiar.

"Oh, crap."

# Chapter Twenty

Before Alex could figure out his next move, his cell phone chimed again. Detective Spitz returning his call with just a quick "Down to the house. Now." No use arguing he needed to check out the old wineries.

Hold on, Bette.

Now, here he was. Spitz ushered him into a small office and told him to wait. Hurry up and wait. Oldest game in the book. He settled in a guest chair and drummed his fingers on the padded arm.

No time for this shit.

He stood and paced. Checked his watch. They'd already kept him waiting for almost an hour. Time was flying by, and he was hung up here. Time he needed to find Bette and his family. He stepped outside the office, glanced up and down the hall. "Where's Detective Spitz?" he asked a passing uniformed officer.

She shook her head. "Don't know. But he said you were to wait." She jerked her head toward the office.

"I've been waiting. Dammit." He went back inside and sat, fists clenching and unclenching. Should've never come down here. Should've gone looking for Bette and Jackie.

After another eternity, the door opened. He glanced up, expecting to see Spitz. Instead, the newcomer was male, tall, and moved with an attitude of authority. Alex noted the navy suit, tie, and starched shirt, but it was the attitude more than anything else which marked the newcomer as one of his federal counterparts.

"Tom Hixson, Buffalo field office." He gave a grim smile. "Sorry to hear about your troubles, Agent MacGregor."

Alex acknowledged Hixson with a nod. "I'm just glad the local LEOs finally requested federal intervention." He leaned forward. "Maybe now we can make some real progress. There's been a ransom demand. I'm telling you, I've got a good lead, and no one's doing shit about it."

Hixson sat behind the desk. "You understand you can't be a part of the investigation?"

"Would keeping me up-to-date on developments be too much trouble?"

"We can do that," Hixson said, nodding. "What's this about a lead?"

"Bette—Miss Smithson—left me a voice mail sometime before I heard from the kidnapper. I was in the shower and missed her call. Somehow, my sister got to a phone and called Bette. The connection was terrible, but she made out something about a deserted winery. Might be the old Massamore Winery. I was headed up there, but Detective Spitz caught me before I could leave. I've been cooling my jets for nearly an hour."

"Good thing he did. We don't need you going off precipitately." Hixson's expression took on a contemplative note, as if considering whether or not to reveal something. "In the interest of full disclosure, as soon as we were called by the local department, we subpoenaed your brother-in-law's financial records and discovered something interesting. He makes regular monthly payments to an escort agency in New York City."

"What!" A burst of anger flashed through Alex. Fists clenched, he stood. "I knew that bastard was hiding something."

"Now, hold on." The agent held up a delaying hand. "What we *didn't* find was any indication he'd hired anyone to kidnap your sister. He submitted to a polygraph yesterday. It was inconclusive. As expected, there were some areas of deception noted when he was questioned about his alibi."

*No money trail. And no alibi.* Alex scratched his head and sat, wishing his present nightmare would go away quicker than the itch. "What about the escort agency? Could it be a front for a killer-for-hire business?"

The agent's mouth quirked in a half smile. "Hire a hit man...on a monthly payment plan?" He shook his head. "Doubtful. We're still investigating the escort agency. It's definitely a shell company and backed by money out of the Caymans. We don't know who owns it yet, but it appears to be exactly what it purports."

"While my sister was being kidnapped, my brother-in-law was in the Big Apple playing hide the salami with a hooker. Bastard still has a lot of explaining to do." He clenched and unclenched his fists, envisioning what he wanted to do to the sorry son of a bitch his sister had the poor judgment to marry.

Hixson shot him a sympathetic look. "Know how you feel, MacGregor, but you need to hold off...for the time being."

Alex took a deep breath before answering. "Could you? If it was your sister?"

The agent shot Alex a sideways glance. "Probably not."

"What are we going to do about the ransom? You've seen the financials. Does Brad have that kind of money lying around?"

"You know we don't recommend paying any ransom."

"What choice do we have? We have to at least make him *think* we're going to pay it. Set up surveillance. Catch him when he comes to pick it up." Crap! This was taking too damned long.

"More than likely, it won't be a simple drop. If the unsub knows what he's doing, he'll have multiple check points to make sure you aren't followed. Don't suppose *you* have that kind of money, do you? Better not, since that would trigger an automatic investigation of *your* finances." The agent shot him a wry smile.

Not amused. "Hell, no! I don't have that kind of change in my piggy bank or anywhere else. You never answered my question. Does my brother-in-law have it?"

Hixson offered a grim facsimile of a smile. "Given his

propensity for engaging prostitutes, he might only want to pay the ransom for his son."

"I'll take it from his hide if he doesn't."

"In any case," Hixson continued, "we've placed a trap and trace on both his home line and his cell phone."

"The kidnapper called *my* cell phone. He could've only gotten the number from my sister or Bette."

"Hm." The agent frowned, then let out a sigh. "We ran background checks on everyone involved. Bette is really…"

"Yeah, yeah. I know who she is, and her brother too."

"Any chance she's involved in this?" Hixson rested his elbows on the desk and steepled his fingers in a thoughtful gesture as he spoke. "Maybe your Miss Spinelli is shaking you down, pretending she's been kidnapped? Her brother could be a part of the scheme."

"No." Alex leaned forward. "She left New Jersey after her parents died. She has no part in the family business. Her brother doesn't even know where she is."

"You sure about that? Do you really want to trust a woman with mob connections with your sister and nephew's lives?"

"*I* trust her. Whoever did this is trying to get to *me*. Someone has a grudge and is trying to hurt me by taking the people I love."

Eyebrows shot up. "You're in love with this Spinelli woman, or Smithson, as she's calling herself now?" Hixson shook his head. "You're aware how your career will be affected?" He paused and raised a quizzical brow. "If you choose to pursue a relationship."

Alex swallowed the impulse to tell the agent to mind his own damned business. "Let's just find them. Then I'll sort out that particular relationship when I have time."

"No offense. Just a friendly warning." Hixson made a small washing-hands gesture.

"None taken."

"Now, I'm going to follow up on this winery lead of yours with the detective. I'm sure he'll want to assemble a team to check out the place." He stood and indicated with a frown that Alex should remain seated.

"It's about time someone did something." Alex nodded. Besides, he needed to have a man-to-man with Brad and see what he could do about the ransom. He waited until Hixson was out of earshot, then rose and pulled out his cell phone. He seldom had any reason to call his brother-in-law, but the number was in his call directory for emergencies. And this was a freaking emergency.

While it rang, he waited and sucked in a deep breath. Damn! Why wasn't he picking up? Then, as Alex was about to give up, Brad answered.

"It's Alex. Need to talk to you, man. Where the hell are you?"

"Home. What do *you* want?" Bastard's tone was surly. He'd show him surly. Kick his ass too, while he was at it.

Too freaking bad. Sonofabitch was at home when he ought to be out looking for his wife and kid. Alex tamped down the anger and modulated his tone to noncommittal. "There's been a ransom demand."

"What? No one called me."

"Everything isn't about you. Stick around. I'm on my way." Unable to control his frustration any further, Alex snapped the phone shut and sprinted for the rental car.

Alex bounded up the front steps and went inside. He brushed past the two agents, who were minding the trap and trace, and found his brother-in-law standing by the fireplace, drinking what appeared to be a scotch rocks.

*Great. Freaking great.* He grabbed the bastard by the front of his pricy silk shirt and slammed him against the brick wall. "Dude! I know you lied about the hooker. You son of a bitch! You freaking failed the lie detector test. Now either tell me what you've done with my sister, or I'm going to beat you within an inch of your life."

"Man, that's not how it is." The oily sheen of sweat glistened on Brad's flushed face.

"Then tell me *how it is*, Brad. And this time, it better be the truth. Or so help me God…" Alex drew his fist back.

"B-Brandi's my sister."

"That's a good one. Don't remember you having a sister named Brandi." He relaxed his grip on Brad's shirt.

"Yeah, uh—" Brad swallowed hard. "Maybe you remember Susan, the youngest? She moved to the city to go to design school. Got in with some real artsy-fartsy types who got her hooked. Now, she's on the streets. Not on the streets, exactly. She's working for this escort agency. Higher class clientele, I guess."

"First I've heard about it." Not that he'd bothered to keep track of his brother-in-law's siblings.

"I'm the only one in the family who knows. Jackie doesn't even know. I tell her I've got a conference, and I go up there periodically to see if Suze's all right. I go through the agency, pretending to be one of her out-of-town johns. I pay her so she won't get in trouble with her bosses. That's where the money goes. And I promise you, every single time I go up there, I do my best to talk her into going into treatment and coming home, but she's not having any."

A familiar story. But was it the truth? "You better not be bullshitting me. And don't think I won't check it out. I want the name of the escort agency, how you contact her, the whole works."

"All right! Now take your damned hands off me."

Alex released his hold. Brad sagged against the wall and let out an exasperated grunt. "You slam me against the wall one more time, and I'll have your special-agent ass arrested for assault."

One of the agents stuck his head into the den. "Everything all right in here?"

Alex glared at his peer. "Family matter. Everything's fine." He redirected his attention to his brother-in-law. "What about the three million ransom? Are you going to pay it or not?"

"Three million?"

"He wants a million for Jackie, a million for your son...and for Bette. Did you even know she's been kidnapped?"

"No, but you've got some damned nerve, Al. First you come in here, slam me around, and then have the nerve to ask me if I'm going to bankrupt myself to pay a ransom for your sister and your girlfriend."

"Your *wife* and your *son*, dickhead. Bette wouldn't even be involved if—"

"If you hadn't sent her up here to work. How the hell do I know she's not involved in the whole scam? Hell, Jackie might've cooked this up herself to get back at me. They're probably both sitting somewhere, laughing at us and tossing back mojitos."

"Why would she want do something like that?"

"Jackie already accused me of being unfaithful. Guess she got suspicious of my trips to New York." He shrugged. "But I had to check on Suze."

"Oh, you couldn't just share the truth with your wife. Somewhere along the line, did you find time to cheat too?"

"No." Brad's head twitched to the side. "Not really."

Alex took a step forward, ready to slug his brother-in-law. "That's like being a little pregnant. Either you were faithful or you weren't. There's no in between."

"It's none of your damned business." Brad's face grew red, and his gaze shifted down and to the left. "I know my wife a hell of a lot better than you do. How long's it been since you bothered to show your face around here? You breeze in here after not seeing your sister for years, acting like you're some kind of Fed big shot."

"You can't lay this on me, man. Jackie wouldn't scare us to death like this, and you damned well know it."

"I don't *have* three million. Now that the FBI's involved, they can just catch this kidnapper. I mean, that's what you guys do, isn't it?"

"Make up your mind, dip wad." Alex held his clenched fists close to his sides to keep from knocking Brad a good one. "Which is it? One minute, she's laughing at you and drinking mojitos, and the next you want to sit back and let the FBI find the kidnapper. Can't have it both ways, man." Jaw tensed, he dragged a hand through his hair.

"For all I know, it's somebody after you. Looks like *you're* the one who needs to come up with two-thirds of the ransom."

"I don't freaking have two million dollars. You're the financial whiz—ah, hell! Who gives a flying fuck—" Alex stormed from the room. Killing his brother-in-law wouldn't bring any of them home. Come to think of it, Hixson had probably told Alex about the escort agency to divert him on a wild-goose chase. A freaking monumental waste of time.

He stopped at the front door long enough to say, "By the way, Bette heard from Jackie. She was still alive a few hours ago."

"I-I'll do what I can," Brad called after him. "Gotta stall for time."

Stalling for time and obtaining proof of life were two things he had planned. All he had to do was wait for the kidnapper to call again.

Waiting wasn't his best sport. But something was about to break. It had to.

# Chapter Twenty-one

The kidnapper's sandy beard threw her for a second, but not the blue eyes. Nor the smile. Yes, the bastard was smiling. He was a bit bulkier, but if the kidnapper wasn't Alex's twin, he was a blood relative. "Andy? You're Alex's brother, aren't you?" *Okay, play nice with the kidnapper, Bette.*

He nodded a little uncertainly. "I prefer Drew."

Obviously, Alex's twin wasn't dead at all, which begged the question—several questions, in fact—whose body was found all those years ago, and where the hell had Andy, or Drew, as he preferred being called, been all these years? "Drew's fine with me. My family used to call me Tina, but my name's really—"

"Bettina and now you go by Bette," he finished for her, still smiling with Alex's smile, although his teeth weren't quite as perfect. Maybe Alex had braces and Drew's kidnapper hadn't bothered. But how did he know her birth name? Maybe Jackie mentioned it. "This certainly is an interesting turn of affairs. I never thought to meet you. Alex will be thrilled to know you're alive."

Drew's gaze narrowed for a second when she mentioned Alex's name. Her last word trailed off. How had he survived? Mouth dry as the driest Chardonnay, she swallowed the rest of her questions.

"You've a very interesting background, Miss *Spinelli*. Yes, I know who you are. After Jackie so graciously joined me, I had some time to dig into your background."

Bette swallowed the ever-growing lump in her throat. Creep must be handy with his computer. Her background wasn't all that visible—at least she hadn't thought so until now. Like she had nothing better to do than Google herself.

He motioned for her to have a seat. Since her knees were about to give out, it seemed like the sensible thing to do, so she sat. Her mind whirled with options…actually, with the lack of them.

"Most of my family is here now." He continued with his gracious-host act. "Do you think Alex will arrive soon? I'm looking forward to seeing him after all these years, as you might imagine."

"Um, yes, I suspect he will." Difficult man to read. Was he really looking forward to seeing Alex again, or did he have something else in mind? *Stall for time.* What else could she do?

"I've followed his career, you know, waiting for the right time and circumstances for us to get *reacquainted.*"

Again, a brittle edge crept into his tone. Not that she was any expert, but Drew seemed a few bricks short of a load. She glanced around the finished basement. Not a rough cellar like she'd first feared. The floor was painted concrete, but here and there, several small area rugs were scattered about, plus a few pieces of comfortable furniture…and toys. "Where's Cody?"

"I asked Jackie to put him down for a nap. I thought it best to give you time to get used to your surroundings. I tried to make it homey. I hope you approve."

Like she was going to live in his basement the rest of her life? No freaking way! "So, Jackie's okay?"

"Of course. I know my method of arranging a family reunion is a little unorthodox, but I wouldn't harm a hair on her head. I missed her and Alex so much, and my adoptive parents too, although I didn't get to spend much time with them before…" He glanced away quickly, then met her gaze again, ignoring the elephant in the room. He held out his hand. "Come, I want to show you your quarters. I thought you'd like to be close to Jackie. Is that all right?"

She nodded, rose to her feet, and carefully took Drew's hand. It felt so much like Alex's. In spite of his bulkier build and the beard, his voice was dead-on almost the same, except his upstate accent was more pronounced. Only the transitory wildness in his gaze unnerved her. Wasn't everyday a woman was kidnapped and treated like a guest at the kidnapper's warped idea of a family reunion.

He led her around the corner of the huge basement. Had to be one hell of a house upstairs. If she could just get up there and get to a phone… She'd left hers in the car when she got out and opened the gate.

"This is your room, right next to Jackie's. There's a full bath— you'll have to share. Sorry 'bout that."

"Not a problem." Oh, no, the problem was right beside her: all six feet three inches and two hundred plus pounds of problem.

He tapped on a closed door. "Jackie, our company's here."

The door opened, and a wide-eyed Jackie stepped out somewhat slowly. Over her shoulder, Bette made out Cody asleep on the bed. A rush of relief flooded through her. "Hi, I'm so glad you could make it." Jackie put her arms around Bette's neck and whispered, "Sorry, but he made me call you. Threatened Cody. Play along."

Bette nodded her understanding and said aloud, "I think Drew has a great idea. A family reunion. And I'm really, *really* glad you invited me, even though I'm not exactly family. I suppose that was you at Jackie's?"

"Sorry." He nodded slowly. "But you're the key to getting Alex here. Y'see he—uh, never mind." His eyes went all funny again, and his hands clenched at his sides.

Uh-oh. Maybe Alex'd be better off if he missed this particular reunion. They all would.

"So, what have you been up to since…?" Bette broke off when she noticed Jackie shaking her head, as well as her panicked expression. *Okay, then, try something else.* "Uh, does Alex know where to come?"

Drew smiled. "Oh, *Alex* was always the smart one. He'll figure it out. You did."

"Yes, I did, but…" Bette chewed on her bottom lip.

"Something wrong?"

"My dog. I'm afraid she ran off when we—uh, met. She's not used to the woods. She's more like a city dog. That's what she's used to."

Jackie's brow furrowed at the mention of Bette's dog, then she shook her head and eased back into her room, leaving Bette alone with Drew.

Drew shrugged. "If I wasn't expecting Alex to show up soon, I'd go look for her myself."

Wringing her hands, Bette tried again. "No, I really think *I* should go. She's a little shy. She'll probably hide from anyone but me. She's really not used to being around men." God, she was babbling like the village idiot. How long could she keep it up?

"How's Alex get along with her?" Drew snorted with laughter. "You know, he got himself chewed up pretty good by a neighbor's poodle when we were just kids. He never cared much for dogs after that."

"He's not crazy about her, but I hope that'll change in the future." If they even had a future.

"Alex seems crazy about you. Never knew him to get involved with anyone before, especially someone with a dog."

How the hell did he know anything about Alex's life or his involvements? Had he been cyber-stalking his brother? She glanced toward the stairs. "D-do you think I could go out and have a look around? Her hearing's sharp. She'd probably hear me and come running. I'm not really sure how far we came after you—uh, picked me up."

"Don't worry about that." His dismissed her worries with a wave of his hand. "Your dog'll be okay until there's time to have a look."

"But Alex isn't here yet, so there's still time."

Drew smiled, then gave a chuckle. "Wouldn't want *you* to get lost out there too."

Not that she expected him to let her go. He was crazy. Crafty. But definitely not dumb.

"Your room—I'm afraid it's not as well furnished as Jackie's. I've been planning this reunion for a while, but I didn't know until recently that you'd figure into my plans." He gave an eerily familiar smile. "The more the merrier, I always say." He opened the door with a flourish.

Inside the small room was a bed with a discount-store quilt folded across the foot. Two pillows. Not even a side chair she could use to whack him over the head. "I'm sure I'll be very comfortable." Like hell she would.

"No trouble at all."

"I don't have a change of clothes. I don't suppose…"

He smiled, and somehow it didn't have a pleasant effect on her jitters. "Check the closet. I picked out a few things when I bought the bedding."

"That's so thoughtful." She opened the door. Jeans, flannel shirts, and a pair of boots. Great, she could go hiking and roast to death in the June heat. "How long did you plan for us to stay? They really miss Jackie down at the office. The temp is looking forward to working part time again."

"Why don't we play it by ear? Surely, you're not in a hurry to leave. Not before *Alex* joins us."

Every time Drew mentioned his brother's name, his squirreliness grew more and more apparent. His tone changed and grew edgy as if his throat tightened.

"But I promise I'll—"

His gaze widened, his fists clenching at his sides. "Don't talk to me about *promises*! People don't keep them. Never. Ever!" He whirled away from her and stomped up a set of stairs which apparently led up to the house. A door slammed, and Bette heard the loud click of a deadbolt.

Damn. Somehow, she'd set him off. What was it? All she'd said was, "I promise I'll—" That had to be it. *Note to self: erase that particular word from your vocabulary.*

She knocked on Jackie's door. When the door opened, she said, "He's gone upstairs. Has he ever let you up there?"

"No. And he never fails to lock the door."

"Are you really all right? Has he hurt you?"

Jackie shook her head and slipped her arm around Bette's waist. "I'm sorry you've been dragged into this, but selfish as it is, I've never been so glad to see anyone in my entire life. Although Alex and a squad of FBI agents are right up there at the top of my list."

Bette giggled, then sobered. "I did something to set him off."

"That's easy to do. His fuse is on the short side," Jackie said with a tight smile. "I tried to warn you."

"I know, but I had to test his gracious-host façade to see how far he'd let me go. Guess I found out."

Jackie wrung her hands. "We've got to get a message to Alex. I think Drew means to get even. His body language, his tone of voice—both tell me he's angry."

"Yes." Bette nodded. "There's no telling what his kidnapper put him through. Is he here alone? Have you seen or heard anyone else?"

Jackie glanced upward. "No one." She closed the door behind her. "Let's talk in your room. I don't want to wake Cody."

They entered Bette's room and sat side by side on the bed. "And Cody's all right? Isn't he scared?"

"He was very upset when Drew brought him here. I've tried to make it a game." Jackie's bottom lip started to tremble. "But I don't know how much longer I can keep him pacified."

"Okay, so Drew seems to be alone and in charge now. Why didn't he come forward before? Why carry on with this whacked-out reunion BS?"

"He's not quite sane. There are times when he seems normal, but at others, it's very clear he's on the brink of a total breakdown. I've heard him shouting and talking to himself upstairs. But that's just this vet's opinion."

"I don't doubt you for a minute. We've got to get out of here. Does he ever leave?"

Jackie nodded. "Yes, sometimes for several hours at a time."

"Is there anything we can use for a weapon?" She glanced around the room. "There's nothing in here." She got to her feet and left the small room, giving the remainder of the basement a hurried once-over. Poking in several boxes, she found nothing of use. Where was a MacGyver, or more specifically a MacGregor, when you needed one?

"I've already gone through everything." Jackie's voice grew faint. "At least we're warm, and he feeds us regularly. Good food too."

"*Great,* our kidnapper is a chef." As she talked, she ran from one of the high windows to another. All of 'em sealed shut. Dammit. "Don't give up. Alex knows I heard from you. I left him a voice mail telling where I was headed. Drew must have some deep pockets, 'cause a house like this takes major bucks to maintain."

"I can't imagine where his money comes from," Jackie said. "It's not just the house. There's all the land surrounding it. It's so secluded. I mean, I haven't heard anything or anyone, not since he brought us here."

"Did you see anything at all when he brought you in? I was in the trunk of a car and blindfolded, to boot."

"No, it was dark, but of course, I knew the general direction, and I could tell when he took the High Road. I was just guessing about being beyond the deserted winery."

"It was enough of a clue. It led me here. Now, we have to give him a reason to let us out of here. What if one of us gets sick? He'd have to do something, wouldn't he? In his crazy logic, we're his guests, so it stands to reason, not that anything he says or does is reasonable, that he wouldn't deny care if one of us got sick—would he?"

"Your guess is as good as mine." Tears welled up in Jackie's eyes and her shoulders slumped. "I'm just so ready for this to be over."

"We're going to get out of here." Bette slipped her arm around her boss's waist. "Alex will find us. You did say something about a deserted winery." She shook her head. "You know this doesn't look anything like an old winery."

"Oh, no. You misunderstood. The connection was horrible, but what I was trying to say we were in the hills above the old Massamore winery."

"So it's going to take a little extra time for Alex to find us." Bette stood with her hands set at her waist. "Which one of us is going to get convincingly sick?"

"I will," Jackie said. "I'm halfway there already, if sick at heart counts."

# Chapter Twenty-two

Alex returned to the CPD and found Detective Spitz and Agent Hixson standing in front of a local area satellite map. "This is the place." Spitz tapped an area with his finger. "Bound to be. Went out of business in the mid-nineties. It wouldn't be Widmer's. There's still too much going on up there—tours and such." Spitz turned and glared when Alex entered. "Where the hell have you been? Thought you were told to stick around."

Alex shrugged. "Needed to talk to my brother-in-law about the ransom and a few other things."

Spitz let out a raucous laugh. "I bet you did."

"Look, guys, I have to be in on this raid." He glanced from the detective to the Buffalo field agent. "I can't just sit here and wait. You couldn't—not if it was your family."

Hixson nodded. "You can tag along, but you'll be restricted to the surveillance van. There's no telling what we'll find."

"No telling what you'll find?" Alex sputtered. "Hell, as of a few hours ago, Bette and Jackie were still alive."

Hixson cleared his throat. "You're too close. Can't risk your getting in the way like Detective Spitz says you did at the lake. By the way, the coroner determined that woman was a suicide. Documented history of severe depression. Her sister ID'd her."

A suicide. Alex hung his head, still ashamed of his earlier relief that it wasn't his sister.

Hixson shook his head. "But we don't have a profile or anything to tell us about this unsub's state of mind. How likely he is to panic, for instance."

"We can't afford to wait for the Bureau to send a profiler." Alex looked toward the door, his body tensed, ready for action. "We gotta act *now*."

"I'd prefer going in under cover of darkness, but it's June." Hixson glanced at the detective. "What about it?"

"It's not going to get good and dark until after nine or so, but as a matter of strategy, it's better to start an assault in the early morning hours."

"Are you nuts?" Alex strode to the door, but Spitz stepped in front of him.

"Not so fast, MacGregor."

"That's too long." Alex's mind reeled with what could happen in the hours before dark settled. "Fuck it! We know where they are. Let's go before he moves them or—" He broke off, unable to finish.

Hixson frowned. "Like I said, we don't know enough about the unsub to make a determination."

"So when *are* we going in?"

"We're going as soon as the team is ready," Spitz said, his expression softening with apparent pity. "The SWAT van should be pulling up and the team assembling for a briefing any minute. Think you can hold on that long?"

Alex nodded and sucked in a ragged breath. Soon. *Very* soon he'd know something. His heart pounded with the surge of adrenaline; his breathing increased. "Don't forget he's holding three innocent people."

"Not likely to forget." Spitz rolled up the satellite map and inclined his head, first at Hixson, then finally at Alex. "You on board?"

"Rock 'n' roll!"


Alex sat in the back of the CPD SWAT van and fidgeted with the straps on his Kevlar vest. The van was parked at the base of the hill that led to the winery buildings. Peeking over the surveillance equipment tech's shoulder, he watched the assault team slowly advance toward the main building. It was a large shabby structure and looked like a good wind might topple it. Several smaller outbuildings had already been cleared. "Any sign of them?"

The tech scratched his neck and yawned. "Nah. I think this is a bust. Nobody home."

"I'm sure this is the place she meant."

"Didn't you say the original message was garbled?" The surveillance tech kept his gaze on his monitors.

"Yeah, but…"

"There ya go." The tech shrugged. "Your lady misunderstood."

"But now *she's* missing and isn't answering her cell."

"Out of range. Not surprising with all the hills. Or maybe her battery's dead."

Antsy and irritated by the tech's so-what air, Alex stood. "She would've come home, then," he muttered and opened the van door.

The tech turned his attention from the screens long enough to raise a single brow. "You're supposed to stay with me."

"Getting stuffy." Alex shrugged. "Think I'll get some fresh air. Stretch my legs."

The tech shrugged. "You're a big boy. Suit yourself. No skin off my nose if you get your ass in trouble."

Alex clenched his jaw and resisted the impulse to tell the tech to kiss off. Instead, he sucked in a breath of fresh upstate air. This wasn't his first time at the Massamore Vineyards. When he was a kid, he'd come on a class trip and toured the winery before it closed for good. What a god-forsaken, dilapidated place it was now, with peeling paint and a roof ready to implode. He walked around the back of the van and checked his vest.

It was then he heard the radio squawk, but he couldn't make out what was said.

"Agent," the tech said, "they're about to call it a day. They haven't found anything."

Alex's heart sank. He'd been so sure this was the place Bette meant in her message.

Bette nodded. "You're his *sister*. Drew'll be more inclined to take you to the hospital. Me—I doubt he'd care if I were in pain or not."

Jackie's blue eyes filmed over with tears. "Maybe so, but I can't leave Cody. It'll upset him if I pretend to be sick."

"Tell him it's a game." Bette leaned forward and gave Jackie's shoulder a bit of a shake. "We've got to do something. You've been strong this long. You can do this. One way or another, we've got to outfox him."

Jackie went into her and Cody's room while Bette considered their situation. Her boss was obviously at the end of her emotional tether. And no wonder.

When Jackie returned, lines of worry creased her face. "I talked to him. He understands it's a game. And a secret." She chewed the corner of her lip for a second. "But he's so young and not very good at keeping secrets."

Bette slipped her arm around Jackie's waist. "Maybe not, but it's our only chance. We have to risk it. Nothing ventured, nothing gained—right?"

"R-right."

Bette held a hand to her ear and said in a low singsong, "I couldn't *hear* you."

"Right!" Jackie said with a growl.

"That's more like it. All right. Now I'm going up to knock on the door and tell him you're sick. So get in character. We need an academy award-winning performance."

Jackie nodded and pinched her cheeks until they were reddened, then went into the bathroom and splashed her face with hot water. She grabbed her belly and started a low groan.

"Lights. Camera. Action." Bette bounded up the stairs, then banged on the door. "Drew! Open up. You've got to do something. Jackie's sick. She's in pain." Was the basement soundproofed? What if he couldn't hear her?

After what seemed like forever, the door opened. His tall, broad form filled the space. "What?" His gaze peered over her shoulder. "Jackie?"

At that moment, Jackie moaned and fell, then, for good measure, rolled around clutching her belly.

Without warning, Drew shoved Bette aside and thundered down the stairs. His sudden, swift movement slammed her head against the wall. Pinpoints of light and a wave of dizziness set her reeling. She grabbed the hand railing and clung to it until her vision cleared and her head stopped pounding.

Maybe this wasn't such a good plan after all. He was big, fast, and strong. His gracious manners were barely skin-deep. The fierceness of his shove was so reflexive she might as well have been a fly buzzing around his head.

Cautiously, she descended the stairs; the handrail had loosened when she grabbed it. Drew was standing over Jackie with his fists clenching and unclenching. "Stop rolling around like that. You were fine a few minutes ago." He spun and advanced on Bette. "What did you do?" He raised his fist. "If you hurt her—"

"No! Drew!" Jackie wailed, continuing to thrash. "Bette didn't do anything. I'm *sick*."

Bette backed away. No point in being within his reach. "That's right. First she turned pale, then red, and she started having stabbing pains in her stomach. She needs a doctor. It sounds like appendicitis to me. You've got to get her to the hospital."

His facial expression morphed blindingly fast from one of rage to one of sadness. "Can't you see," he said, as if explaining something to a not-so-bright child, "the hospital would ask questions. Besides, we have to be here when Alex arrives." He gave a deep sigh. "We don't want him to think we're rude, now, do we?"

"Alex would understand after we explained. He wouldn't want Jackie to be in pain either."

"Don't care what Alex wants." He swung around and slammed his fist into one of the metal support columns. "Alex. *Alex.* It's always about Alex." His tone took on an angry muttering quality that sent chills up and down Bette's backbone.

"Careful." With a great deal of caution, Bette approached him. "I think you've hurt yourself."

Drew glanced down at his bleeding fist and frowned, as if puzzled by his injury. "I'm fine."

"No, you're not, and neither is Jackie. Now you *both* need a doctor." Bette shot a frown at Jackie, whose performance had momentarily stalled.

"Drew! I'm sick. I think I might be losing my baby." Jackie clutched her lower belly and moaned.

*Way to go, Jackie.* A miscarriage was even better than appendicitis, since it would nudge Drew back into family mode.

"Baby? You didn't tell me you were having a baby." Drew kneeled beside his sister and wrung his hands.

"It's very early. I wasn't sure. But the pains feel like a miscarriage. I had several before I had Cody."

And that wasn't a lie either.

Drew looked over his shoulder, his face sickly pale. "*You* have to help her. I don't know what to do."

"Hold on. Do I look like a doctor? I don't have a clue. I've never had any kids whatsoever."

"But you worked in her office. Surely—"

"As a freaking *receptionist*!" Damn, but this guy was hard to convince. "Before that, I studied interior design. But I'll tell you this, I know enough to know she needs to get some pain meds on board, *and* she needs a doctor. She might even need a transfusion if she starts bleeding. Miscarriages are serious business. Dammit. She could die!"

Their captor rose to his feet, his face a blank but frightening caricature of Alex's. He paced from one end of the basement to the other, muttering. She could only make out part of what he said, and none of it was reassuring.

"Not supposed to happen like this. Supposed to be easy. Just bring the family together. Jackie. Cody, Bette, and *Alex*. A real MacGregor family reunion. Of course, Bette's not family yet, but she'll help bring Alex here." He stopped, and a smile broke. His eyes not quite so scary, he pulled what looked like her cell phone from his pocket and handed it to her. "I'm tired of waiting. Call him!"

# Chapter Twenty-three

Back inside the van, Alex drummed his fingers on his knee. The tech was adjusting his equipment and appeared to be ready to shut it down.

Just then, Alex's phone signaled an incoming call. He pulled it from his pocket and read the caller ID. *Bette*. His heart rate escalated. Hixson and Spitz were making their way down the hill. He gave them a *hurry-up* wave. "Hold on," he told the technician. "It's from Bette. See if you can trace and triangulate this." He nodded at the equipment. "I'll keep her on as long as I can." He jumped down from the van before answering, "Bette? Where are you? Is everyone okay?"

"Don't interrupt." Her tone was hushed and brusque. "Just listen. I have to make it quick. He could come back at any time."

"I'm listening."

"He's keeping us in the basement of a big house. We're in the hills above and beyond Naples. Please, look for Shadow as you come up the drive. She got away when he grabbed me. You know her *brother* will pine away if she goes missing."

Her dog was the least of his worries, but he kept his mouth shut since it would only infuriate her, and they didn't have any time to waste.

"Just hurry. We heard him leave, and there's no way to tell when he'll come back. Oh, no—"

He picked up the sounds of a struggle, and then the connection broke off. "Bette?"

He looked up when Agent Hixson and Detective Spitz reached

the van.

Agent Hixson rushed to Alex's side and asked the tech, "Get anything?"

The tech shook his head. "Just a general area, and we're already in it."

"Damn. Okay, she said big house in the hills *beyond* and *above* Naples. Any ideas?"

"Pull out those area satellite maps," Alex said. "Compare them with tax records for big houses."

"Got quite a few of those. Most of 'em rented out in summer. Tourists, y'know?" Detective Spitz said with a frown. "What else?"

"Just some garbage about being on the lookout for her dog, but the next bit didn't make sense. Makes me think she was trying to tell me something."

"Think, man."

"Being kept in the basement of a big house. The kidnapper was gone, and they didn't know why or where he'd gone or when he'd be back. And then the stuff about her dog's brother pining if she went missing. That dog doesn't have a brother that either one of us knows about. Hell, Bette just adopted her the other day. I was there. Guy who gave it to her didn't say anything about it having a brother."

"Then that has to be significant. Maybe she *was* trying to tell you something."

"But this is more ominous—the call ended suddenly. The kidnapper was there, or she would've told me more. This reeks of being a trap. He has my family, and now he wants me."

"You sure pissed off somebody," Hixson said. "Has anyone looked into your old cases?"

"No. And now there's no time." His gaze darted from the agent to the detective. "We've got to find them now." If he had to get down on his knees and spit-shine the detective's shoes, he would.

"Still a pretty large area," Spitz offered. "Shouldn't have to tell you we don't have the manpower or resources to launch an all-out search."

Days too late. A search should've been done already. He bit back the words. Alienating the local LEOs at this point wouldn't accomplish a damned thing. "What about bringing in dogs? Now that we have a general area?"

"I'll call the sheriff's department. This is his jurisdiction, anyway."

"Call that Rigby fellow with the bloodhounds," Alex said, restless to get something done.

"Main thing for you is to settle down and let the locals take care of this situation. They know the area." This self-serving statement came from his fellow agent.

Traitor.

He'd never been one to act off profile, but damn, it'd never been his loved ones involved before. Gave a guy a new perspective. And not a pleasant one.

Hills above Naples. Big house. Something nagged at the back of his mind. One of his freshman high school teachers lived in an old sprawling house which had seen better days. He made a practice of having all the boys in his class up there every year for a campout. More than likely the teacher had sold it to someone who'd either torn it down or remodeled it to take advantage of the great lake views. Real estate with a view raked in premium prices.

He pointed to the satellite map showing on one of the tactical monitors. "What about that place? Used to belong to a teacher."

"Current owner listed as a D. K. Rideout."

"Yeah, Robert Rideout was the teacher's name. Must belong to his son. Don't remember him having a son, though. He was single last I remember."

"Could be a nephew or some other relative," Agent Hixson suggested.

"Check your DMV," Alex said. "What does he drive?"

The tech accessed the DMV database. "2005 Black Ford Excursion and a 2010 Cadillac CTS." He finished by rattling off the plate numbers.

"Damned close to what Bette described. I say, let's check him out."

"Need to get a warrant," Hixson reminded.

Alex nodded. If they went up there unprepared, they'd tip their hand and lose the element of surprise. *If* this Rideout fellow was the kidnapper, no telling what he'd do. "Do we have just cause for a search warrant?" He cut his gaze to Spitz, who nodded sharply.

"It's close, but if I call the right judge, we can get one."

Tension built in Alex's gut. He fisted his hands and clenched his jaw. Search warrants took time, even with the right judge. What if they were too late? No, that didn't bear thinking about. He shut his eyes, fighting the onslaught of negativity. Nightmarish possibilities. But negativity wasn't as easily banished as a bad dream. He swallowed the bile building in the back of his throat.

He gazed from Spitz to the agent and back again. "Where's this house? I'm kind of hazy on the location." Maybe if he'd come home more often, he wouldn't have forgotten.

The detective looked up and answered, "We're about two and half miles southwest of there." He pointed to their present location. "Now if you'll excuse me, I need to get hold of the DA and a judge." He pulled his cell phone from his belt, jumped down from the van, and walked away from Alex and Agent Hixson.

Alex shook his head. "Don't know how much more of this—" He broke off and cast his gaze to the northeast hills and jumped out of the van.

Hixson was right behind him and clapped a hand on Alex's shoulder. "Forget it, MacGregor. You're not peeling out of here on your own. You might not care about your career with the Bureau, but I'm damned fond of mine."

Alex spun, ready to deck the agent, but pulled the punch just in time. "Fine," he said, not really meaning it.

Damn, he'd give a month's pay to have his former partner, Jake LeFevre, on hand right now. Good old Jake would've already commandeered a vehicle and damned the consequences.

The detective returned, all smiles. "Warrant's on the way. Suggest we set up a recon some distance from the house and wait for the go-ahead."

"I don't blame you," Hixson said. "If I were in your place, I'd be ready to bust out of here and go running to the rescue. But we both know the rules and procedures are there for a reason."

Alex met Hixson's gaze with a glare but nodded, albeit reluctantly. "Yeah." He pulled at his collar. Seemed like it grew tighter the longer this ordeal lasted.

Without warning, a lancing pain across Bette's forearm knocked the phone from her hand. Drew jerked her around so they were face-to-face. He squinted, and his face flushed with rage. "I *told* you exactly what to say. Why didn't you stick to the script? And what was that crap about the dog and her brother?"

She rubbed her wrist where he'd struck her. Alex's brother was strong. Luckily, it wasn't broken. So she'd tried to give Alex a clue. Surely, he was smart enough to figure it out or at least figure out that something was fishy. She didn't want him walking blind into a trap. "My dog—the one you left running loose in the woods—Jackie has the brother. You know, littermates. They're devoted to each other."

Drew pulled a gun from the back of his pants, the first weapon she'd seen since being kidnapped. "All three of you, get into Jackie's bedroom."

Bette frowned at Jackie, who seemed to have forgotten she was supposed to be in severe pain. "What about a doctor? Jackie *needs* a doctor."

A quick "duh" expression flashed across her boss's face, and she doubled over once more with a groan.

With a wide smile so like Alex's, Drew shrugged. "You're playing me. Understand you needed to try, but it isn't going to work. Been there. Done that. Doesn't matter."

Was he referring to things he'd tried when he was first kidnapped?

She tried an understanding smile. "Was it bad when you were first taken? How long did it take to get used to being away from your family?"

His muscular hands clenched. His back stiffened, and for a second, she thought he was going to hit her again. She ducked, anticipating a blow.

"I won't hurt you, not as long as you do as I tell you."

*Keep him talking. Keep him engaged.* "Who took you?" she dared to ask. "Where he is now?" Hopefully Drew's kidnapper wouldn't be an unknown factor in their situation.

Drew's jaw clenched, the muscle jumping like a demon. His gaze averted quickly. "He died a few years ago."

"I don't understand." Planting her feet apart, Bette set her hands on her hips, but she tried to keep her voice calm and soothing. No point in setting him off again. "Why didn't you contact your family then? Why all this kidnapping rigmarole? I'm sure you didn't mean to, but you've upset a lot of people."

"By then, my *family* had forgotten about me, Besides, I had the business to run." His gaze flickered away from her and toward the stairs.

"What business?"

"Doesn't matter, but it takes some work now and then. All computer, though. Amazing thing, the Internet." A wide smile wreathed his face. Unsettling, given the circumstances.

"Yeah. Yeah. I get it."

"Oh, it is. There's all sorts of ways a guy can cash in, if he's smart." A single brow shot up. "And I am."

"Tell me about it. What kind of business can you run on the Internet?" Not that she cared. She just wanted to keep him talking long enough for Alex to arrive...preferably with the FBI version of the cavalry in tow.

He turned and narrowed his gaze, sending a chill up Bette's spine. A very real urge to run almost overwhelmed her. If she were alone, she'd give it a go. But she wasn't about to leave Jackie and her son alone with this creep who looked so much like Alex in spite of carrying an extra forty pounds of muscle. Good old Drew was seriously whacked-out. No doubt he'd suffered God-only-knew what kind of abuse for years. Maybe his personality wasn't as strong as Alex's. Whatever...

Drew preened, running a hand back through his hair. "I run an escort service."

"Canandaigua has an escort service?"

"Not here. You're thinking's too provincial. In the *city*."

"As in New York City?"

"None other."

Great idea, the Internet. Now pervs could run their business hundreds of miles away, somehow keeping their proverbial hands clean. "How did you learn to use computers?"

Briefly, his brows drew together, but he couldn't keep the corner of his mouth from twitching. "Bob taught me to run the business."

"Why didn't you use the computer to let your sister or brother know you were alive? I still don't get it."

"After all this time, what was the point?"

His fists hung at his sides. Was it her imagination or was his body tensing? His gaze bored into hers. It seemed as if she could feel his rising agitation. "Oh-kay..." She drew out the word, still stalling for time. "So what's the point of having a family reunion now?"

"Shut up!" He swung at her, but she dodged out of his reach.

"Don't ask so damned many questions." He took a deep breath, his massive chest rising, and lumbered forward.

Holding up her hands as a sign of surrender, Bette stepped back. "Chill out, big fellow. I just wondered. No biggie."

She felt a soft touch on her arm. Jackie moved in closer, supporting Bette.

"We're just happy to be here now, Drew," Jackie said in a mollifying tone. "You can't blame us if we're a little upset with the manner of your invitation."

*Invitation, hell. Kidnapping plain and simple.* Bette's gaze ricocheted between the two siblings.

Jackie continued in soft, nursery-school-teacher tones. "I'm sorry we tried to trick you. It was *my* idea, not Bette's."

"No." Drew shook his head and clenched his fists. "You weren't any trouble until *she* showed up." His gaze narrowed to slits as he glared at Bette. "Damned if I know what Al sees in you."

*Showed up? Yeah, right.* Bette swallowed the annoying lump in her throat. He took two steps toward her. Omigod. What now?

# Chapter Twenty-four

With one ear, Alex listened to the assault plans for his old teacher's residence. While the other agent and detective pored over details and schematics, Alex eased away from the group. Granted the plan included time-tested tactics, but would they work with whatever nutcase had Bette and his family?

His mind kept going back to her aborted phone call. Bette's giving him a partial location was a trap. Had to be, because as soon as she digressed from the kidnapper's script, he ended the call. So what *else* was she trying to tell him?

All that nattering about the dog's *brother*. Made no sense, unless...

No, but the idea that popped into his head made even less sense. Maybe it was her way of telling him the kidnapper was the same person responsible for his brother's death, after all.

The location wasn't all that far. As the crow flies, about a two mile trek, northeast uphill through forest and brush. Much farther if going by the twisty-turning roads. By the time the authorities obtained a warrant and moved the team into place, too much time would've passed. Time Bette and his family might not have.

His gut tightened. Too many images of too many bodies found too late to do any good crowded his mind. The first—his brother's bones lying bleached in the sun. What could be worse?

Several things. But thinking about them only paralyzed him. No way could he stand by while the local LEOs debated with the Buffalo field office over a mission plan, objectives, and feasible outcomes.

If it meant screwing up his career with the Bureau, so be it. He had to find Bette and the rest of his family. The very fact he put Bette before his family in his thought processes was scary enough, but he couldn't stop any longer to consider the ramifications.

First things first.

After glancing in both directions, he ducked around the next van. Good. No one was paying any attention. In spite of his special-agent status, he was a tagalong on this op and clearly of no consequence. Twenty yards to the cover of a stand of trees. Once he reached the perimeter of cedar, he had it made.

As if taking a Sunday stroll, he moseyed toward his goal. Checking over his shoulder, he heard the sounds of the SWAT team as they clambered into their vehicle.

He ducked behind an outcrop of fieldstone and held his breath. Would they miss him?

"MacGregor!" Detective Spitz bellowed, then shook his head.

*Guess so.* Even so, doubtful they'd waste time looking for him. Again he heard Spitz. "Let him walk back to town. Serve him right." One van left, then the other. He eased his head over the outcrop and realized he was finally alone.

He stood, stretched, then sprinted for the trees.

Fifteen minutes later, he was deep into the woods and constantly heading northeast. His second wind kicked in and breathing eased. Muscles warmed up and loosened. Damned if he wasn't in almost as good condition as when he graduated from Quantico. Still, this uphill trek through old-growth hickory, pine, and cedar was considerably more difficult than his daily morning runs on Chicago's flat city streets.

He ducked low-hanging pine branches and muscled through the thick undergrowth. Another fifteen minutes and he should hit the perimeter of Rideout's land.

Damned lucky it wasn't deer season. Someone would be bound to take a shot with all the noise he was making. Once he was closer to his target, he'd proceed with more caution.

He stopped and caught his breath, listening.

Ahead of him, a rustle of leaves. The snap of a twig.

He waited. Not loud enough for a large animal. Probably a raccoon.

Then a bark.

Damn. Just what he needed: a feral, possibly rabid dog.

He held his breath. Stupid. The creature could already smell him. And it was getting closer.

Fight or flight. He chose the latter and took off east as fast as his long legs could carry him.

Another yip of a bark. Damn. It was closing in.

Then more excited yips. Come to think of it, *familiar* sounding yips.

He stopped. Waited. Exhaled. Of course, none other than a certain canine. Shadow, her thick coat matted with burrs, leaped into his arms. Startled, he grabbed and held on tight to the panting creature. Her dark eyes bore him no malice but gazed intently into his. Maybe she was engaging in an attempt at the canine version of ESP.

What could it hurt? "Okay, girl, where's Bette?"

Good thing no one was watching. How asinine. Asking the freaking dog as if she was Lassie and could lead him to Timmy in the mineshaft.

The Sheltie licked Alex's cheek as if he were a nice bowl of Alpo, then squirmed.

"All right. All right. Down you go. Not like I asked you to wash my mug." The dog barked, then headed uphill and northeast.

Might as well follow her. After all, she came from where he was headed. Must be the right direction.


Drew loomed over Bette, his face a mask of determination. The expression in his gaze, however, was freaking scary, not to mention how he kept repeatedly clenching his fists. She backed away. "Sorry. I speak without thinking sometimes. If it's any consolation, Alex hates that about me too."

He grunted, averted his gaze, then pointed at Jackie. "You and Cody, back in your room."

"What are you going to do, Drew?" Jackie nudged Cody back into the room, but then stood her ground with her hands on her hips. "Bette's my friend..." she faltered, perhaps trying to think what would mollify her volatile brother. "I *need* her. It's lonely down here with just Cody. You don't spend that much time with us, so it helps to have another woman around...if you know what I mean."

During Jackie's plea, Bette eased away from Drew's reach and made herself as small and nonthreatening as possible. She didn't do meek well, but if acting meek would keep him from bashing her again, she'd give it a go.

"No more funny stuff. I got business to attend to. And Al should be here soon." A wolfish smile creased his full cheeks into an expression more grimace than smile. "I have a nice reception party waiting for him. Just wait and see." With that ominous statement, he bounded up the stairs, slamming the door at the top.

Relief rushed through Bette, leaving her weak in the knees. At least breathing came easier, and she didn't have to wonder if it was going to be her last. "Finally. We've got to get out of here before Alex shows up." She rushed to stand below one of the high basement windows. "I don't know what Drew has planned, but it won't be hots, brats, and tall cold ones." She jumped and tried to grab hold of the windowsill but missed.

"Damn, I hate being short. Come on. Maybe you can stand on my shoulders and reach it." Bending over, Bette laced her fingers together. "Come on. Quick. Before he comes back."

Jackie shook her head. "I won't leave Cody. Besides, you weigh less than I do. Let me hold you up." She bent over, lacing her fingers. Bette hiked her leg and set her foot into the cup of Jackie's hands, then jumped for the ledge. "Hup!"

The added boost was enough for Bette to reach the sill. She used her forearms on the ledge to hang on, halfway clinging to the wall like a drunken spider. "There's an opener, but it's rusted tight." She banged on the glass with a clenched fist and let fly with a string of expletives. "Sorry, Cody can't hear me, can he?"

"Don't worry." Jackie shook her head. "He's in our room, and I made sure the door was closed."

"If we just had something I could use to break this window…" The muscles in her forearms started to jitter. "Ack!" She lost her hold, slid down the wall to her feet, and plopped on her butt. She muttered another expletive. "Let's look again. There has to be something down here I can use to break the glass."

"But we've already gone over everything," Jackie said. "Looked everywhere at least twice."

Bette motioned for Jackie to follow her into the other room. "What about taking this bed apart?" She yanked off the quilted spread. "See? The frame's metal. Maybe we can break the glass with that." She folded the spread into a square. "I can use this to pad the broken glass and climb out. If I can just get to the main road, I can get the cops out here in no time flat."

"What if he hears us?"

"I'll have to be quick. No hesitating." Bette looked around. "He can't hear us, can he?"

"I don't think so. I've never been able to hear *him* walking around upstairs. The only thing I hear is when he unbolts the door."

"Good. It's a risk, but it's our only chance to get help before Alex comes waltzing into Drew's trap." She shoved the thin mattress off the bed. "Let's do it!"


Alex stopped and crouched low as he reached the line of trees bordering the old Rideout place. Only it didn't look so old anymore. Whoever had it now had restored the place until it looked brand new. Formerly an old saltbox style farmhouse, it was freshly painted, and gingerbread molding had been added, unnecessarily. Tarted the place up, all right.

The Sheltie squirmed beside him but remained in place. "Hush. No barking. Think you can remember that?" he muttered.

Fuck. He must be losing his mind, talking to the dog like she was human.

From his current vantage point, he made out a root cellar door and small basement windows along the back of the two-story farmhouse, but he couldn't see the driveway or if there were any vehicles. He'd have to work his way around toward the front. And naturally there wasn't a single sign of the local LEOs yet, or his Bureau counterpart. No doubt they were still waiting on the sheriff or a judge who would sign off on a search warrant.


By the time Bette dismantled the bed, perspiration had collected on her neck. Her hair was a sticky mess and wouldn't stay on top of her head, no matter how often she rearranged it. She blew upward, but her bangs clung to her forehead as well. "If we ever get out of here, I'm going to shave my head."

"Why? Plan on getting kidnapped again?" Jackie asked, her tone more good humored than the situation called for.

Bette made a face and huffed. "Tearing this bed apart was a little more difficult than I thought."

"Who knew the headboard was screwed to the sides?"

"And us without so much as a freaking screwdriver."

"Good thing we're women and determined."

Bette nodded, then hefted the metal-side frame over her shoulder. "Just be ready to help me with the comforter. I'm not anxious to shred my body parts trying to get out of here." She propped the metal frame on end in front of one of the high windows. "Here goes nothing." She sucked in a deep breath, then jabbed the frame against the glass.

Cringing at the sound, she held her breath.

Nothing.

Maybe if she backed up and ran, momentum would do the trick. The glass cracked but didn't break through. "One more time." She backed up as far as the space would allow and hoofed it like an Olympic pole-vaulter going for the gold.

Success. The end of the frame jammed through the glass. "Quick. Throw me the comforter. No, wait. I'll shinny up the frame; then you can throw it to me."

Bette attacked the pole and swung upward, hand over hand, just like she had so many years ago on the school playground. Reaching the top, she wrapped her legs around. Damn. Not comfortable at all.

"Here!" Jackie tossed the comforter, and Bette caught it with one hand. She wrapped it around her fist and knocked the majority of the jagged glass fragments from the window frame. "Sure could use an extra hand to refold this thing." She grunted and managed to cover the ledge and bottom of the window and started the process of working her way through the window.

Her elbow scraped against a fragment of glass still in the frame. She swore under her breath. The warmth of the blood oozed down her arm, but she inched forward.

"Are you okay?" Jackie asked.

"I've been better, but I'm taking it easy."

The sound of a door opening. She whipped her head around trying to see over her shoulder, but the angle was wrong.

"Hurry!" Jackie cried, panic rising in her tone. "He's coming. Oh, no."

A bellow of outrage emanated from their captor and echoed through the basement. His heavy footsteps pounded down the stairs.

Bette's elbows dug into the concrete well outside the window while she tried to wiggle the rest of her body up the makeshift pole.

Alex stood in a stand of pine trees and watched the farm house. As before, he couldn't see anyone moving about either inside or out. A black Ford Excursion sat in the front drive. And just beyond it was a dark red Cadillac. SUV had to be Rideout's. Certainly fit the description of the vehicle Bette had seen when she'd left Jackie at the office. And the Caddy fit too. Walking up and knocking on the front door was out of the question. Instead, working his way behind the house seemed a more viable solution. There were several small basement windows, but fitting his shoulders through one of those suckers was doubtful. What about the root cellar door?

And how to keep Shadow from barking and giving away his position was another problem. Fortunately, she still had her leash. "Okay, girl, you need to wait right here." After a couple of false starts, he managed to loop the leash around a bush. "Not much slack, but it can't be helped," he muttered. "Just behave and you won't choke."

Crap. While Alex himself might be considered expendable, Bette would kill him if anything happened to her dog.

"Sit. Stay. Whatever..."

The sound of breaking glass fractured the quiet countryside. He searched for the origin of the sound. Something had broken through one of the basement windows. Crouching, he scrambled through the brush until he reached a spot perpendicular to the window. Still hidden in the cover of the trees, he waited. And watched.

Some kind of thick blanket or spread was shoved through, and then miraculously, a head—Bette's. His heart thundered as adrenaline surged through his body while he watched her struggle to escape.

He broke from the tree line and raced toward her. "Bette," he called in a low voice, hoping she would hear and no one else.

She glanced up, her eyes widening with surprise. "Hurry. He's back." Then she squealed and disappeared from the window.

He stopped, straightened. A door slammed, and he heard the ominous clicking of nails on the side porch. The sounds of a large animal rushing accompanied by heavy breathing and growling.

A dog. A big dog. The creature racing around the corner of the house was the size of a small elephant. A freaking Rottweiler with lips curled back, showing some massive teeth. Massive, *sharp* teeth.

Alex shuddered. Phobia or not, that snarling creature stood between him and the people he cared most about in the entire world. One way or another, it was going down.

Not a nine-year-old kid anymore. Simple as mind over matter.

But first, put some distance between him and the Rottweiler.

He ran the fastest one hundred meters of his life. Ahead, a low-hanging branch looked as if it would support his weight if he could just reach it and swing up...

He leapt and grabbed hold, but not before he felt the searing pain of those bone crushers ripping through his jeans and into his calf. His momentum carried him upward. The Rottweiler hung on for several seconds longer than Alex was comfortable with, then dropped to the ground with a yelp. Undaunted, the dog stood its ground, snapping, growling, and baring his teeth.

Alex clasped his legs around the branch and held on. Based on the animal's snarls, it wasn't going anywhere soon. Somehow, he had to get rid of the dog and find out what happened with Bette.

Again the door slammed, and his gaze immediately went toward the sound. Son of a bitch! Around the corner of the house came a tall, bearded man, dragging Bette in front of him, his arm around her neck in a choke hold...and what looked like a 9 mm pointed at her head. Blood trickled from her forearms.

"Simon, *sitz!*" the man ordered. The dog ceased and sat, then went into the down position as promptly as a Westminster show dog. "Come to the party, Al, or I'll have to put a bullet in this broad's head. I'm tempted anyway. Dude! How do you put up with her?"

*Al?* The sound of the man's voice was eerily familiar. Like listening to his own on voice mail. Andy? Could it really be, after all these years?

"Alex! It's—"

The man's arm tightened around Bette's neck, cutting off her reply. "Told you to shut the fuck up!"

"Come on, Al. Haven't you guessed? I'm having a family reunion, and if you want to keep this broad of yours alive, you'd better throw down your weapon."

"I-I don't have one." Unless you counted the hideout in his ankle holster. "I'm not here in an official capacity."

"Right." His brother laughed, a harsh and ugly sound that ripped from his throat. "And the pope doesn't live in the Vatican."

Alex glanced down at the now calm dog. "What about him?"

"He won't hurt you—unless I tell him to."

"Reassuring—not." Alex's grip involuntarily tightened around the branch. His gut twisted. His mouth grew dry. Cooperate. No other way. Only for Bette.

"Come on, brother. Don't be such a chicken-shit. Should've thought you'd outgrown your fear of all things canine by now."

Childhood phobia or not, that muscled Rottweiler would make anyone stop and think twice.

# Chapter Twenty-five

Bette choked back fear and ignored the pain from where she'd sliced her forearms on the broken window. Drew's viselike hold around her neck tightened. Her vision dimmed. She tried to shake her head, a warning not to trust his twin brother, even as Alex dropped to the ground in a crouch.

Drew's grasp relaxed slightly. He backed up, dragging her with him. "Come on. You first." He waved the gun toward the door.

With his loosened grip, her vision cleared. Alex took one step forward, then another, casting a wary glance over his shoulder at the Rottweiler. "It's a trap," she managed to call out before his hold tightened again.

"Told you to keep your mouth shut. Told you this is a long overdue family reunion." Bette felt her body weakening, and her vision grow spotty.

"You're killing her!" Alex's voice sounded farther away.

Fading. Falling into a black well of nothingness.


Alex's hands trembled. The sight of Bette collapsing in his brother's grasp had him off-balance. After steadying himself, he cast one last glance at the attack dog and rushed toward Bette.

"That's far enough!" his brother shouted, then barked an order in what sounded like German, "*Platz!*" The dog dropped to his belly but looked like he would gladly remove one of Alex's legs if given the appropriate command.

Alex stopped but remained upright, squaring his shoulders in a position of dominance he certainly didn't feel. Bummer. Figured the dog would only obey German commands. Why hadn't he taken that as one of his languages?

Andy backed up and motioned with his weapon. "Inside."

Unable to tear his gaze from Bette's limp form, Alex raised his hands in surrender. "All right. All right." His brother must've loosened his chokehold a bit because the color was returning to Bette's waxy white cheeks. Relief flooded through him as he marshaled a renewed sense of determination. Maybe he could still talk their way out of Andy's freaked-out idea of a family reunion.

Reunion, hell.

Expecting any moment the attack dog would pounce at him from behind, Alex moved slowly. Too slowly, apparently.

"Move it!" his brother yelled, then followed with a sneer. "Some hero to the rescue. I think your girl, here, picked the wrong brother. Not that I'd ever put up with her smart mouth."

Alex eased through the side door, then glanced over his shoulder. Bette's color was almost normal, but she wasn't moving. Still unconscious? Faking it? Who knew with Jersey? Unpredictable should've been her middle name.

"Next door on your left. Open it slowly. No heroics. I still got your girlfriend."

Nodding, Alex opened the door to what turned out to be the basement and peered down. No sign of Jackie or his nephew.

"Ugh!" Alex grunted.

Without warning, Andy shoved Bette's body into Alex's, and they tumbled down the stairs together. Desperate to control the fall and protect her from further injury, he grabbed her with one arm and the handrail with his other.

Their momentum ripped his hand from the rail, and they tumbled down the stairs, every step ramming into his spine. He wrapped both arms around Bette. Tucking her head into his shoulder, he tried to slide the rest of the way on his side as he'd been trained. Above him, Andy slammed the door.

Pain sliced through his spine and hip as they landed at the bottom. He groaned. Throughout the fall, Bette hadn't made a sound. That realization alone nearly sucked the air from his lungs. Somewhere, the sound of his sister's screaming invaded his consciousness.

Still cradling Bette, he rolled upright, wincing as every muscle in his back chose that moment to spasm. "Jersey?" She had to be all right.

Had to be.

The barest of flutters of her dark lashes against her pale skin. The muscles in her throat worked as she tried to swallow.

Unable to stand, he inched away from the bottom step, pulling Bette with him. She moaned, then took a shuddering deep breath.

"Is she all right?" Jackie rushed to their side. "Are you?"

Finally, Bette's eyes opened. The warmth of her gaze shot a jolt of reassurance through him.

Jackie let out a sigh of relief. "Can you move?"

Nodding, Bette grunted and elbowed her way into a semi-sitting position. "That's the second time he's had a go at knocking me down those stairs." Her voice was husky, probably from his brother's chokehold. "The first time was a close call. All the same, I've had it with his fists. Like to kick his—"

"Hold on, tiger. You're not quite ready to kick anyone's anything…yet." At least her fighting spirit was back, even if the two of them together didn't amount to one wholly fit person.

"Just hold tight," he said, lowering his voice. "I still have my hideout weapon. Andy didn't bother to check. The worst that can happen is we have to hold out until the locals show up. There's an agent from the Buffalo field office as well," he told her quietly between muscle spasms. The very last thing he wanted to do was use that weapon on his brother. Not when it was Alex's fault they were all in this situation.

"I think I'm okay." Bette shoved herself into a full sitting position. "Can you move?"

"Not unless you're ready to see me cry like a girl."

Bette grunted. "I won't tell. It'll be our secret."

He pulled up one knee and groaned, then the other, but the action seemed to relax the spasms in his lower back. Blood from the dog bite oozed through his jeans.

His sister pulled the shirt from his pants and palpated his back. "You have a massive bruise over your kidney. That's probably what's causing you the most pain. You're definitely going to need follow-up X-rays for that."

"Hmph. Spoken like a real doctor, sis."

"Shut up. I may be a vet, but I bet I know more about human anatomy than you do." She ripped a strip off the hem of her skirt and tightly wrapped his bleeding calf.

He grimaced, then gazed up at his sister and shook his head. "No way." Then he followed with a feeble-at-best grin.

Jackie set her hands on her hips and nodded sharply. "Yes way."

"Okay, guys," Bette said. "Let's stop the bickering and come up with a plan for getting out of here."

Without warning, the door opened. Alex's gaze shot upward. His brother was clambering down the steps, carrying a gun, and—crap—a pair of handcuffs swung from his belt. What kind of sick game did his brother have in mind now? Who was this man who used to be his brother? His go-to guy—before Alex had left him in the movie theatre. What had his kidnapper turned him into?

The corner of Drew's mouth lifted in a grim half smile, his gaze boring into Alex's. "Time for payback, *brother*."

# Chapter Twenty-six

By the time Agent Hixson and Detective Spitz found an amenable judge and obtained a search warrant, the sun was hanging low in the western sky. Hixson and Spitz drove through the winding two-lane road, followed by the tactical team in two of Ontario County's black vans. Hixson pulled at his shirt collar. The upstate summer heat was getting to him, not to mention the biting black flies and pesky mosquitoes. He slapped his neck where one had just chowed down. He cast an irritated glance at the detective. "Spitz, how much farther is this Rideout place, anyway?"

The detective shrugged. "Another mile or so up the next turnoff."

"Hmph!" He loosened his tie and removed his jacket, then set it aside. The regulation vest would be hot enough. "We'd have done better to follow MacGregor's example and struck off through the woods."

"Yeah, you Feds like to show off." Spitz pulled out a handkerchief and mopped his shiny forehead. "I hope one of your superiors kicks this baby agent down to entry level. That's what I'd do if he—"

"Give the guy a break. You ever had a member of *your* family kidnapped? Different ballgame, Detective. I feel for the guy. Don't blame him at all. If we have a positive outcome, the most he'll get is a slap on the wrist."

"Hmph," the detective muttered. "What'll they do about the girlfriend with mob connections?"

Scratching his chin, Hixson stirred uncomfortably in the seat and tried to keep his breathing shallow. Someone in the van had a bad case of BO. "That's a dicey situation," he said. "All depends on what *he* decides to do about *her*."

"Hey, slow down," Spitz said to the officer driving. "The turnoff should be around the next curve."

Hixson unfolded the topography chart. "Looks like the house is a good mile or more off this main road."

"Yeah, at least."

The van turned into the drive and stopped. "Damn!" Hixson and Spitz said simultaneously.

Beyond a wooden gate, an ancient pine tree lay across the lane, effectively blocking their progress. "Didn't think there was that much storm damage the other night," the detective said.

Hixson jumped from the van to check the tree. It was a big mother. Must've taken quite a storm to bring it down. Then he glanced at the base. "Son of a gun must've been expecting us. It's not storm damage. It was cut down. Recently too."

Spitz shook his head. "We'll have to continue on foot."

So not looking forward to that, Hixson mused. He felt sorry for the SWAT team that would have to carry all their equipment for over a mile. And from what he could observe, the majority of it was all uphill. "Better hurry before it gets dark." He felt another sting on his neck and slapped at whatever vampire of an insect that relished more of his good old Type A.

"Enough!" Alex grunted and sat up as straight as possible. Time he asserted some control over this situation. No matter it was obvious to all he had none whatsoever.

"Just wanted you to have a taste of what it was like, *Alex*. You missed out on a lot of interesting experiences."

His brother's eyes grew a little crazy when he said Alex's name. Alex hid the uh-oh shiver. Whatever his brother had suffered, he was definitely damaged. No happy endings here. No, the possibility of a happy ending had vanished a long time ago. If Alex hadn't left him. If the authorities had kept looking for Andy after he disappeared. If everyone hadn't believed him dead.

"This is between you and me, Andy." Maybe by invoking his brother's childhood name, he could bring back some vestige of the brother he'd once known. "You've got what you want. Let the others go. Don't make this any worse for yourself."

He leaned down in Alex's face. Bette was easing away, trying to make her body smaller. Less of a target. "Andy's dead!" Then his mouth pulled into an approximation of a smile…a ghastly evil leer that boded good for no one. "But *Drew* wants a family reunion, and *now* he has one." He straightened and turned to Jackie. "Get Cody. He should join us for dinner."

Jackie shook her head, her blonde curls bobbing. "I'd rather not. He's napping."

Alex watched his sister straighten her back and jut her chin. Her tone was rock solid. She had that mom-thing going on, as in she meant business. "You *have* to do something for your brother, she said. "He's hurt. He needs some muscle relaxants. Surely you have something…?"

"I'm fine. Everybody just calm down," Alex said, gesturing with both hands.

Fast as a striking cobra, Drew grabbed Alex's right wrist and cuffed it to the stair railing before he could react. Not a lefty or remotely ambidextrous, having his gun hand out of commission sort of upped the complication factor.

Bette licked her lips and patted her tummy. "You mentioned dinner?" She eased to her feet. "You know, I could do with some dinner. What's on the menu, anyway? Jackie said the eats were pretty good." She finished with an impish grin as if Drew wasn't waving a gun around.

"You aren't going to be around long enough for a meal, smart mouth." He turned from Alex and lumbered toward her.

Unable to keep her mouth shut, no matter what he threatened, Bette continued, "Have you ever considered laying off on the free weights? Or maybe shaving the Grizzly Adams beard? Honestly you wouldn't look half bad." Bette paused, hoping to give Alex time to free himself from the handcuffs. "In fact, you'd look just like your brother." She shrugged and smiled up at Alex's twin. "Then how would I ever choose between the two of you?"

Drew's eyes widened, and the muscles in his jaw bulged with tension. "I'm going to rid you of this aggravation, brother," he said, towering over Bette. "She's nothing more than a pesky mosquito and needs to be swatted...at the very least. But I have a more permanent cure in mind. Extermination." He drew back his fist for a mighty, swinging blow.

Prepared for such a response, she ducked and heard Alex suck in a deep breath. Then the basement reverberated from a loud yell of fury and the sharp crack of wood breaking and being ripped from the wall.

Bette scooted back. Drew whipped around, coming face-to-face with his brother, who brandished a three-foot length of handrail. Drew ducked Alex's first blow, spinning and landing a back-fist strike into Alex's jaw.

Bette gasped as Alex staggered from the brute force of his brother's blow. A red bruise appeared immediately on his jaw. Blood trickled from his mouth. *Please don't let anything bad happen.* Alex was their only chance.

Alex recovered his stance and swung at his brother, but the blow bounced off his back. Drew yelled with rage and attempted a head-butt. Just in time, Alex stepped aside and pounded his brother's lower back with the handrail.

Drew grunted, stumbled, but recovered and punched Alex in the gut. Seemingly unaware of the blow, Alex kneed Drew in the groin, collapsing him to his knees.

Alex's chest rose and fell rapidly. His gaze was unfocused as he swung the handrail and bashed the back of Drew's head. He drew back again and knocked his twin flat to the floor, then kicked him in the ribs. But in spite of all that punishment, Drew scrambled to his knees. Alex took another swing at his brother's head. The blow knocked him down into a massive heap. An unmoving heap.

"Alex, stop it! That's enough. You're going to kill him." Bette tugged on his elbow. He whirled to face her, his gaze wild and unfocused. "He's not moving. You've beaten him unconscious."

"Don't care." Gasping, he lurched forward with the broken handrail still attached to his wrist. "He's a dead man."

Using the full weight of her body, Bette dragged him back while pleading, "Jackie, do something. He's lost it."

Jackie gazed at her younger brother. "Alex will be all right. I'm not so sure about Drew." She kneeled beside him and checked his pupils, then his pulse. "Definitely unconscious, but his pulse is steady." She bit her bottom lip. "At first, when it was just Cody and me, he was pretty much holding it together. Then when Bette came, he became much more erratic."

"It was a personality conflict. That's all," Bette said.

"But when you showed up, Alex, Drew's deep anger took over. I think he's had some kind of psychotic break. I'm afraid any remnant of our brother is hiding deep inside, if at all." The vet shook her head.

At that moment, Bette heard a tiny voice say, "What's going on? I heard loud noises." The child stood in the doorway of his and Jackie's "room." Eyes wide, Cody looked over at Drew. "Is Uncle Drew dead?" His blue gaze turned to his mother. "Can we go home now?"

"No, he's just sleeping." Jackie took her son in her arms and hugged him close. "And yes, baby, we can go home now."

Bette busied herself with gingerly rifling through Drew's pockets for his handcuff key. "I've got it." Quickly she unlocked

Alex from the steel cuffs. His breathing was rapid, and he still didn't seem quite present.

Still, first things first. While Drew was still out of it, she ran back to his body. Tugging his hands behind his back, she cuffed him, then fished his cell phone from his jeans pocket.

"Bingo. I'm calling 911."

"Good. Drew needs an ambulance." Jackie rolled him to his side. "We need to maintain his airway while he's unconscious."

"I know he's your brother, but I'm more worried about the good twin. Something's wrong. He's not himself."

The vet cast a worried glance in Alex's direction. "He's pale. Have him sit down. Take some slow, deep breaths."

"Alex!" Bette snapped. "Sit." She backed him, still unsteady, until he sat on the steps.

"Screw it. He's not going to touch you again."

"I'm *all right*." Somehow, she had to get through his fog of rage. "Take some deep breaths. You have to calm down. We're all okay." She held up the cell phone. "See, I'm going to call 911."

"Yeah, 911." Still pale, he nodded and did as she instructed.

After a couple of breaths, his eyes grew focused. "It's over."

"Yes."

Overhead, there was the thunder of footsteps. Many footsteps.


Above Alex's head, the door to the basement burst open, the wood splintering from a battering ram.

"Un-freaking-believable. Now the troops arrive." Alex leaned against the wall, his chest heaving. He nodded toward the unmoving figure bundled on the floor. "Gently. He's nuts, but he's my brother."

"Your brother?" Agent Hixon and Detective Spitz said in unison.

"Yeah. You know"—he paused for another breath—"the one

the CPD decided was dead and didn't bother to investigate further." He winced with pain and braced his side with his elbow.

"What about the others?"

He glanced over his shoulder and observed Bette leading what remained of his family up the stairs. "They're fine." He gasped again. "On the other hand, I could use some medical assistance," he got out then collapsed into a swirling red-and-black well of pain.

# Chapter Twenty-seven

Alex struggled to open his eyes. Tried to sit. Arms wouldn't move. He tugged. Someone had tied him down. "Wha...?"

"Careful, Double-O." Bette's soft voice drew him to consciousness and away from feeling imprisoned. "You're in the hospital. There's an IV in your arm, and they're giving you blood."

This time he managed to raise his lids. Dear sweet Bette's face hovered over him. Maybe he was dreaming. He looked over her shoulder and made out an IV pump. Tried again to sit. Too dizzy. Sank back onto the pillow. He swallowed and spoke, "You're safe? Jackie and Cody?"

She caressed the back of his hand, the comfort of her warm touch centering him. "Don't you remember? You were a wild man. Your brother didn't have a chance once you got free."

He cleared his throat. "I don't remember anything except he went after you."

"You lunged and pulled the handrail out of the wall. It broke from the force, and you bashed Drew's head with it, then again and again, until Jackie and I pulled you off him. He wasn't moving."

After all Drew'd been through, had Alex killed his own brother? "Is he...?"

"No." She shook her head. "The doctor said Drew would recover physically, but his mental condition is another story. By the way, he's down the hall...with a guard, of course."

"Good." He managed to lever onto one elbow. "I want to see him."

Bette shook her head. "Uh-uh. The doctors agree it's better if you don't—for now, anyway."

He let his gaze travel up the IV tubes to the bag of blood and another of fluids. "What's with the blood? Was I shot?"

"Nope. You know—your sister is a pretty smart lady. Your kidney—it was bruised. Not too bad, though. Your real problem was a bleeding ulcer. That's what the blood's for. Plus the other bag has antibiotics to heal the ulcer. Your Rambo attack increased the bleeding. Fortunately, the cops arrived and got you to the hospital. The doc in charge says you'll be on bed rest for a couple of days."

He grunted, "Bed rest, huh?"

"Yeah, doll, real rest." She gazed down at him, her eyes glimmering with humor. "That means no monkey business."

He gazed up at her, cocking an eyebrow. "Sure about that?"

"Very." She nodded for emphasis. "The doc also says your kidney and the ulcer need some time to heal. He's ordered more tests to make sure there's no permanent damage." She rose from the bedside chair. "Sorry, but I gotta go. The office is hopping with patients and their curious owners. Honestly, I never saw so many pets brought in early for their annual checkups."

*Shadow.* "Oh, God, I left Shadow in the woods behind the house. Tied to a bush."

Bette giggled, a happy sound that warmed his heart. "I found her. She's fine. I wouldn't let them take me away in the ambulance until I looked for her. And Drew's Rottie has been taken to Finger Lakes Rottweiler Rescue."

"I don't think anyone's going to want that ugly brute," Alex said, tamping down the impulse to shiver.

"At least he'll have a chance of being rehabilitated." She picked up her purse.

"Any *chance* you'll ever get over being a dog lover?"

"Not one in a million, Double-O." She leaned over and planted a measly kiss on his forehead. "See you after office hours."

"Don't leave on my account." A solemn-faced Agent Hixson

stood in the doorway.

"I'm not. I *really* have to go to work." She shot an uneasy smile in Alex's direction and mouthed *good luck*, then zipped from the room.

"Attractive, if you like that type," Hixson said.

Alex glared at the agent and tried to lever up to an elbow, but collapsed back onto the pillow, grimacing from pain. "And what type would that be?" he asked with a growl.

Hixson gave him a knowing expression. "You know, Jersey Shores bimbo. More hair than brains."

"She's no bimbo," Alex said through clenched teeth.

"Whatever." The agent shrugged. "I've debriefed everyone but you. They say you're going to live, so I'd like to tie this up and get back to Buffalo."

"No thanks to you."

Scowling, Hixson settled on Bette's recently vacated chair. "What transpired after you took off from the winery?"

"I headed to the Rideout place and found Bette—Ms. Spinelli—trying to escape from one of the basement windows. That didn't work too well. A minute or two later, I saw someone—my brother, it turns out—come around the house. He had her in a choke hold with a weapon pointed at her head." He continued with what he remembered. "My brother threatened her. Exterminate was the word he used. As for the rest, you're out of luck, pal. I don't remember." He shrugged. "Whatever the others said I did, that's what I did."

He took Hixson's stony expression as a sign the fellow agent wasn't thrilled with the response. "Seriously, dude, I don't remember what happened. The doctor would probably say my memory loss is due to trauma or blood loss. But if I remember anything beyond what I've already told you, I'll give you a call."

The agent rose stiffly, his jaw set. "If you can't remember, you can't remember."

Alex frowned. Before he could say anything else, there was a tap at the door. A short, stocky man dressed in blue scrubs entered. "Got an order to take Mr. MacGregor to Medical Imaging," he said, looking from Alex to the agent and back again.

"Fine. I'll hold you to your word, MacGregor. You damned well better give me a call when your memory returns."

"Said I would...*if* it does." Guess Hixson didn't really believe Alex's memory loss was real. Jerk.

The patient escort's brows shot up, but he made no comment and set about transferring the bags of blood and IV fluids to a pole attached to the gurney.

"Thanks for dropping by, Agent Hixson." Alex gave a royal wave as the agent nodded curtly and left.

"So what are they going to do to me in Medical Imaging?" he asked the orderly.

"I'm just a patient transporter. They don't tell me anything."

Nodding, Alex moved gingerly onto the stretcher. "Yeah. Like that all over." The patient transporter aimed the gurney through the door and started down the hall.

All Alex could think about was how Bette's beautiful face was all he ever wanted to see first thing every morning when he opened his eyes...for the rest of his life.

He spent the next day and a half being transported hither and yon. If someone wasn't poking tubes into places best not mentioned and radiating his insides, someone else was drawing multiple tubes of blood. The only bright spots in his boring life as a hospital patient were Bette's visits before and after office hours.

Finally, after the rest of the tests were negative and his blood counts were stable, his doctor told Alex he could discharge in the morning, but he finagled the physician into signing a discharge order for that evening.

Glad to be free from IVs, tests, and tasteless hospital food, he headed over to his sister's house. Bette should be off work by now, and he wanted to surprise her.

# Chapter Twenty-eight

When Alex reached his sister's house, neither she nor Cody were home. He headed downstairs to Bette's apartment. He knocked on the door. It opened slowly, and she gave a squeal and started to jump into his arms but stopped and hugged him very carefully. Shadow wasn't so inhibited. Yipping gaily, the Sheltie ran in circles.

"I thought you weren't coming home until tomorrow. I was going to take a shower, then bring you some dinner."

"No need." He reached down to scratch the Sheltie's ears. "I've been officially released from the hospital. Cleared for duty."

"Does that mean...?"

"Yes, cleared for action." He gave her a cheeky salute.

"You should've warned me." Her hands went to her hair. "I'm a mess."

He took in the sight of her tousled hair and skimpy halter top. Skinny jeans that struck just below her belly button. "A beautiful mess," he said with a laugh, then nuzzled her neck and nipped at her ear lobe.

Squirming free from his arms, she rushed into the bedroom and grabbed a brush. He followed and watched while she brushed her long, dark hair, the silken strands caressing her tanned back. She turned from the mirror and gazed over her shoulder. "What about your brother? What will they do with him?"

He sat on her bed and toed off his running shoes. "After he's ready to leave the hospital, he'll undergo a psych eval to see if he can stand trial. That'll determine where he goes next."

She set the brush on the small bureau and walked toward him. "Three kidnappings and the attempted murder of a federal agent. They'll put him away somewhere for a long time, won't they?"

Swallowing the huge knot in his throat, Alex nodded. "Yeah." If he just hadn't left Drew at the theatre all those years ago...

"It wasn't your fault, y'know. It was that Rideout guy who took him and abused him." Bette stood knee to knee with him and brushed the hair back from his forehead, her touch gentle and comforting.

"Yeah, but..." He rose from the bed and paced over to the small high window and gazed out at the backyard. Regret weighed on him like a stone around his neck. "I left him. Told him I'd be right back. Meant it too, but..." He shook his head. "My fault. Mine."

He felt Bette's arms ease around his waist as her head rested against his back. "You were a kid. Even worse, a teenage boy with hormones. All you did was follow a cute girl to the arcade. Normal, natural behavior."

He turned to face her, not willing to accept her comforting words. "My *twin* went through years of abuse and God only knows what else because of my teenage hormones. *He* didn't know the meaning of natural or normal."

"And it's still not your fault. That's on Rideout." She frowned. "What about the body with Drew's ID bracelet? Did your brother reveal anything about that?"

"Another kid. Rideout picked him up hitching on the Turnpike and ended up killing him when he tried to escape from the basement. Rideout put Drew's bracelet on him. He must've figured by the time the kid's body was found, everyone would assume it was Drew's."

"Which they did."

"Yeah. The authorities didn't bother to check DNA." Alex shook his head. "It was fairly new back then and not routine. As far as everyone was concerned, the case was closed."

"I'm so sorry. I don't know what else to say." She reached up and wrapped her arms around his neck, offering her lips to his. For a second, he surrendered to their softness. Heat suffused his body, and he grew uncomfortably hard. He shook his head. "No. It's not fair." As much as he wanted to give in to Bette's heat, he didn't deserve the gifts of her tenderness and passion.

She gazed up at him, her warm eyes shimmering with emotion. "I don't care about fair. I care about *you*. And if now is all there is, I'm fine with it."

"Jersey, I'm not worthy."

"Probably not." Her tone was casual, but her gaze was mischievous as she led Shadow from the bedroom, shutting the door. "We don't need an audience," she said, wrinkling her nose.

God. The radiant woman before him was all that was good and right in his life. For now. Forever was a distant illusion. A mirage. Beckoning, drawing him closer, then evaporating at the last possible moment.

He'd found love at the worst moment in his life with the woman most likely to ruin his career—at least as far as the Bureau was concerned. But maybe not. If—and it was a big if—they accepted her assertion she had no part in *the life*.

She took his hand and pressed a tender kiss in the palm. He stiffened and shook his head.

"Don't pull away." Her eyes glistened as she gazed into his. "I meant what I said. No expectations. No promises. I can't think of a nicer way to say good-bye."

What was a red-blooded man, who was head-over-heels in love with a woman who wouldn't take no for an answer, supposed to do?

His determination melted away like snow in the sun. Taking full advantage of her warmth and selflessness, he pulled the halter over her head. At the sight of her firm breasts, he sucked in a deep breath. His mouth grew dry. "You know you're freaking beautiful, don't you?"

She cupped her breasts and gave them an evaluating glance. "Since you seem to think so, I guess I'll have to consider your opinion as valid."

She moved to unzip her jeans, but he covered her small hands with his larger ones. "No, let me."

"Okay, but..." She gazed up at him, her brows pulled together in a frown. "Are you *sure* you're all right...physically? Jackie will absolutely freaking kill me if your ulcer starts bleeding again."

"We'll be careful." He leaned over, lifted the hair from her neck and gently placed a kiss just beneath her ear. "Very careful." He unzipped her jeans and helped her step from them. He slid white lacy panties over the delicious curves of her round ass. Then, kneeling, he eased the panties down her trim thighs and buried his nose in the crisp dark curls where her legs met. A whiff of her female musk rocked his senses. Reeling as if drunk on her scent, he groaned aloud.

"Are you all right?" Her eyes widened as she pulled away. "Did I hurt you?"

He laughed at the sudden note of concern in Bette's voice. "No. Just the opposite. I want to make love to you. If this has to be our last time—"

"You know it is." Eyeing him severely, she raised her chin a defiant notch. "You're going back to Chicago. After that, you'll be involved in whatever the VCTF does. I have a life here. I'll be working with Jackie, helping out however I can, so don't be making me any promises." She nodded as if to say, *end of discussion.*

As far as he was concerned, there were two people in the room, and he'd have his say...if he could get a word in edgewise. Shaking his head, he set his hands on her shoulders and eased her down to his level. "Just shut up. We're wasting our last night together. Honest to God, Jersey, you talk too damned much."

Her mouth opened to protest, but he stopped her flow of chatter with a kiss.

\*\*\*

Bette struggled, tried to push away, to resist, but only for a couple of seconds. After all they'd been through—dammit, her defenses were next to zero. Her arms went around his neck, her breasts pressing against the hard muscles of his chest, so closely the rapid beat of his heart startled her. Try as she might, she couldn't ignore the sense of loss already sweeping through her. This truly was their last night together. The last time they would make love. The last…anything.

She surrendered and opened to his sweeping tongue. He rose to his feet and gathered her in his arms. Rather than let him try to pick her up and possibly injure his bruised kidney, she took his hand and led him to her bed. Behind closed doors and away from the rest of the world, she would have to make this night last a lifetime.

Just the two of them together, they tumbled onto the bed. Alex shed his shirt and kicked off his jeans. That he wanted her was obvious. His cock was rigid and sleek as it arrowed upward. She pressed her belly against him and rubbed back and forth.

"See what you do to me," he said with a groan.

She took his hand and slid it into her cleft. "See how wet I am. That's what *you* do to me. I want you…" Her voice cracked, and the gut-wrenching need to have him shook her through and through. This "one last time" deal was a mistake. How could she let him go when all she wanted forever with him? This one night would never be enough.

"Mm." He slipped two fingers inside and back out again, then rubbed the head of his cock up and down her slit. Her inner muscles clenched. She reached to guide his cock—

"Uh-uh." He nudged her back onto the bed and lifted her legs over his shoulders. Once again he buried his face in her core, licking up and down her slit, lavishing attention on her clit, nipping and sucking.

A kaleidoscope of sparks burst beneath her closed lids, and a moan ripped from her throat as his masterful tongue quickly brought her to a shattering climax, her inner muscles shuddering.

"More," she gasped, though, with every cell in her body afire, how she could stand more she didn't have a clue. She grabbed a condom from the nightstand and slipped the foil packet into his hand.

"Your wish is my command," he murmured. He lay back on the floor, sheathed himself, then pulled her with him. He supported her hips over his as she took his cock and centered it between her legs, inching down, enveloping him easily with the wet warmth of her body. Her muscles stretched to take all of him. Once he was fully inside her, she rotated her hips to give them the pleasure they both craved.

Raising his hips clear of the floor, Alex drove into her slippery heat, harder and harder, his body blazing with an inner fire. More and more, deeper and deeper as if the harder he thrust, the more he could possess her, body and soul. His knees jittered as his groin tightened, the urge to come overwhelming. Not yet. Not yet.

"More. Don't stop," she begged. Her raspy breath warm in his ear, she rode him, her high breasts bouncing with each thrust.

He reached for her breasts, pulling on the nipples until they were tight chocolate buds, imploring him to taste. Pulling her upper body closer, he captured one nipple and sucked and gently raked it with his teeth.

Her breathing quickened, and her silken skin flushed pink and hot against his chest.

Almost there.

Her inner walls tightened around his cock—oh, God, the sweetest sensation.

Now.

He bucked hard, driving them both over the edge. She cried his name and collapsed on his chest. Slick with sweat, he shuddered beneath her. "I love you," he gasped. "I—"

Shaking her head, she placed a finger to his lips, stopping him from saying more. "*No* promises." Breaking the bond holding them together, she slid off him and curled into the crook of his arm. Her head resting on his shoulder, she fell asleep.

His eyes stung. This was really it. The end.

How could he bear to leave her? In what seemed like the blink of an eye, this one woman had changed him. Made him think of someone besides himself. This was the one woman he didn't want to love and leave the way he had so many others before. Maybe there was a way?

Later, Bette lay spooned in Alex's arms. "I don't want to say good-bye," he said, gently brushing a strand of hair back from her forehead. "I don't want to leave."

A sense of peace and comfort spread through her. Just the words she wanted to hear. Needed to hear. But it could never work, so the next step was bound to hurt them both. Good medicine always tasted bitter. Best to rip off the bandage quickly. Wasn't that the conventional wisdom?

Gathering her courage and determination, she wriggled up to her elbows. "You *have* to go back. That's all there is to it." She watched as he swung his legs off the bed and set his feet on the floor. Glancing over his shoulder, his gaze riveted to hers, he stood, then pulled on his jeans.

Why did she have to sound so selfless when she certainly didn't feel that at all? Devastated, yes. Selfless—not by a long shot. Still she had to try. "You have a job to do. And it's important. You can't give up everything you ever wanted and worked so hard for. My family will cause you nothing but trouble with the FBI. And I refuse to be responsible for ruining your career."

Unable to watch him leave, she turned away. Her chin started to tremble, and tears welled in her eyes, threatening to spill down her cheeks. She sucked in a deep breath, hoping she could keep from shattering into a thousand pieces. If he would just leave. Like *now*.

"Just go," she said, squeezing her lids tightly and with all the calm she could muster.

"I'll call you as soon as I'm situated."

"No!" She yanked the sheet up, covering her chest. "No! I told you no promises."

He walked around to her side of the bed, then sat beside her. "Things are different now, Bette." His voice choked with emotion, his chest rose and fell rapidly with his quick breaths. "Before, we were strangers who passed in the night, but now, we've shared too much. I can't leave you like this. I don't *want* to leave you, at all."

Dammit. How much more torture could she take? Somehow, short of physically kicking his fine posterior out of her apartment, she had to make him leave. "You don't have a choice. Don't you have some task force to get back to in Chicago? Now get out and leave me in peace. I'll be fine. It's not like this was anything more than a glorified booty call."

Disbelief spread across his face.

"A booty call? Is that what the time we just spent together was? Not for me. And not for you either. Act as casual as you want. What we had—have—is a heck of a lot more than a freaking booty call."

Bette swallowed hard—or tried to, but the muscles in her throat wouldn't cooperate. Mouth dry and speechless, she shook her head and held up her hands, warding him away. "No. It isn't. We're two healthy adults whose hormones got the best of us. Just go. I don't have time for all this emotional nonsense anyway. I have my job here. Jackie really needs me now. Did you know she kicked Brad out last night? She found out everything. She needs all the support I can give her."

What would it take to see his backside out the door? A freaking stick of dynamite? "You're going back to Chicago to do your secret agent thing. Nothing's really changed. We had some laughs. Some good sex—"

His brows spiked, and his nostrils flared. "Laughs and good sex? That's it?"

Summoning all her Jersey-girl bravado, she shrugged. "Okay, so it was laughs and great sex? You got over your fear of dogs—one of 'em, anyway."

Please, just go.

His jaw clenched, the muscles jumping. "Yeah, I guess I did at that." His tone came across as sharp and bitter as wine turned to vinegar. He bowed grandly. "For the first time in my life, it was more than sex—a lot more." He let out with a harsh laugh. "Happy to have obliged your libido, Ms. Smithson-Spinelli, whoever the hell you are." He spun and grabbed his go-bag. Over his shoulder, he said, "Don't call me. I'll call you."

Unable to control her temper, she yelled at his back, "Fuck you!" Then she shot him her best smirk. "No. Been there, done that."

"You said it, lady." He squared his shoulders. And left her.

She heard Shadow give a quiet *yip* as Alex blew past. Holding her breath, she waited until she heard the front door slam, and then she dissolved in tears. The sense of loss threatened to suck the life from her very soul. Knowing she'd done the right thing for *him* didn't ease the pain. It merely sharpened it.

Dying couldn't hurt any worse.

She ran from her apartment and bounded up the stairs, Shadow at her heels. Too late. She couldn't call him back. He was gone.

That was it. Done deal.

No more laughing blue eyes that sparkled with humor and glittered with desire whenever she caught him watching her. No more teasing. No more seeing her love reflected in his eyes.

No more promises.

Now get on with your life.

A wet nose pressed against her calf. Shadow gazed up at Bette with big beautiful eyes. "It's all right, girl. I'll be fine…in about thirty or forty years."

# Chapter Twenty-nine

*One week later, Chicago FBI Field Office*

Alex paced from one side of the SAC's reception area to another. The longer his superior kept him waiting, the more the pit of his stomach churned. "Let's get the show on the road."

"Agent, did you say something?" O'Riley's AA looked up.

Had he said that out loud? "Sorry, just talking to myself," he said, hoping like hell she hadn't heard exactly what he'd said.

She smiled as if she had, or maybe she'd just seen other agents about to be handed their asses in a sling and sympathized.

Maybe.

Her intercom buzzed. "You may go in, Agent MacGregor." This time, she kept her gaze averted.

Not a good sign at all.

Time to suck it up. Either his ass was fired or assigned to somewhere like Juneau. Either way, any upward advancement was off the table.

Squaring his shoulders, he strode into O'Riley's office. "Thanks for taking time to see me, sir." Like he hadn't been summoned—and none too politely.

O'Riley motioned for Alex to sit, which he did, in spite of the urge to continue pacing. He forced his body into a relaxed position. Image was everything.

*Don't let 'em see you sweat.* Whoever came up with that bright saying never stood, or sat, in front of Chicago's Special Agent in Charge, John O'Riley. His dark eyes and hair coupled with a grim-faced expression sent a chill up Alex's spine.

Bad enough, until O'Riley smiled with a full set of white shark-like teeth. Alex swallowed the boulder-size knot in his throat. Any second, his superior would tear into Alex's career and leave it in shreds.

O'Riley spread a sheaf of papers across his desk. Alex's file, no doubt. "MacGregor, your personal life is of grave concern. Connections with a daughter of the Spinelli crime family, and let's not forget your brother's mental instability that brought him to kidnap two members of your family as well as this Bettina Spinelli. Or Smithson—I believe that's what she calls herself now."

"Yes, sir. But surely you don't blame me for my brother's kidnapping by a predator?" Why *shouldn't* the Bureau blame him? His brother blamed him. Worst of all, Alex blamed himself.

"You didn't conduct yourself according to regulations during the search for your family. Your position on the Violent Crimes Task Force is compromised. An agent who doesn't follow procedure can't be expected to be an effective leader. Until this incident in New York, you showed a great deal of promise; however, I now have no choice but to reassign you."

"Reassign me?" Meaning he wasn't fired. There were worse things than being kicked out of the FBI, although he'd never expected to learn what they were.

"After much discussion, you're being assigned to an area where your former mistress's crime connections don't reach."

"My mistress? Are you seriously calling Ms. Spinelli my mistress? We fell in love." Now, he sounded like a total sap—not the way to go.

O'Riley scowled. "Nevertheless, her brother is becoming more of a problem than her father ever was. And your relationship, whatever it is or was, is a severe conflict of interest."

"She's had nothing to do with her brother for years."

O'Riley neatened the stack of papers and set them aside. "Nevertheless, you will present yourself to the field office in Salt

Lake City tomorrow."

"Salt Lake City?" Swallowing hard, he resisted the urge to salute…barely. "Yes, sir."

The Salt Lake City field office merely covered the states of Utah, Montana, and Idaho, where the memory of Ruby Ridge was still fresh. Didn't take a genius to figure out Salt Lake was a step or twenty down the career ladder from the VCTF in Chicago.

Back in his apartment, Alex zipped his go-bag and set it aside. His flight to Salt Lake left in four hours. The landlord let him out of his year's lease since he understood agents didn't have any control over when or where they were re-assigned.

And what had he done to deserve this bump in his road to success? Fall in love with a freaking Mafia princess was all. Bette pretty much told him to go back to Chi-town and forget he ever met her. Not so easy.

Who could forget their last angry words? Once his sanity returned and he cooled off, he realized she'd kicked him out for the right reasons. Feisty and sexy—nah, no way to forget her. And no way to keep her in his life and also keep his career with the Bureau viable. Hell, even viable was a relative term.

Face it. Bette's family connections weren't any worse than his. He had a brother who was a serial kidnapper and in a mental hospital for the thankfully foreseeable future. A brother who, in his more lucid moments, blamed Alex for not keeping his promise to come back at the movie. A brother who blamed Alex for every unmentionable thing that had happened since.

Two strikes against him. Why bother?

He strode into the bathroom and checked for anything left behind. Shaving gear already packed. Hell, maybe he'd grow a beard just to fit in and not look like such a white-bread city boy.

His phone chimed. Fishing it out of his pocket, he glanced at the readout. Who the hell was *D.C. Security Services*?

"MacGregor."

"Dude. How's it going?"

Alex recognized the familiar voice. None other than Special Agent Jake LeFevre. "Not so hot. You?"

"Can't complain."

"How's your new baby girl?"

"Already spoiled rotten."

"And Caitlin?"

"She's a wild woman—no change there." Alex heard his old partner take a deep breath. "Got a proposition for you. Join me at my new firm."

"You *left* the Bureau?" Jake had always been Bureau all the way. Never would've thought he'd leave before retirement age.

Jake chuckled. "Decided I wasn't cut out for profiling. Too much time away from home and my family. Wasn't fun anymore, dude."

"Sure could've used a profiler in upstate New York."

"That's what I heard. That was some tough shit. Sorry about your brother."

"Yeah, well. You know how it goes. Good news and bad news." He paused to take a breath. "Anyway, got a new assignment—Salt Lake City, *Utah*."

"Whoa. You really screwed the pooch. Did they even buy you dinner?"

"Not even close." *Proposition?* That's what the man had said. "So what's this about a proposition? Make it quick. I'm supposed to be at the airport in two hours, heading for parts west."

"Remember Clint Eastman? He retired from the Bureau a couple of years ago and opened a security firm. Last week, he offered me a partnership. I took him up on it and immediately thought of you. Maybe you'd like to stay on the East Coast for a while."

Mind racing, he asked, "What kind of services do you offer?"

"Lot of corporate services, some bodyguard work, industrial espionage—preventing it, not doing it." Jake laughed. "You interested? With your qualifications and my recommendation, you're a shoo-in."

"I'll give it some thought." Hell, yeah, he'd give it some thought. Just give him a line to sign on.

"Don't think too long, or you'll find yourself hunting grizzlies in the wilds of Utah and Montana."

"Just one little complication." Might as well get it out in the open. Jake needed to know.

"I'm listening."

"Any problems with my being married to a gen-u-ine Mafia princess?" Alex held his breath. This job offer could be the answer to everything.

"You married a *what*?" The rising note of surprise was evident in his friend's voice.

"Not married. Not yet, anyway. Long story, dude."

"That why they sent your butt to Utah?"

"Yeah. Pretty much."

"Then change your flight from Salt Lake to DC. You won't be sorry."

Alex laughed. "That's what you told me about New Orleans too." He took a deep breath. "I need to talk to someone else first. Can you give me that much time?"

"Sure thing. Talk to your woman. Hope she's more manageable than mine." Jake let out a deep chuckle, then broke the connection.

Alex punched in a number he'd memorized but hadn't called until now.

# Chapter Thirty

Bette ushered out the last patient and turned to Jackie. "That's it for another day."

Jackie nodded. "Yeah, I have to take Cody over to Brad's new place tonight."

"How's Cody adjusting to the split?"

"So-so." Jackie shrugged. "You know how it is. Brad's doing his damnedest to be the fun dad. As a result, I'm mean old Mom who makes Cody brush his teeth and pick up his toys."

Bette nodded her agreement. "Divorce is tough on kids, but with you for a mom, I'm sure he'll be fine." The phone rang. "Sorry, I'll have to get it. I haven't switched the phones over to the answering service yet." She picked up the receiver and answered, "Animal Hospital. This is Bette."

"Bette."

No mistaking *his* voice. Alex. There was no stopping the insistent racing of her heart. Or the flare of hope bursting in her chest, making it difficult to breathe. "Hold on. Jackie's right here."

"No. I'm calling you."

Her throat constricted as she held back the tears. "What for? We've already said everything there is to say." And way more.

"Don't be too sure."

"What's that supposed to mean?"

"Need to see you. *Talk* to you."

"Why prolong the agony? Or do you just get a cheap thrill out of breaking my heart?"

"You're the one who sent *me* away. Remember?"

"What else was I supposed to do? Ruin your career? Your whole, entire freaking professional life?" She gathered her courage, ignoring Jackie's wide, questioning gaze. "I'm hanging up now. Bye." She set the receiver on the phone.

"Well, that's that." She smiled at her boss. "How 'bout we share a slice and a beer after you take Cody to his dad's?"

"Sounds like a...winner." Jackie's manner was hesitant. Her mouth twisted to one side. "Okay, are you going to tell me what my brother said or not?"

Bette shook her head. "Nothing new. Meet you at Pontillo's at seven-thirty?"

She glanced down at Shadow, who was curled up in a basket under the desk. "That should give you time to drop off Cody at his dad's and time for me to feed and walk Shadow."

Jackie flashed Bette a quick smile, but the look of speculation was still written across her face. "Deal."

Bette reached Pontillo's before Jackie. She spotted an empty table and sat facing the door. Since the kidnapping, she was still a tad too paranoid to sit with her back to any door. Besides, she wanted to see Jackie when she entered. She picked up the menu. Ordering was simple: a small white pizza with mozzarella and veggies for Jackie, and a red and ditto on the veggies for Bette. She gave the order to the waitress. Hopefully, Jackie wouldn't be too late. Shadow hadn't been happy to see Bette leave for the evening. A single lifted paw and her eyes said, "Please don't go."

When the waitress set the two pizzas on the table, Jackie still hadn't shown up. "Stood you up, huh?"

Bette shook her head. "She's just a few minutes late." She drummed her fingernails on the table, the tension starting to grow and collect, knotting her midsection. She snagged one slice and took a bite, quickly discovering she couldn't swallow. What if Jackie and her soon-to-be ex got into an argument? What if something had happened? No. No point in borrowing trouble. She sucked in a deep breath, trying to tamp down her impatience. And her apprehension.

She rummaged in her purse for her cell phone and sent Jackie a text.

Her phone dinged. She quickly opened the message. Just a cryptic response that something had come up and that Bette should come on home. And Jackie had a surprise.

A surprise? Bette motioned for the waitress. "Could I have a couple of to-go boxes instead?"

The waitress rolled her eyes but nodded and flounced away.

A few minutes later, Bette was speeding down Eastern, her hands tight on the steering wheel. What kind of surprise? A surprise didn't sound like something bad. Surprises were supposed to be good.

Nothing like being a nervous Nellie. *Take a deep breath. Calm down.*

She hung a right on Main, keeping a watchful eye for one of Canandaigua's finest. No point in getting a speeding ticket.

Another right on Gibson and just a few more blocks. In spite of taking several deep, calming breaths, and telling herself there was nothing to worry about, her heart thrummed along at a dizzying pace.

She slowed and turned into the driveway. A dark four-door sedan was parked behind Jackie's SUV. So Jackie *was* home. And *who* did the sedan belong to?

She pulled in behind the Intrepid, grabbed the pizza boxes, got out, and checked the license plate. Sure enough, there was a rental car sticker from a Rochester agency. Her steps slowed. Should she check on her boss? Maybe she should just go in the back way. Jackie might have company. Well, obviously she had company, but maybe—nah—not a date.

Curiosity and more than a little concern won out over

discretion. She bounded up the front steps and gave a quick rap on the front door. Without waiting for a response, she entered. "Sorry, I couldn't get around—"

Her breath caught in her throat.

Alex wandered casually into the living room, carrying a beer and wearing a smile. "Hey, Jersey. How's it going?"

Her chin dropped. Mouth dry, she tried to form a coherent thought. "Alex," she managed to croak. "What... I mean—"

"Didn't have much choice. You wouldn't talk to me on the phone." He shrugged and flopped casually on the sofa, his lanky body looking entirely too comfortable. "Face-to-face is always better."

"But you're supposed to be on your way to Utah." She darted a questioning glance at her smiling boss. "At least that's what Jackie said."

"Yeah." He nodded with a wry quirk of a smile. "That was the Bureau's plan, all right. Sending my sorry ass to Salt Lake City." He shrugged, then shot her a smile that blazed through her body and shook her to the core. "Got a better offer."

"A better offer?" she managed to ask, her mouth gone suddenly dry. Unsteady on her feet, her thighs wobbly as rubber bands, she grasped the back of a Queen Anne chair. Wouldn't do to fall on her face, or worse, her ass, now, would it? Either possibility was imminent if she didn't pull herself together.

Braced by the furniture, she stiffened her knees and wondered if she ought to attempt a step or two. Yeah. What was she—some kind of a wimp to go all girly at the sight of six feet three inches of male hunk?

Yes.

She straightened her back and stepped away from the protection of the wingback. "A better offer? Better than the Bureau?"

"Depends on *you*, Jersey."

She chewed her bottom lip and considered whether or not to

breathe. "On *me?*" Another quick glance at Jackie, who was now doing her best imitation of the Cheshire Cat. What was that about?

Alex held his breath. The signs of confusion on Bette's beautiful face touched him, convincing him he'd made the right decision—at least, if her response to his big question was a yes. He was so nervous at this very moment, his knees were probably weaker than hers.

"On me?" Her expression grew more uncertain. Bottom lip trembling, she gestured with her hand on her chest.

"Oh!" Jackie sprang from her place on the sofa. "I've got something on the stove."

He winked. His sister wasn't exactly on speaking terms with her stove.

"What's going on, Double-O?" Why was she gripping the chair as if it were about to escape?

"Sit down"—he patted the sofa beside him—"before you fall down."

Her full upper lip lifted in a sneer. "Cute."

She closed the distance between them, somewhat hesitantly, in his opinion.

"What does your better offer have to do with me?"

"If you'll sit and stop staring like a deer caught in the headlights, I'll tell you."

"Fine." She sat uneasily at the far end of the sofa, folded her arms across her chest, and favored him with a bored-to-death expression. "I'm waiting."

"You've heard me mention my old pal Jake LeFevre? He's the one who met his wife during the undercover op in New Orleans."

"Yeah." She nodded slowly. For all her attempts at nonchalance, he could see her toe tapping nervously.

"He recently retired from the Bureau, and he's a partner in a private security firm in D.C. Wants to know if I'd be interested in working for their firm."

"Cool." She shrugged as if it were nothing to her. "I guess anything is better than Utah."

"I'll be based in DC and—"

"Makes sense." She gave another little shrug.

Damn the woman. Could she care less when he was trying to propose? "For Pete's sake, stop interrupting." He stood and walked stiffly to where she sat. Could she make this any harder? Or him, for that matter.

She gazed up at him, a quizzical expression flickering in her dark chocolate eyes. "So what's stopping you? You're taking a job with your old pal. I'm happy for you."

"For one thing, he doesn't have a problem with your—uh, family background. And *I* never did." God, he was making a total balls-up of his proposal.

"What does my family have to do with anything? It's not like he wants to hire me. I already have a job."

"Dammit, Bette. He's not... What I'm trying to say so poorly is he doesn't have a problem with my *wife* having a mob connection, however slight."

"You're getting married? You certainly don't waste—" She broke off as a glimmer of understanding widened her eyes. "Oh—"

"Yeah. I'm not too good at this proposal business, am I?"

A tiny smile flickered at the corner of her mouth. "You really suck it."

He went down on one knee, took her hand in his, and swallowed hard. Her eyes glistened as she blinked rapidly.

"What about the Bureau? That's your whole life. You really want to give up your career for me?"

"I love you, Bette. I can't imagine spending the rest of my life without you." He hadn't heard what he needed to hear yet. All she needed to say. One freaking word.

"But my job?" She bit her bottom lip and glanced toward the kitchen. "I'm really settled in with your sister. She depends on me."

He rocked back on his heels. Damn. Not what he expected at all. "You're choosing your *job* with my sister over marrying me?"

"It's just she's going through a divorce—in case you've forgotten."

"My *sister* can replace you. I can't." *Think fast, man. Don't let her get away.* "In case you didn't hear me before, I *love* you. If you want to stay here in Canandaigua, I'll commute. Hell, maybe in time, they'll open an office in Buffalo or Rochester." Okay, he was stretching it. Desperation did funny things to a man. Was groveling out of the question?

She wrinkled her nose and shook her head. "Never cared for the idea of a long-distance marriage."

Hope blossomed in his chest. "Then come with me to DC. You'll love it. We'll find a great apartment, condo, house— whatever you want." In fact, he already had a real estate agent on the lookout for a place, but she still hadn't said what he needed to hear. Confidence flagging, he finger-combed his hair. Could he convince the woman he loved to marry him or not?

Fluffing her hair, she exhaled with a small sigh. "I'd really like to hear more about how you love me and can't live without me." Her lips parted expectantly.

"You'll hear it every day of your life if you make me the happiest man in the world and just say yes."

She squeezed his hand and leaned forward, smiling widely. "Yes, Alex," she said in a breathy whisper, "I'll marry you."

"Just to make sure, you *are* saying yes? That's your final answer?" He pinned her with his gaze, wanting to tease her a bit since she'd already said yes. "And all that stuff you said when we said good-bye was bogus?"

"Hell, yes! I've cried myself to sleep every night for the past week. Missing you and hating myself for the things I said." Her eyes started to glisten with tears.

With his forefinger, he raised her chin a notch. "Your acceptance isn't bogus, then?" He shrugged as if wary. "But how can I be sure?"

"I'll show you *sure*." Smiling, she slipped her arms around his neck. "Right now. Right here. Downstairs. Upstairs or up against a wall."

"She's convinced me," Jackie called, peeking in from the hallway. "Go on. Get out of here. I've got to get busy and start looking for your replacement."

He swept Bette into his arms. "Jersey's irreplaceable, but you keep on looking, because I'm not going to let her get away again."

A wide smile wreathed Bette's face, her eyes glittering with happiness. "Damned straight, Double-O. And that goes double—no, triple—for me."

## The End

# ABOUT THE AUTHOR

Romantic suspense author Marie-Nicole Ryan has had a life-long love affair with books, so one could say it was only natural for her to start writing some of her own. She was born in Kentucky, but lived in Nashville, TN, for more decades than she cares to admit.

When she has time, she loves to read murder mysteries, browse antique shops and meet her friends for lunch. She's also very fond of her Sheltie rescue, Kelsea, who tries to help her write by walking on the keyboard.

She loves to hear from her readers, and she's never too busy to respond. You can e-mail Ms. Ryan at marie@marienicoleryan.com.

## LINKS

Web site: https://marienicoleryan.com
FaceBook: https://facebook.com/MarieNicoleRyan.author
Twitter: @marienicoleryan
Newsletter:marie-nicoleryannews-subscribe@yahoogroups.com

# ALSO BY MARIE-NICOLE RYAN
## NOVELS

*Measure of a Man, Music City Heat 3*
*Hunted, Hill Country Lawmen 1*
*Because of You, Music City Heat 2*
*Mastering the Marshal, Loving the Lawman 3*
*Pleasuring the Pinkerton, Loving the Lawman 2*
*Love Me if You Can, Music City Heat 3*
*Seducing the Sheriff, Loving the Lawman 1*
*Holding Her Own, FBI Guys 2*
*One Too Many*
*Love on the Run*
*Too Good to be True*
*The Man for the Job*
*See You in My Dreams*

### SHORT STORIES
*Valentine's Gift, Holiday Interludes: 3*
*Pillow Talk, Holiday Interludes: 2*
(Prequel to *Broken Promises*)
*Mistletoe and Mario, Holiday Interludes: 1*